THE GUARDIAN HILL/ /AGA

MARK-JOHN /CHMITZ

PublishAmerica
Baltimore

First printing

ISBN: 1-4137-5625-5
PUBLISHED BY PUBLISHAMERICA, LLLP
www.publishamerica.com
Baltimore

Printed in the United States of America

TABLE OF CONTENTS

Happy Birthday

To all victims of terror—those actions great and small—this,
I give to you.

Russell

Mark Ornch

markisz@msn.com

MURDER IN GUARDIAN HILLS

A storm began of streaky lightning, hesitant thunder, and pesky winds.

And amidst such a clatter four men ran amuck. Deep within a great forest of pine and birch, halfway up the side of a small valley, and away from the sleepy little town of Westcreek, Minnesota four men went in search of treasure—Indian treasure that is, a sort of secret vault filled with supposed gold, jewelry, and splendid art. In the early morning and under a growing mass of black clouds, they ran single file along a curvy deer path, dodging puddle after puddle, and jumping log after log. Nothing, it would seem, would stop them from reaching their goal. And just in case—in case of a physical confrontation unforeseen—all four men were loaded down for bear. High-powered rifles were slung over shoulders. And packs, jumping about on backs, not only contained food rations, toiletries, and a couple of days' worth of clothes, but also boxes and boxes of heavy ammunition. The journey was a serious one.

Lives might be lost, you see.

Bernie was the first in line. A widower, man of fifty, and wearing a flannel hunter's cap holding down flyaway gray hair, he appeared terribly cautious in regard to the thievery being imbibed in. Months of planning—refining of those plans and mock ambushes went into this night—this one night, so nothing could be left to chance. It all came down to a matter of where *he* was, how powerful *he* was, and how vengeful *he* might be, should their mission prove fruitless. Running down the deer path, his arm outstretched and holding a near useless lantern, he tried to catch a glimpse of his surroundings and with the help of flashy lightning. He was almost sure the forest was coming alive.

Did something rustle in the bushes, he thought? How about near the top of that fir tree? Why were the winds increasing so? Was *he* on to us already? Was *he* out there just waiting to kill? *Maybe the timing was wrong,* Bernie thought. Maybe it was best to turn back and refine plans once more. Bernie showed a near panic attack.

Bull was the second in line, a mountain of a man, and not looking too happy. Carrying bulging biceps and bouncing pectorals, he seemed the strength of the group. A bit younger than Bernie and wearing a plaid hunting jacket with the sleeves ripped off, he was growing frustrated with Bernie's over concern about myths and legends: he didn't believe any of 'em. He simply wanted his riches and he wanted them... now.

And it was best not to frustrate Bull. Back in town, and as Bernie recalled, Bull could be tough on people. Visions appeared to the senior: of conflicts with others—even those that were minor, like those related to a subordinate on a lumbering call that was behind schedule, or those related to slow food or drink service at the local diner. All were responded to with angry scowls, a shouting, foul mouth, and many times a belt in the gut or a slap across the chops— particularly if Bull had been drinking whisky. The big man often acted first and thought later, especially under an intoxicated state. Only Bernie was given any kind of respect. Most times, that is.

Pounding his heavy boots into the yielding earth, Bull bumped into Bernie, accidentally at first, you see, but a bump nonetheless and maybe it would speed up the pace, Bull thought. Maybe he'd even do it again, this time on purpose—anything to get quickly into that Indian vault.

Two brothers brought up the rear. Balding, identical twins and with babies' faces, they were the sort of packhorses of the group. This search was a last ditch effort to recoup losses incurred from their joint business in Westcreek. The two owned a small hardware store, you see, and the place was failing, miserably. Too few customers generated too few dollars, and it was getting close to the time when they'd have to soap up windows. The brothers' wives and children had already moved back to the Twin Cities because the prospect of survival had looked so grim. The twins would have joined them, had Bull not been so pressuring in regard to joining he and Bernie. Indeed, the twins had a hard time saying no to the big man, most people did.

Running lightly, the twins had an even harder time keeping up. Their meager, skinny frames didn't seem conducive for such a hectic trek through the wild. Hearts were beating rapidly but not entirely due to physical exertion. They also appeared fearful: of the unknown. The brothers felt like they were being watched by someone or something or both. Were the *tales* really true, they wondered? Was Bernie right about the danger?

CRACK! and a bolt of lightning tore up the sky. *CRACK-CRACK!* and a couple more incursions seemed to compete for vibrancy.

And Bernie suddenly stopped the procession of four. At the edge of a great clearing, surrounded by tall, tall Jack Pine, he held up his hand. "Wait!" he yelled. "No farther! Check the area! *He* could be anywhere!"

And his cohorts did. Each slowly turned in circles, as if robotic, eyeing the nearby greenery for anything out of the ordinary— anything that might be human or nonhuman and the range of possibilities just scared the brothers even more. But still, from what they could see the forest seemed natural—seemed normal, albeit increasingly windy and combustible.

"There's nothing here, you old fool!" Bull snapped. "Now where's this damn vault?"

Bernie reluctantly pointed ahead. "There. To the north of The Great Rock."

Lightning stuttered terribly. Shown was a small, abandoned mine within the side of a hill and with spindly vines dangling in front, as if forbidding entrance. The sort of cave was at most six feet high, four foot wide, and with worn metal, rusted railings on the floor and for transporting once-useful heavy ore cars from deep inside. Such ore cars were elderly in appearance, you see, and most likely discarded somewhere deep inside, collecting of blanketed dust and encumbering spider webs. A bountiful harvest of granite seemed ancient history and out of reach.

Bull rudely pushed Bernie to the side, taking a couple of steps forward, his eyes bulging. "Ooohhh! It's just as you described: out here, far away from everyone, just waiting to be cleaned out. Let's go!" He lunged forward.

"Wait!" Bernie shouted.

Something was heard.

Amidst the now howling wind and more assertive claps of thunder was the faint sound of hissing. It was hoarser than that of snakes, intermixed with almost a sort of gibberish language, and it seemed to be coming from all around the men.

The evidence Bernie was looking for seemed close at hand.

"The Indian is here," he whispered, and with a paranoid look. "With his creatures. Thinks he's got us in his web, he does. He's probably laughing. We best turn back!" he raged.

Bull bit his lip and dropped his eyes to the cold black earth. "It's just some damn wild animals! We've come too far to go home! I want my share of the riches!" He pointed to the mine like a father ordering his children to their rooms. "Now come on, let's go!"

"Maybe it's not safe," the oldest of the brothers, by seconds, mumbled, taking a step back, "like Bernie said. Let's come back— back another time."

Bull thought for a moment, a short moment. Then he grabbed his rifle, cocked the hammer, and headed toward the mine. "There'll be another day for you three. Go back to Westcreek and cower over fairy tales. I've got a job to do."

"No!" Bernie said, running after him and grabbing a big arm. "We came together. We leave together. I can't let you go in alone, it's almost certain death."

Bull jerked roughly away, but to no avail. "Let me go, dammit!"

"Listen to me as someone who knows the *old man's* mystical ways! Listen to me as a friend! It's not worth the horror!" Bernie seemed not to give an inch.

Lightning veined its way across the sky... kettledrum-like thunder vibrated the earth, occasionally... winds stung red cheeks, and the brothers nervously waited for Bull's reaction, their hands sweaty.

And the big man pondered more deeply. He thought about options. Glaring into Bernie's big, blue eyes and breathing terribly, he grinded his teeth.

"Feel the storm around us and know what I say is true," Bernie said. "There will be another day."

Bull pulled his look away from Bernie and with a sigh. Then he nodded. "Perhaps you're right. I'm being selfish. You know more about these matters..."

Bernie smiled. "Good choice, friend! Believe me, you will have your wealth! Just not tonight." He patted Bull's shoulders and then turned his attention to the brothers. "Our mission is over, my friends. It's time to go home!"

And yet it wasn't.

"THUMP!" and the butt end of Bull's rifle connected viciously with the back of Bernie's head. The big man growled terribly as his friend's suddenly limp body dropped to the earth.

"The mission has just begun!" he spat.

Bull was enraged and frightened—all at the same time.

"What have you done?" the youngest brother screamed, rushing to Bernie's side. "My God... Bernie? Bernie!"

The fallen man was unable to answer.

"He grabbed me!" Bull tried to explain, surprised by seemingly even his own actions. "Nobody grabs me! Nobody!"

"He's your best friend, dammit!" the oldest twin scolded, meekly. "You don't do that to your best friend!"

Bull watched the sympathy being paid to Bernie and for a short time. He breathed deeply. But then, succumbing to the return of a pressing want, and gaining back all of his confidences, he slowly pointed the barrel of his rifle at the oldest brother. "We're still going into that mine. All three of us. Without Bernie."

"I'm sorry."

"Are you crazy?" the kneeling twin cried, cradling Bernie. "He's bleeding! Bleeding bad! He needs medical attention!"

"All in good time. All in good time. But right now I have a treasure to get. And I need your help hauling it out."

"No!" the kneeling twin whined, clutching Bernie more tightly. "I won't leave him here! Damn you!"

"The longer you stall, the longer he hurts." The big man sighed with impatience. And he juggled his pectorals. "On our way back to town it will be me that carries Bernie. Knee deep in riches. All will be forgotten. Even by Bernie. You will see. Bind his wounds and let's go."

"No!"

Bull's face turned red. He let off a warning shot into the night. "God dammit, I'm not gonna tell you two again! Now let's go or Bernie won't be the only one carried out!"

The oldest twin had seen Bull like this too many times before, and the consequence for not following orders was always the worst of brutalities; like at the café, not more than two days ago. Liquored up and looking for trouble, Bull assaulted a short barkeep for denying him further shots of whisky, this after a regiment of six straight slams. The attack was quick and fiery, sparked simply by "No."

A cracked jaw, a torn ear, and a bloody nose were the damage done. It took five lumberjacks to remove Bull from the barkeep's person. The clearing could surely not afford such assistance, and so out of control anxiety would seem to call for a much humbler resolve.

"Do as he says, brother," the standing, older twin droned, lost in Bull's intense stare. "We have no choice. The faster we find what he wants, the faster we can get Bernie home. Now come on. Get up." He crouched down to his younger, slowly and with lifting arms. "Come on."

"But Bernie needs our help now," the younger tried to explain, rocking with the fallen man, almost oddly and institutional-like. "We can't leave him. Look at the blood! The blood."

"I know, I know," the older answered, "but we must. Bull's in control here."

He pulled his weaker half to a stand, prying shaking fingers from Bernie's heavy coat.

Then the older grabbed for the lantern.

"But he's a bastard, brother!" the younger said.

"Yes. But let God sort it out. It's out of our hands."

The two huddled together like mice caught in the mighty gaze of a lion—a lion with a rifle, that is, and the sudden leader kept a bead on them both as they all stumbled toward the north end of the clearing and toward a dark, dark opening in the side of the valley. Bernie was left behind like roadkill, near a huge rock, the hissing growing louder.

The brains of the group had been compromised, it seemed.

And then the winds picked up to advisory levels. As the three ascended, swirls of air danced about the clearing, tossing tree limbs to and fro, and dust every which way. It was like tiny tornadoes sprung from the earth to sort of protest Bernie's treatment, and the rest of the forest was going to hear about it, via subsequent high-pitched humming.

Then consciousness came.

Bernie awoke. He bobbled his head off the ground like a newborn on its tummy, his sight blurry, at best. Faculties returned in stages, coaxed first by the wind, then by the sound of what seemed to be little person gibberish, and then finally by a kind of rotten odor. A sixth sense came to Bernie, and he was sure he was being watched. By someone. By something. By both—and a solid sort of panic attack seemed to hit.

"Has the old Indian got me?" he babbled out loud. "Have I fallen under one of his spells? One of his tricks? Where are the others? Are they in danger? Where are you, old man?" He readied a heavy breath in order to scream. "Help! Help, I say!" But there was no response, and Bernie's heavy eyes could find little life in the southern part of the clearing, his vantage point. Things were just not making sense.

The so-called leader felt for his bloody head, trying to remember the sequence of events leading up to the present. "We packed our gear. We checked our guns. Ran through this damndable forest, we did. Decided to turn back… and then…" He stroked his gray hair. "But then what?" He screamed at the unknown. "Where are my friends, you demon? What have you done with them?" He was determined to find the three, no matter what treachery they had succumbed to.

So he spun around. Like a turtle suddenly shifting direction on its bulky belly, he spun 180 degrees, The Great Rock just a short distance away and to his northeast. "Bull! Brothers! Answer me! We are in danger! The old Indian is here!"

Some sporadic breaths—some slight wheezing, and then he located his men through a snowstorm of dirt. They were climbing atop a sort of apron to the mine. Bernie's excitement could not be contained.

"Over here, friends!" he bawled. "Bull! I am here! And hurt! Help me, friends!" But they kept going. Seemingly unaware. And as the brightest flash of lightning—as the loudest clap of thunder occurred overhead, Bernie attempted to remember.

Again.

"We packed our bags. We checked our gear. Ran through this damndable forest, we did. And then turned back for home." His wrinkled face became puzzled. Just momentarily. "And… I was hit. With my back turned. By Bull." The pain in his head fell to his heart, and a hot feeling flooded most of his chest. Anger, you see, the size of two Bulls came upon him. "Not attacked by any old Indian," he groaned. "No. Attacked by my very own friend, so that he could get his treasure. And the brothers… they, too, are caught up in his greed. Look at them! Look at them search for a treasure I told them of." His fuzzy eyes narrowed. His mind became active with recourse possibilities. Deadly ones.

"Oh, my friends," he said to really no one. "You shall find more on this night than a vault of wealth." Floating a bloody hand down to his waist, he dug in his worn hunting pants for a small metal handgun with grips of quartz. "You shall find tragedy, as well." And he sought a sort of higher power. "Dear father, just show me the light. So that my aim may be true. Friendship, dear friendship, has found a bog, one where trust and brotherhood not tread." He squinted his eyes and drew a bead. And Bull and the brothers were about to enter the mine. They stood upon the apron to the mine, catching their breaths, Bull pleased with the progress. He smiled. "All that life could offer is upon us." And yet there was still opposition.

"I hate you for this, Bull!" the youngest brother said with tears. "I hope you rot in hell for what you did to Bernie!"

"On the contrary," Bull replied calmly. "We'll all be brought to something much greater with the contents of this vault. Just you wait and see." He shook the barrel of his rifle toward the interior of the mine. "Let's go."

But they'd get no farther.

The sky—it lit up.

"BANG!" and a hunk of lead cracked harshly, the skull of one of the twins. "BANG-BANG!" and two more penetrated the back and leg of the other. Both fell quickly to the ground and without so much as a moan—maybe a palsy-like quiver, at best, thereafter.

"Have you found what you've been looking for?" Bernie mumbled. "Is the wealth all you hoped it would be?" He giggled.

Bull whipped around. He searched hard for the source of gunfire and through the visual turbulence. "Bernie!"

With a ghost white face, he hastily brought his rifle up to eye level. His aim was with appall and somewhat at his old friend. "Die, damn you!" he yelled.

The sky lit up again.

"CRACK-CRACK!" went his rifle. "CRACK!"

Bernie countered, letting loose with all he had. Blindly. "BANG-BANG-BANG-BAng!" Then, "CLick-Click-click," the gun jamming. Only one shot hit its mark.

Bull clutched his chest. Ripping through dense muscle, the bullet found a home in the northeast corner of his heart, sending the big man flailing into the side of the mine. Then warm, red fluid bubbled up gradually atop his chest. There against the mine he slid down like an invalid, muttering softly, helplessly. He flopped around a bit like a Walleye out of water, and until only slight movements prevailed, until only a gasp was let out, with a spit.

Then nothing.

Bull would never seemingly find his riches.

Bernie was still pumping the trigger, his eyes getting fuzzier and fuzzier. Just one of Bull's shots connected, a deflection off The Great Rock, and to that which lodged within his larynx. But one shot would be quite enough, and Bernie's time became terribly limited. He wheezed. He spat. Survival was an impossibility, and he knew it. In a queer turn of events, his greatest fear had materialized: that death comes quickly to the living in Guardian Hills. He spat with sort of mucous and blood, and then came a congested chortle.

"So this is the last chapter in our friendship," Bernie said to his murdered friends, his blood dripping into his larynx. "Death by way of greed… and in the backyard of the devil. Yes. Yes… and it could have been so different. Together we four could have been rich off this valley. Instead we die alone. In anguish. How ironic."

Bernie still felt there was another hand in things, a sort of wispy entity lurking in the darkness.

Watching.

"Have we entertained you, old man?" he called out to the swirling air. "Are you happy with what you see? Your treasure is once again safe and there are no new plans to be made. No modifications… no preparation for future trips. Knowledge of your Indian vault dies with us. No one else knows." Choking briefly on blood, his head bobbled again like a newborn, and off the hard earth. He became upset. "Show yourself, dammit! Grant me one last wish! A meeting between us! You owe me at least that." Bernie started wallowing a bit in self pity. He muttered some sort of prayer, scanned the clearing like a drunk, and then rested his aching head upon the cold dirt.

That's when the hair on the back of his neck stood up. That's when a sharp gaze was felt from somewhere—everywhere, and yet somehow just right in front of him.

Lightning stuttered terribly. A multitude of flashes occurred, and the result was a washing of brightness over the clearing. As if for Bernie. And as if to see by.

With all his muscle, Bernie looked to The Great Rock. "Ohhhhhhh," he sighed with both terror and excitement. "It is you... old man. You do still live. The tales are not exaggerated..."

Atop a sort of podium stood a sort of specter. Engulfed by a heavy, heavy-hooded robe of earthen tones that seemed to meld with the rock, the sort of being was man-like and still. Just standing. Its skin was not visible, or even its limbs, and the only hint that a possible mortal existed beneath the ancient fabric was found within the large hood. There a pair of brown eyes, a nose, and a small mouth could be seen—just barely, mind you, set back deep within the garment and as if just a casual observer in it all.

And one could see such features only during the brightest paths of lightning.

The weather and forest seemed to respect his anonymity—he seemed one with it all. Indeed.

Bernie smiled oddly, his teeth red. "It's so good to see you one last time... to battle you one last battle." He felt a pulling in his stomach that jolted his body. "Before I leave this world I must rid the valley of you. Only then can our town have a fighting chance at survival. You know it to be true." With borrowed strength, he hoisted his handgun into the air. "To the last I grapple with thee... long live 'the war!'"

"CLIck-CLick-Click... click," went the jammed weapon, doing nothing more. It was as powerless as Bernie, himself.

"No," he labored psychotically, feeling detached and yet somehow online with his surroundings. "Darkness... lightness... all of it."

Then came a greater, ascended drunkenness.

His hand flopped to the ground, soon followed by his head. A lifetime of treasure seeking had come to an end. Bernie's eyes shut slowly and his body became numb—became stone and diminishing of heat, it did. The last feeling felt within Bernie's core was that of a tingling sensation in his gut. Such tingling rose symmetrically with the fall of his last breath. Then nothing more; then there came over-stimulation, anxiety, panic and a sort of light. Intoxicating, somber, at first it was, then sort of placid and yearning—it was both bright in vision and hot in terms of sudden body sensation.

Indeed.

And then the sort of specter was alone. With his robe rustled playfully by a suddenly much lighter wind, he looked down upon the little town of Westcreek in the base of the valley. His brown eyes shifted from east to west... east to west—as it were—over and over again. It was as if he was waiting—waiting as if something were to happen, and this based on his anxious, rhythmic fingering of a large, wooden staff. Over and over again he played an unknowable tune, like he was playing an upright oboe, and without timing, the melody recognized by only him and lacking in catchiness, the specter's consistency in playing the only observable oddity...

Just watched and played, he did. Just watched, played, and waited, he did. For something. Something to happen.

Just something...

ONE LITTLE INDIAN

The storm continued, though much less violently.

And a soft rain suddenly fell upon Westcreek. Its cool, yet cleansing droplets moistened the dirt roads, the old wooden buildings downtown, and the many small homes and 5th wheel trailers that dotted a valley floor of mostly pine and ash trees. The whole scene resembled a Terry Redlin painting, save the vibrant color and inherent magic. The little Minnesota town appeared dull—rather ghostly, and anyway no one probably would have noticed. It was the middle of the night, and most of Westcreek's four hundred inhabitants were in bed, trying to sleep, but with little or no luck.

Men, women, and children were preoccupied in thought, you see. Concerns and interests from the previous day, and the previous day before that, had infiltrated dreamworld, and virtually no one could rest peacefully. Men wrestled with the prospect of unemployment running out. They hashed over the probability of going broke and the probability of finding work, and then the probability of going broke all over again. Tired women thought about food. They wondered if existing resources could be stretched. Could a few potatoes and a pound of hamburger be carried over into two, maybe three meals? And how about tomorrow's lunch? Could a simple rice dish be substituted for the usual meat sandwich, soup, and fruit?

Options seemed few.

And finally, the children of Westcreek were consumed by thoughts of their own. Few and mostly boys, they tossed and turned with excitement under their thin bed sheets, for tomorrow was another day of make-believe. Together with friends, cowboys and

Indians would reign supreme as a favorite game, and like the day before and the day before that, straws would have to be drawn to determine who would play what roles. Fingers were always crossed in regards to being a cowboy.

A cowboy was a wonderful thing to be, you see.

But not everyone in town had turned in for the night. At the east end, in the large attic of a modest, one-level dwelling, a light shone through a small window. There an almost man was about to perform magic and for no one. There one little Indian yearned to touch the past.

Inside the attic a single bulb dangled from the ceiling of an A-framed space. It swung stiffly from a teasing wind that muscled its way through the nooks and crannies of the roof and insulation. Back and forth, it swung, back and forth… and then back and forth, again. It glowed warmly, yet softly, and just mainly upon an old black chest that sat in the middle of the floor. Warmly, yet softly, it swung, it did… warmly and softly…

Then a keeper of the chest was noticed.

A stepping sound was suddenly heard… and then a slide… a step… and then a slide… a step, and yet still another slide.

From the shadows and into the light walked Steven. Tall and scrawny, he was, neither fully White nor fully Red—somewhere in between, and he hobbled like a cripple, pulling a bum left leg and a lazy left arm that pressed hard against his side.

But still he moved with intention, to the black chest and a shiny metal clasp for which he tinkered with, removed, and then flung cover and all open. The contents exposed brought a brief smirk to his otherwise tight features.

You see, it was time to honor a hero. It was time to remember. Indeed, it was time to celebrate.

The almost man reached into the chest for a top hat, heavy black cape, and cane, items stored with care and in a certain place of their own along the bottom. From such a position each was held proudly and under a sort of spotlight. The top hat got placed gently upon Steven's jet black hair, and he had to bend slightly in such cramped quarters to get the complete effect. The cape was twirled Parisian-style around his shoulders—with finesse, nonetheless. And the white cane, dulled and marred, was gripped with sure fingers and in his one good hand.

To be certain, the look had to be perfect, so Steven gave himself the once over. He adjusted a wrinkle here and a wrinkle there upon the cape, but for the most part the result was pleasing. And so the stage was set.

It was time to remember.

And he closed his eyes and opened his ears. A warm feeling soothed his stiff body, starting with his gut, and as he pictured a birthday party many years ago. It was in the town park, in and around a little White Gazebo, and children of all shapes and sizes ran happily about on a day of glorious sunshine. Red and White played together, you see. So did White and sort of Black. So did sort of Black and sort of Yellow, and all other combinations, therein. Playing games of tag, Simon says, and Marco Polo, all colors shared joyous laughter that echoed throughout the trees. That is until an Indian elder stepped to the center of the gazebo, and then silence seemed to naturally follow as everyone scampered to get a good seat, even climbing the stair railings—anything to get the best view.

The Indian elder was Steven's grandfather.

And his magic show was about to start.

Steven breathed deeply within the attic. He could see his grandfather so clearly: red as the earth, standing tall, and smiling to all. A man of no more than sixty, he was a bit stout, but jolly nonetheless as he moved atop the gazebo floor and with little reservation. First he'd entertain his audience with comedy. He'd dance around like a crazed bumblebee, his arms flapping and rhythmic and to the sounds of giggling. He'd play the buffoon and fake a series of trips, as if clownish, almost tumbling into the children. Then he'd catch a sort of cold, sneezing shiny gold confetti into the air and to even more laughter. But it was all just a prelude to the mysticism to come, some of which defied explanation—most of which defied explanation.

Another dance ensued, the children hushed. The entertainer in top hat, cape, and cane brushed the air with his old, yet gentle hands. He stroked back and forth across a canvas of nothing until a hundred or more silver lights dropped to the floor like a sparkler burst on the Fourth of July. And they didn't disappear. They became somewhat like crickets, jumping into the audience and causing quite a ruckus. Each child tried to pocket the magical light, though it wasn't easy. The light would zig and zag and to the sheer delight of the little ones as they bumped each other again and again. Meanwhile, the magician was prancing about in circles and with a hum, though not entirely rhythmic. Each of his rotations brought at first small gusts of air, then larger ones, then finally huge gusts, causing hair to mess and Minnesota Twins' caps to go flying.

And Steven's grandfather became concerned about safety, for some of the children had been bowled over. He raced to their sides in dramatics, his top hat falling and left behind. In an effort to comfort, he touched many of their snickering faces and ears. Nickels then dropped from lobes like water from a faucet, some long after the magician's hands had been taken away. Audience members collected their gifts, batting at their ears for each and every last coin. The magical light, the playful winds, and the abundance of money thoroughly captivated the youngsters.

And suddenly, a little Indian girl gasped. She pointed to the far end of the gazebo, the show interrupted. The magician's top hat seemed to have a mind of its own.

Brim side down, it waddled across the floor like a penguin. Steven's grandfather frantically tried grabbing it. Faking exasperation, and while his audience sat in awe, he chased after the incantation, getting only so close before it would spring to the left or right, or just plain forward. Around and around the gazebo the two went, like a Laurel and Hardy routine. 'Round and 'round, and until the magician had had enough. He became winded. Planting his stout behind upon the floor, Steven's grandfather apologized to the children, emphatically. That's when the hat flew back atop his dark head and in perfect form. The children let out with riotous excitement, jumping to their feet. Clapped again and again, they did, the birthday party exceeding expectations.

And the magician took a bow. Rising to a stand with a wider than wide smile, he tipped his hat, twenty or so doves flying out. Snow white, they headed off into every direction. Feathers from their flight floated down like big flakes in a deep winter's storm, and the children tried to catch them all, adding just one more trinket to their already bursting pockets—adding just one more memory to a seemingly most memorable day.

"More!" they all cried. "Please, do more!"

The Indian elder would not disappoint. And his finale would have almost everyone soaring.

Steven's grandfather stood ghostly still. With the winds changing direction, he closed his eyes and held his hands high—high into the air, his lips reciting some kind of mantra. But nothing followed. No trick occurred. The last few light feathers floated peacefully down to the ground, the children exchanging bewildered, if not impatient, looks, and it was as if a fuse to a huge firecracker had been lit but fizzled out just before the explosion. Had the magician tried a trick untested and doomed for failure, one might've thought?

Had the magic simply died away?

Then tummies began to feel ticklish.

And the children began to rise. One by one, they were slowly levitated and twirled about. Girls and boys became feathers themselves, blown gradually to all points around the outside of the gazebo. Each was a bit scared; at first, anyway. They pawed and kicked at nonexistent supports, some tumbling end over end, but nonetheless held between sky and earth. They were flying. Dearly, flying. With time and safety seemingly assured, smiles began to reemerge, and each and every child was paired with a complimentary other and floated to sort of seats on a sort of merry-go-round. Wind gusts would help facilitate positioning by moving each pair to almost exact spacings around the hexagonal-shaped structure. And there they hung, just a few feet off of the ground. There they waited, just a few feet from the pointed rooftop. All the ride engineer had to do was flip a sort of switch to get things going. And he did.

The boys and girls circled around the gazebo. Slowly. As if straddling horses or donkeys on poles, they rose... then fell... rose... and then fell again, with symmetry—with rhythm and while opposing their chosen neighbor. 'Round and 'round, they went, giggling uncontrollably and carrying on in great fun. Though a bit wobbly and somewhat inconsistent in speed, the ride proved airworthy, with little streams of vertical wind forming seats under each patron. The sorcery was virtually self-sufficient with just that one flick of a switch. But the engineer wasn't about to sit back—content. He worried.

Steven's grandfather scrambled to all points inside the gazebo. His cape bouncing, he hurried to peek over the railing and upwards, his mouth muttering still more mantras. Are they high enough, he wondered? Is it the correct speed and the right amount of spacing? So many variables were to be considered in the magic. So many calculations to keep track of, and the old man began to sweat. He began to pant, and so a quick break was in order. The children seemed well taken care of. Grinning, he turned his attention to one little boy left on the ground, watching with pride. He turned to Steven. It was his birthday, you see.

Steven was just eight years old and yet he could've cared less about flying and circling about. The greatest gift received was just being near his grandfather—to witness a master, at work, wielding a powerful force of joy and love. Steven wanted to cling to his grandfather—he wanted to be his grandfather, and a simple touch upon the boy's slightly red cheeks was enough to fill his belly with all that was good.

All that was good...

The past faded into the present, and within a cold little attic, the memory of that day was kept alive. Steven performed a magic show of his own. In a lonely spotlight for one, he danced a dance he fashioned himself. With clumsiness—without rhythm, he stepped to and fro. One, two, three, he stepped. One... two, three, and it was to some inner music, a peaceful melody coupled closely with the vision of his grandfather and that glorious day. His hands painted the stuffy air with uncertain color. His hands played in the cool drafts like a tired orchestra conductor leading a lullaby. Strokes were tentative and constricted, at best, but conveyed a soft mood, nonetheless. And he could imagine the results of his movements.

Steven imagined shooting stars falling around the gazebo. He imagined breezes flowing in patterns of figure eight and small animals of the forest, like badger and martin, dancing on their haunches and to his direction—he was in control, mind you. And he imagined an audience of young and old, cheering.

Steven's performance in the present resembled that of a drunken ballerina, his steps still one, two, three and then one… two, three. But his face showed something deeper. Long and mostly dark in complexion, it denoted an admirer seduced by what was yesterday and no longer today. Steven would have given anything to be a part of that past show again, to be near his grandfather just once more. Indeed, he would have gladly given his life to turn back the hands of time.

"CRACK!" and both thunder and lightning rode each other directly over the attic, halting Steven's performance. Such a clatter caused a shock back into reality and present matters, and a belly full of all that was good began to sour…

Steven left the spotlight to enter darkness. To the little pane of glass, he hobbled, and to peer out upon a world he barely knew. With the help of a few glowing lamplights he saw through the rain to the very center of town. On both sides of a muddy Main Street were thin wooden buildings scrunched together, some one-story—some two-story—but all in desperate need of moist stain. At the far end were a couple machine shops, a white church, and a small park with a half-demolished gazebo, and it was this last sight that soured Steven's stomach even more. It was an ugly reminder of what Westcreek had become, and the little Indian's heart began to hurt. And when he thought of the town elders—when he thought of those responsible for vandalizing the sort of theater—his gut boiled with acid. Such an uncomfortable feeling branched out like lightning, heating his chest and neck, his heart answering with faster beats and occasional palpitations. Stupid fools, he thought.

Stupid, drunken fools...

Steven had to calm his body. With his pulse almost pounding out of his chest, he had to swallow it all down, with heavy gasps of air, a clenched fist, and a gnarled face doing nothing to stem the tide of overpowering sensation. To vomit or not to vomit—that was the question. Steven felt out of control. And sudden anxiety would only murk up his state.

Tomorrow, you see, was an anniversary. Tomorrow he'd visit his father at the far end of town, and he'd have to walk past many of those same elders he so despised. He'd have to leave the sort safety of his attic, his simple home, and be subject to their quiet comments and long, long looks—he'd have to become a discolored and misshapened fish in a bowl of sorts, and such a journey would have to be made alone.

But he felt it was his duty to go. To comfort. To remember some more.

Steven sank to his knees. Drained from the commotion of emotion, he rested his little meager body and to take a second look at tiny Westcreek. He forced himself to remember a simpler, more gentler time, when the sun shone brightly in the valley and hoards of children scampered to hear the tales and see the sorcery of one great man—the last true Chief of the Ojibwe First Nation. He forced himself to remember what life was like and might be like again, and pretty soon that fire down below began to die out. As he rested his head against the scratched windowpane, a sense of peace washed over him, his eyes becoming heavy. The fight was gone. His meager strength resembled Jell-O; he fell asleep in a top hat, cape, and cane, the storm outside continuing and hassling the window.

And Steven's dreams would be wonderful. They would be of his grandfather...

Then lightning flashed and thunder rumbled.

Gloria, a Mother
A door flew open.
Downstairs, in a kitchen small and broken, Gloria and her late-night date returned from a café downtown. Drunk and giddy with laughter, they staggered through the doorway arm in arm, and then began to dance on the cracked linoleum floor, she in a sundress of paneled colors, he in a stained T-shirt and faded jeans. Both were soaking wet. Both were terribly excited.
"Are we crazy, Danny?" Gloria asked, twirling about and to her man's whistling. "I mean, is it happening too fast?"
"It's not happening fast enough," Danny answered, his eyes bloodshot. "If I had my wits about me, I'd gather up the justice of the peace and be done with it all tonight. The ceremony is unimportant. To me, it's our love that matters."
"But are we rushing into things? After all, we've only known each other a few short weeks. I feel like a schoolgirl who needs to be set straight. I mean, I love you dearly, but I'm scared my heart is blinding me. It has in the past, you know. It's like I need someone else to tell me what I should be feeling. So I can be right this time. I know I'm not making much sense." Gloria was dipped.
Danny held her close, stumbling a bit in his next few dance steps. "You're making perfect sense, my dear. You want assurance and I wanna give it to you. Do you remember when we first met?"
"Yes, how could I forget?"
"You just began work at the café. I had rolled into town, looking for lumbering work. And there you were, behind the counter stuffing napkins into a rusted metal holder. God, I was taken by you. All I could see was your beautiful face—I swear. I fumbled over my words just ordering a damn cup of coffee!"
Gloria laughed, gingerly covering her mouth. "I remember."
"I didn't tell you, but from that moment on I wanted to kick the shit out of everybody in the place!"
"What?"
Danny slowed their movements. "I got insanely jealous of all the other men. If they even looked at you—them with all their cheap

come-ons and fancy talk, I wanted to hit 'em. You woke within me an instinct. To protect. To take care of you—not that you need taking care of, okay? I just wanted to put you on a pedestal where no one else could touch. My feelings have only grown since then. Sometimes ya just have to go with your gut instinct. And my gut instinct tells me to marry you. I love you deeply."

"Are you sure?" Gloria asked, vulnerably.

"Without question… now tell me what your gut says…"

Gloria didn't answer. She laid her head upon one of Danny's massive shoulders and began to cry. "Marriage. I never thought I'd be at this point in my life again. I thought Steven's father would be the only man for me. After him, I thought I was doomed to live a life of loneliness in this God-forsaken town."

Danny pulled back, trying to reestablish eye contact. "This is a whole new chapter in both of our lives. A whole new book for that matter. It'll be you and I."

"And Steven, too," she remarked with shyness, her gut stirring a bit. "You forgot Steven…"

"Yes, yes, Steven, too!" he replied in haste. "I want you both on that pedestal. As if all three of our lives had been together from the start. Sincerely." He kissed her lightly on the forehead.

Gloria smiled innocently. "I want him to be a part of our celebration, Danny. Right now." She pushed away and headed for a rickety ladder, beneath a small trapdoor, and in the middle of small hallway. "He's probably in the attic again."

"No!" Danny jumped, grabbing her arm. "Not right now. Please. There'll be plenty of time for the three of us. I swear. He's a wonderful boy. But let's just keep this moment between man and wife. Okay?"

Gloria paused. She looked deep within Danny's eyes for something sincere. "Okay," she said finally. "Later, then…"

"How 'bout just one more drink to toast our future. Before I wash away in all this bliss!" He guffawed and with a flinch, a few dirty white teeth showing.

"All I've got is old gin."

"You're in luck, old gin is my favorite. At least it is now."

Gloria smirked briefly, and then meandered her way passed a Formica island. To a pull-string kitchen light and row after row of mostly chipped cupboards, she went, opening door after door and until she found a little cloudy bottle and two cloudy water glasses.

Her beau was taking a long, hard look.

"Ooohhh," he said with a heavy sigh. "It is a vision of loveliness that stands before me. I can't believe you're gonna be all mine. God has truly blessed me on this night."

And, indeed, Gloria was heavenly. With the body of a sort of Godiva, and yet the stance of a woman who blossomed too soon, she filled her wet sundress with perfect curves and roundness. She appeared soft and tender in the pale kitchen light—almost like a sexier Snow White—and she had the thick black hair to match. Her nipples jutted slightly out as if timid. And her eyes. Her eyes were an alluring blue… but tired.

"Gloria J., Gloria J.," Danny muttered, stumbling his way to her. "I'm finding it hard to wait for the honeymoon. Please forgive me, but I'm having thoughts of making love. Like man and wife. I can't help it."

"We… shouldn't."

Gloria nervously poured a small amount of booze into each of two cloudy glasses. "Tell me again—what our lives will be like. After we leave Westcreek."

"We'll move to the Twin Cities. We'll get a place in the suburbs, that house you've always dreamed of. Small, a huge yard, and surrounded by a white picket fence. I'll scrounge up a good job, maybe at the local lumberyard. You don't have to work another day in your life, if you don't want to. And we'll get Steven enrolled in school. It's his junior year, right?" Danny clumsily grabbed for one of the glasses. As his bloodshot eyes turned more bedroom-like, he cornered Gloria between a rusty sink and a clattering fridge. "Our lives will be perfect."

Gloria hugged the big man with tenderness. With dearness. "When I was a little girl I used to hope that someday, someone would touch my soul, get to the very heart of who I was. See me for all that I am." She paused. Then whispered, "Is it you?"

"Here's to us," Danny slurred, raising his blurred glass. "To a new beginning and a happy home." He gulped the gin down in one swig.

Gloria spoke plainly. "Make love to me…"

In a plain and simple kitchen, two sort of lovers held each other. One overpowered the other, groping body parts and biting flesh like there was no tomorrow; the other just sort of taking it all, hoping and praying for a solid flesh future. The physical show of emotion built in such a way as to send both bumping hard against the sink again and again, one moaning and yet the other wincing. Over and over, this happened, and eventually man and woman retired to a room of white walls and an unmade bed. There a pedestal was touched. There a honeymoon took place.

And in the morning, Gloria awoke without her man. She was all alone, her husband-to-be having left without not so much as a good-bye. She'd spend some time crying. She'd throw verbal tantrums and carry on in self-reproach, her son upstairs and having heard everything.

Again.

THE DEPUTY AND HIS SHERIFF

Just after dawn… after the last of the rain moved out of the valley… and in a clearing busy with activity, a quiet Sheriff Waters stood off by himself near the eastern edge of a massive treeline. He was deep in thought. Appearing chubby in a tan uniform, his badge askew, and his jowls sagging, the man tried to make sense of a most grizzly discovery. Four good friends were dead, you see. Murdered.

But when, he thought? And why?

Eleven men and women cleaned up what remained, carrying out official police business. Most came from the county seat about forty-five minutes from Westcreek and to gather evidence, take pictures, measure distances from body to body and body to gun, and to just mainly bag up the corpses for later autopsy work. The initial investigation was thorough—it went like clockwork, and the whole scene to Sheriff Waters resembled something he remembered from his earlier training back at the academy.

There a documentary was made about a triple homicide that took place in Chicago during the early 70s, showing, quite explicitly, proper police procedure from beginning to end. It was a helpful film for he and the other cadets in his class, and yet the whole premise seemed far-fetched—a big city problem, at best. Surely a small town in North Central Minnesota would not have to deal with such a situation, he thought. Not three murders.

But the real world would do him one better: Sheriff Waters had to contend with a quadruple homicide.

"Jesus Christ," he mumbled under his breath. "What the hell happened here?"

A gray-haired, little man in a heavy black coat approached from the southwest. He was the Pine County Coroner. "We're almost done, Nat. A few more pictures and we'll start back to town with the bodies. Should have autopsy results for you in about forty-eight hours."

"What would you estimate the time of deaths to be?"

"About two, maybe three a.m."

Sheriff Waters sighed and shook his head. "What do you think happened?"

"I don't know. I mean, it could have been internal. Body positioning suggests that the group could've shot each other up. A preliminary wound analysis shows that Bernie was killed by a high-powered weapon. It could've been Bull's rifle."

"And Bull and the twins?"

"Their deaths present a problem." The Coroner looked away.

Sheriff Waters narrowed his fuzzy brows. "What do you mean?"

"He means we're missing key evidence." Deputy Jake Flint, a tall, scrawny man with freckles sauntered down from the northern part of the clearing, his hips swaggering and his hands resting comfortably on a gun belt. "It looks as if a small handgun was used to kill the other three. Maybe .38 caliber. We've combed the whole area and found nothing. Not even shell casings."

Sheriff Waters bit his lip. "Any idea as to why they were here in the first place?"

"Nobody knows," Jake answered confidently. "Their families weren't even aware that they had gone. It's like they just snuck away in the middle of the night. Maybe they were out poaching animals."

"What, a herd of moose?" Sheriff Waters snapped. "The twins alone had enough ammo to start a war, for God's sakes!"

"Maybe they were trying to protect themselves."

"From what?"

Jake calmly, slowly, pulled out a toothpick from inside his coat.

He slid it into a corner of his mouth. "Bernie was always obsessive about planning ahead. Maybe he expected some kind of trouble if they ventured too far onto Reservation land. The guns, the extra shells—maybe they were all just a precaution."

"Ah, that's ludicrous!" Sheriff Waters snorted. "You're talkin' like Dick Tracy!"

"Perhaps. But I do know they weren't alone out here." Jake held out his hand, palm side up. Gripped beneath his fingers was a broken archery arrow tipped by a quartz head. It was dirty and appearing very, very old, colored by three red feathers that dangled, limply. "We found about twenty of these in the area, along with hatchets and other Indian relics. Just inside the mine, by the bodies, was a wooden spear sticking out of the ground. It was covered with eagle feathers."

Sheriff Waters began to panic. Turning to the Coroner, he suddenly felt an overwhelming need for just a conversation between two. "Bill, why don't you start on down. I'd like talk to Jake in private."

"I'll verify the rounds of ammunition used," the Coroner explained. "Send the guns and everything else we've got to the Twin Cities for a ballistics check." He nodded and headed for the center of the clearing.

"Thanks, Bill," Sheriff Waters called after. "Keep in touch."

Both lawmen watched the little man depart, and an uneasy silence lingered. Then Sheriff Waters questioned Jake, suspiciously.

"What are you thinking?"

"Indian shit scattered around a crime scene—it's like Deja Vu. Almost eerie."

"Be specific!"

Jake threw his toothpick into the other corner of his mouth, and then he took a few steps to the north. He peered deep within The Great Forest. "A few years ago a crazy old Indian was suspect of burning a family's home to the ground for building too close to sacred land. Paraphernalia just like this was found near the ashes. The old Indian was known to have a huge collection of ancient artifacts within his home. He had no clear alibi in that case."

33

"Nor a clear motive," Sheriff Waters yelled under his breath, pointing at Jake. "And it was never proved that he did it. We never even had a chance to question him. Mob rule chased him out of town. Lead by you, as I remember, Jake."

"He dabbled in black magic. He cursed people—scared people, posed an immediate threat to our children. We didn't know what he was capable of."

"Aw, shit! Your fears were unfounded!"

Jake turned to face his superior, his nose in the air. "Besides, he didn't go too far, did he? A softhearted sheriff dropped all pending charges. Helped him find a cabin in the woods to live in. Far enough away from town, but close enough so that he could keep an eye on family and be near his people." Jake turned back to the north and pointed up the valley where a small light could be seen far, far in the distance. "That cabin is no more than two hundred yards from this clearing. You and I are probably the only ones who knows he's out here."

"Cut to the chase. What are you saying?"

Jake went right up to Sheriff Waters. "I'm saying we have four murders, a missing weapon, and very little to go on. Procedure in any investigation calls for creating a pool of suspects—a pool of witnesses, at the very least. Decoreous fits in there somewhere. Now I'm not saying he had anything to do with these deaths. Maybe the four did kill each other for some unknown, Godly reason. I don't know. But I'm betting the old man saw something—heard something, and maybe even knows where the gun is. It's a place to start."

"Go easy, Jake," Sheriff Waters cautioned.

The deputy tilted his nose back up into the air. "Do *you* have any theories as to what happened up here, Nat? Any suspects, any witnesses?"

Sheriff Waters said nothing.

"Then work with me. Don't let *skin color* blind you this time. I want the truth. They were my friends, too." Jake left his superior's side with dramatics. He headed for the middle of the clearing where the initial investigation was all but over, his body sway exaggerated.

"Jake!" Sheriff Waters called after him. "Jake, look at me!"

The deputy turned with reluctance.

"I want this done by the book. Nothing less."

"By the book," Jake spoke, spitting his toothpick casually to the ground. "Of course, what did you expect?" He didn't wait for a reply. He showed his rear. Walking with even more of a swagger, he headed for a group of county officials only too willing to share what they knew. They looked up to Jake, you see. They sort of pined for his attention and nonverbal accolades.

And Sheriff Waters, again, stood alone. His deputy's parting words did little to lighten the load upon his conscience. He wanted to call after Jake a second time and to clarify exactly what would be done next and according to "the book," and yet somehow the words just wouldn't come out. Something was in the way, blocking his will from deep within. Sheriff Waters had a tumor—a sort of cancer of the spirit, if you will, that had caused indecisiveness and helplessness on more than one occasion. It had emerged many years ago as the result of a personal altercation on a dark summer's eve, and it had pained him ever since. Jake knew about the cancer. The whole town knew.

Fighting back a sudden urge to break down, the chief law authority in Westcreek shifted his attention up the valley and to the small light that glowed somberly through the darkness of the forest. Jake was right. Decoreous would have to be questioned, and such a visit would mark eight years since anyone had seen the Indian Elder. Granted peace in regards to letting him live out the remainder of his life would have to be revoked. It had to be. Too many questions loomed about this tragedy. Maybe he could provide some answers. But the thought of facing Decoreous again arose a certain amount of pain within the cancer of Sheriff Waters. It brought back memories the good sheriff couldn't push out of awareness.

He threw his eyes to the middle of the clearing, and the images captured wouldn't help matters much. A slow procession of bodies made their way down the valley and back toward Westcreek. Near the front, four black bags contained the bloody remains of four good friends. It was like slabs of meat being carried away, for slaughter, he thought. So lifeless. So cold. The good sheriff sighed with heaviness.

He whispered to himself. "What the hell happened here? Where will this investigation lead?" The sort of cancer's pain flared. "What will this investigation lead to?"

Sheriff Waters was the last to leave the clearing, stepping off of Indian land and back onto White. A new storm was building on the western horizon. As Sheriff Waters moved back toward Westcreek—almost with agitation, larger clouds came about, sprung with billowy heat and to seemingly counter cool breezes.

Indeed, the atmosphere became even more unsettled.

In a small office with a small desk and a small file cabinet, Sheriff Waters tried to relax. He was tired—mentally exhausted and looking for some kind of comfort. In a space no bigger than a good-sized kitchen, he plopped his big frame into a squeaky chair, and then he stared into a desk lamp that barely provided enough light to read by. The shades were all pulled. Sheriff Waters was alone, save for the occasional drip that dropped into a bucket near the front door, and maybe being that alone was the whole problem. You see, Sheriff Waters' heart rate was picking up. He began to feel antsy. It was just too quiet. There just seemed to be too much time to think, and in the past such an environment almost invariably lead to a rehashing of sorts—a kind of medley of visions and sounds related to the past, and this morning would prove to be no different.

The lawman tried to focus on some other stimulus as a diversion, and loud conversation through an open window caught his ears. It was coming from the café across the street. Jake and a few townsfolk, those both young and old, were meeting over whisky and vodka and to honor Bernie, Bull, and the twins. It was a sort of wake without the bodies and full of drunken memories and other cheap talk. The good sheriff was asked to be a part of the gathering, you see, but he couldn't stomach attending. It was one decision he didn't have a hard time making. But he wished he could've heard their conversations. As he focused on their mostly muffled words, he wished he could've been a little mouse in a corner—a sort of "non-entity" and in order to hear their topics. Were they truly toasting the dead, he wondered? Or were they all cussing and getting riled up over old matters again? Most importantly, was Jake sharing any privileged information? It was so hard to hear—so hard to tell what they were saying and such an endless array of possibilities only skyrocketed Sheriff Waters' heart rate and worries, his diversion technique gradually failing. The lawman was doomed to remember a personal tragedy—it often crept up on him when he felt the most powerless.

He leaned forward. He removed his tan hat and rubbed his balding temples as if trying to stretch his face straight. Then the vision came... of responding to a break-in at the town liquor store exactly five years ago. It was a call not out of the ordinary, for the little shop had had its share of burglaries. Most times it was just an Indian from the Reservation or a laid-off White miner needing a little cash and a whole lot of liquid spirit, and on this particular night the good sheriff decided to investigate on his own. Without Jake. You see, usually a good scolding was all that was needed to rectify the situation, but sometimes jail, a conversation with the tribal council, if applicable, and/or repayment byway of damages was also required. But not on this night. On this call something went horribly wrong. Indeed.

More visions came: of shattered glass around a broken door... of a busted cash register... of flashlight sweeps... of a frightened Indian face at the back of the store... and, finally, of a fistful of money and a knife, and that's when Sheriff Waters' instinct kicked in. He drew a gun. Adhering to protocol, he pointed the black barrel of his pistol directly at the man, shouting, "Drop your weapon!" and "Get down!"

Both requests were honored.

But then all subsequent happenings appeared as if in slow motion.

Still more visions came to the lawman: of a lightning flash... of the perpetrator cowering... of a pistol hammer dropping without the slightest pressure on the trigger... and of the perpetrator jerking violently as a hunk of metal entered his spinal column. Sheriff Waters had shot an unarmed thief. On his way out. In the back. Dead.

Back in the office, Sheriff Waters rubbed his temples and shook his head. The thoughts just wouldn't subside. They called for present-day understanding. Because of that night, a boy went fatherless and a wife slept alone. He had single-handedly destroyed an entire family. An Indian family, at that, and such a prevailing characteristic caused only a slight grief reaction from Westcreek proper; more for the town sheriff—his mistake, and less for the dead man and his survivors. Sheriff Waters seemed literally alone in his feelings.

He leaned forward in his squeaky chair and opened a metal drawer on the left side of his desk. Inside, beneath notepads, a stapler, and gummy tape, was a black pistol that hadn't seen a holster in almost five years. The good sheriff ruled his jurisdiction with mostly strong words and the occasional billy club, and so the weapon appeared dangerous, as if a snake that might strike out. But uncertain times could call for drastic measures, he thought. A killer in the valley, or more likely, civil unrest that may arise as a result of the ensuing investigation and/or careless words shared in a smoky café, could require law enforcement's most peaceable tool.

And the big man shook. The thoughts—the memories started all over again, and he found himself unable to decide: to carry or not to carry—that was the question, and finally he simply switched off the desk lamp and tried to focus on the slow dripping of water into a half-full bucket. Drip… drip… drip, was heard.

Diversion was given another chance.

Drip… drip… drip.

THE ANNIVERSARY

It was business as usual in downtown Westcreek.

Men and women, about thirty or so, young and old, hung around a muddy Main Street, rekindling friendships stifled by a string of storms that seemed endless. In front of the old wooden buildings and atop cracked boardwalk they talked an ear off or two beneath doorways, near soaped-up windows, and while leaning against wooden railings used almost a hundred years ago to tie up horses. Topics of conversation shifted from the four murders, to job prospects, back to the four murders, and then ultimately, to treaty rights and treaty violations. It was the latter that drew the most heated debate—the most scornful nonverbals, and townspeople were gradually able to get close again. Perhaps even closer than before. Indeed.

But business as usual in Westcreek was about to be interrupted. The whole scene was suddenly about to resemble a sort of "high noon."

Steven hobbled-in from the east end, and it was almost like an outlaw was coming. The little Indian had long since lost his magical attire and now presented himself in a simple gray shirt, a holey pair of blue jeans, and an even holeyer pair of sneakers. In his hand he held a little bouquet of flowers, his eyes staring straight ahead, to the west, and to a little white church. Step... and slide, he walked. Step... and slide, and the closer to town center he got, the more talking ceased and the more a sort of fishbowl effect took over. The thirty or so men and women just stared, suddenly consumed by a myriad of thoughts—some harmless... some hurtful.

Just past the general store, on his right side, Steven attracted the gazes of a rotund man in an apron and a young miner with messy blond hair. Both were surprised by the half-breeds appearance, considering he was thought to be a total recluse—a sort of Hunchback of Notre Dame figure. Few even knew he was still living in town, and anyway, the two men reacted with looks of curiosity, maybe slight suspicion. What did the boy know about last night's tragedy, they wondered? Did he know anyone capable of committing such horrible acts? Could he identify someone with a stash of Native American weapons?

Steven continued on his way.

Between a little hardware store and a soaped up window on the North side of town, three unemployed lumberjacks with dirty white T-shirts stepped off the boardwalk in a show of force-type motion. They walked slowly toward Steven. And then stopped. Crossing their arms and narrowing their eyes, they stood as if expecting some kind of trouble—maybe wanting some kind of trouble, and new questions were raised, silently. How many more Indians do we have to fear, at least one thought? How many from the nearby Reservation would do us harm? And how many do we still have to run out of this valley? The three men kept a watchful eye on their sudden object of mistrust. But the challenge they hoped for would not materialize. Steven went onward.

In front of the café, on the right side, and closer to the western edge of downtown, the little Indian attracted his most intense stares. Jake was there. So was Bull's oldest son, Trace, an almost mirror image of the slain father. And so was a retired trapper in a heavy, plaid shirt. Leaning against one of the old wooden railings, all three emitted varying degrees of emotional heat. And Trace was the hottest. He wanted to bludgeon the boy. Wrenching his hands in the wood and grinding his big teeth, he stared so hard as to almost look through Steven, and yet his eyes were right on the boy. Every solid muscle in Trace's arms, chest, and neck tested the thin fabric of his red windbreaker. Such a hatred spewed from the man that it chilled Steven, and so he picked up his pace.

The old trapper's heat wasn't quite as hot, but it was still unnerving. The White town elder knew very little about last night's events but he was able to fuel his look with past experience. He hated the Ojibwe First Nation. Behind his beady little eyes he kept a firsthand history of Indian injustices: of teenagers breaking into his home and stealing valuables; of property sizes shrinking because of revised treaties; and of trapping, hunting, and fishing rights being limited for Whites yet increased for "Indigenous Peoples." Not even his own government would listen to his concerns. Frequent calls and at least one physical visit to the Pine County Court House resulted in "wishy-washiness"—that is, a sort of tamed political rhetoric that appeased the emotional state of most complainants and yet slumbered any resulting action. Indian-White relations were often considered a "hands off" matter, and so the old trapper bore the brunt of resulting stress put upon he and his family. He felt it was all grossly unfair, and thus the scorn he wafted toward Steven was a strengthening of Trace's emotional heat.

That left Jake. He added very little to the downtown portrait. His bony face conveyed neither like or dislike, his eyes covered by a pair of silver shades. The deputy seemed removed from the situation, like an innocent bystander at the scene of an accident, just watching—just waiting to see what other people would do. Waiting to see what would happen next; waiting for something... something to happen. His chin lackadaisically followed Steven's movements.

At the very western edge of downtown, the little Indian stopped. He glanced back over his shoulder, at the deputy, and with somewhat wanting eyes. He waited for some form of warm acknowledgment—some form of response—and returned to him was neither a frown nor a smile, just simply a shimmer off of a pair of silver shades. But he did have Jake's attention. He could sense it. Steven faced back to the west. He drooped his head and pondered. Just briefly. Then he left downtown. Step... slide, he went. Step... slide.

Conversations resumed amongst the thirty or so, first hushed and then louder. As if someone had suddenly given the order to talk again, men and women discussed the four murders, job prospects, the four murders again, and, ultimately, treaty rights and treaty violations.

But not Jake. His chin continued to follow Steven. Only Steven. And with little consternation or respect. Just simplicity. Just a look.

AMOS

Steven veered from his preset course. Just briefly. He shot off toward the town park, for he wanted to step upon the gazebo again—he wanted to remember a most pleasant birthday just once more.

And the gazebo was in ruins. Only partially intact, and with four broken sets of stairs, chipped railings, and a weathered top being the most endearing qualities, the structure was being overtaken by weeds. The weeds were popping up all over the grounds and underneath, showing through the cracks in the floor and where wood began to rot. The structure had seen many a better day, it would seem. Still, to the almost man it was and always would be a house of magic and beauty that neither time nor neglect could ever erase. Indeed.

With a flush of joy in his cheeks, Steven carefully ascended a set of stairs. The memories returned almost immediately. He could almost see the many feet dangling and spinning around the roof in an orderly fashion. He could almost hear the unbridled laughter. He could almost feel the sudden cool air.

And on this day, he'd be the sort of ride engineer. In a state of deep make-believe, he'd be the sorcerer and have to be vigilant in regards to controlling all components involved. Just like his grandfather. Just like so many years ago. He closed his eyes.

Still holding the bouquet of flowers, Steven spread his arms and danced a sort of broken waltz. One, two, three, he went. One, two, … three, and he moved to the north, to the east, to the south, and to the west, over and over again, in that fashion, stumbling atop broken boards here and there, moist with wear. And the imagined magic was working. The visions were solid. Steven felt connected to the make-believe children and their rising and falling. He felt as if he was one with the winds, dictating proper speed, height, and spacing. Steven was master. *He* orchestrated the fun. The whole experience in reality was intoxicating to the little Indian—relaxing. One, two, three, he waltzed about with an opened-mouth smile. One, two,… three, and then suddenly his imagination and all the children within came tumbling down.

A dirty old hand grabbed his wrist.

"What the hell's ya doin' here, boy!" a hoarse voice yelled. "Ya causin' trouble? Huh? Answer me, boy!" The voice seemed paranoid.

"Who are you?" Steven asked fearfully, recoiling to a corner of the Gazebo. "What do you want?"

Amos stepped closer. He was a short, stout, scruffy old Indian with an emotional forehead. In a greasy pair of bib overalls, he stank of cheap whisky and b.o.

"Don't know me, eh?" he said. "Yer granddaddy never spoke of me, eh? Where is the old fool? What's he up to?"

"My grandfather is gone."

"Sure of that, are's ya?"

Steven pulled his wrist away but to no benefit. "Yes."

"Oh, but he isn't!" Amos jumped with pressured speech. "He is here! Alive and well and's within the valley. Readies to menace, I say!"

"You're lying…"

"Is I?"

Steven looked deep within Amos' eyes. They were big and brown and shaky, as if a man on the edge and waiting for a catastrophe to occur. "My grandfather was driven out of this town many years ago. He's far away. Maybe dead."

Amos puckered his face in seriousness. "They'd likes you to think that, boy. Chasing him away—a great White solution to a mores complicated, Indian matter. Hears me: a great White solution to a more complicated, Indian matter. The man is bounds by ancestral duties. Our people won't tolerates his absence. They need someone to watch over them. He's be just far enough away as to not cause problems. Until now, that is."

"No," Steven whispered, pulling at his wrist again.

"He is here! You know it is true! Search deep within your heart for the answer! He is alive and makings trouble for all of us!"

The little Indian shook his head.

"Now, boy, listen to me. He will tries to seek you out. To be near his kin during this time of great uncertainty. Tells him to stop his crazy rampage! His murdering and carrying on! He's got to leave this valley! There's can be no peace for yous and I with him around. He will bring war where war hasn't existed for a hundred years!" He jiggled Steven, his mucky hands at shoulder height. "Tell him what's I tells you! Tell him what Amos said!"

And Steven just stared, with fright, the seeming crazy words not making sense.

Amos sniffed loudly. He lowered his nose to the bouquet and smiled a smile of brown teeth. "Pretties for the pretty? For your father, I suspect. 'Tis an anniversary? Precious, precious, it is." A winking eye was brought up to Steven. "When yous sees him, gives him a kiss for me. Gives him a kiss from his old uncle Amos!" He ended with a hacking chuckle, insane-like.

With all his wee-like might, Steven busted away from the hold. Terrified and hurt, he fled the beloved gazebo and with a quick hobble, heading further up Main Street, away from the citizenry proper, and away from Amos. Westcreek just wasn't safe. Steven would've given anything to be suddenly back within the attic.

The short and stout, old Indian shouted after him. "Tells yer granddaddy what's I says! Tell him to get out of the valley before it's too late for all of us! He is evil, I say! Evil!"

Amos' look turned suspicious. His forehead wrinkled terribly, and then he ran to a nearby railing to check on a few puffy clouds that passed overhead. Was there a hand in their making besides that of Mother Nature, he wondered? And how about the winds: were they conjured up to the contrary of the jet stream?

Amos sniffed.

Everything must have been within normal limits, for he sighed with disappointment. He was no closer to finding the boy's grandfather, and yet he knew he was very near. He felt him. What treachery was yet to be unleashed upon the valley, he questioned? Was a long-standing peace accord about to be ripped to shreds? And how would his own miserable existence in Westcreek be affected?

The old Indian sort of knew the answers. Indeed.

A dash around a corner… a slowing of speed… a few spastic breaths, and Steven had made a clean getaway. He leaned against the west wall of the church to gather back his energy and realign his thoughts. Meeting Amos was traumatic. On the other side of the church was greater Westcreek, and he seemed distant from it all. In front of Steven lie a small cemetery bordered by a dull white fence. He had reached his objective. It was time to fulfill a duty. It was time to comfort and remember.

Steven headed for a far corner of a plot of land. He passed over old White graves that held pioneers who died of such things as malaria, typhus, overexposure, and wounds sustained during various military skirmishes, some with Indians. Each grave was pristinely kept and marked by either a marble or white sandstone marker. Flowers could be found here and there, but generally most of the cemetery's inhabitants had few surviving relatives, so remembrance seemed a thing of the past—historical past even, and for Steven the place was very much a part of the present and maybe destined to be his future. He needed to be with family, you see.

A good distance away from the other markers, in the remote southeast corner of the plot, he stopped before a simple rock. It was black with white flecks, sitting before a rectangular patch of earth covered with weeds and heavy clover.

Steven quickly felt at home.

He spoke to that rock. "Lazy Boy was always tired. Always sleeping. On the morning of The Great Hunt, he could not be awoken, and so the village men left without him. They were off to track the swift deer and to gather food. They were gone for days. And when they didn't return, the women began to sob."

"The wind spirits," Steven continued, "awoke Lazy Boy and told him that the village men were devoured by a Great White Monster, deep within the forest. Lazy Boy did not know what to do, so he lay back down to sleep. In his dreams the Thunderbird visited and whispered instructions on how to kill the beast. Lazy Boy awoke to find a magical knife within his hand."

The little Indian looked to the sky. "Lazy boy waited until dusk. Then he searched for the Great White Monster, finding it lying upon a lush riverbank. The beast was stuffed. It was much too full from eating. Too full to defend itself. With very little effort, Lazy Boy killed the Great White Monster, slitting its belly wide open and releasing all the men that were lost. Back at the village, everyone celebrated Lazy Boy's courage. Everyone... except Lazy Boy. He simply... fell back asleep."

"That was your favorite tale, father," Steven said, his heavy eyes again on the stone. "One you told me over and over. But I can't help but wonder: Where is the hero for our people? Why won't the thunderbird save us? The village is empty, with some being pushed onto Reservations and others... just fading away. I'm left here with just memories of Grandfather. Nothing else."

He closed his eyes, tightly. "You said that family was the true nature of the soul. You taught me to rally around loved ones in times of pain or loneliness. But that's not possible. I think mother died with you. She spends her days chasing after men without honor. Her soul is muddied by booze and other evils. I don't think she can see through it. I don't think she can see me. So I die with her. Not even Grandfather's magic can change that."

Steven opened his eyes, a small amount of water spilling out. He bent down to the grave and to place his little bouquet upon the weeds and clover. "Father," he whispered, "five years ago today you were gunned down in cold blood. They called it an accident. But there are no accidents in Westcreek. I am here to never forget and to never forgive. And though I know you're at peace, though I know you walk amidst the clouds and play with deer and other animals of the forest, I can't help but to pray for vengeance. A way to pay back their pain, tenfold. Please forgive me, father."

Steven rose with difficulty and to a stand. With his heart racing and his breaths their shortest, he reflected one last time upon the simple black stone with white flecks. *"Nin wanakia,"* he said in the Ojibwe tongue. *"Nin wanakia, nin wâgashkawa."*

He left the small cemetery.

The crippled boy traveled still further north on Main Street. With his fists clenched and his head down, he tottered to the towering jack pine and scattered birch. Following the tree line border back around in a half-circle path, and in an effort to circumvent downtown, he heard hissing and other strange noises coming from deep within The Great Forest. They were unsettling sounds, indeed, even somewhat threatening, but he thought anything was better than facing that fishbowl thing again.

Anything.

A MOTHER
AND SON

Gloria staggered out of her room, looking anything but pretty. It was the middle of the afternoon. She resembled Snow White on a bad hair day, and smudged lipstick, cracked makeup, and a wrinkled nightshirt did little to improve things. Danny was long gone. Visually, and noticed not next to her person in bed, he skipped town—possibly frustrated with the lack of work, and maybe just having gotten what he wanted; Gloria and her son were left behind. Again. And the only comforts within the modest home to ponder over such a turn of events was a pot of cold coffee and a smoke, and Gloria moved into the kitchen for both. Slowly.

She searched for a mug in one of the cupboards. Nothing found. She searched in a couple more and yielded the same results, and that's when she slammed one of the doors. "Shit!" she said in anything but Disney fashion. Her temples began to throb. Rubbing them with shaky fingers only mildly decreased the pain, and so she sought out a cigarette from a nearby broken drawer. She had to try and relax. Her day was just beginning, you see.

Footsteps were heard above. "Steven?" she said with a bit of a whine. "Baby, I'm up. Come on down for some breakfast… lunch… or, whatever the hell time it is. I gotta get back to the café. Seems like I just left that place." She found an old lighter in the bottom of a drawer, low on butane but still able to light a cigarette fiery red. "Steven?" She took a long drag.

There was no answer. The footsteps above seemed to be moving away from the ladder. Toward the little attic window.

"Your mother did it again," Gloria groaned with a confession-like tone. "Fell hook, line, and sinker for a cute face and a lot of words. I thought Danny was different. I thought he really had love and could provide the best for you and I. But we were just a lie. All the men in this town are nothing but a lie, Steven. Guess I reap what I sow, eh?" Taking a bigger drag off her cigarette, she turned and leaned over the Formica Island. "Your father used to always say I solved problems like a child. Guess he was right."

Suddenly losing what little emotional composure she had, Gloria sort of convulsed. She pounded a wimpy fist atop the counter and began to whimper, terribly. "Goddamn it, I hate him for being in that store! I hate the cops being there! Five years… and it only seems like yesterday. It still doesn't seem real. I almost wanna dig up his coffin and see for myself if he's inside. Really—Goddamn it! Or maybe I just wanna crawl in with him, I can't be sure. I'm just tired of this pain. I miss your father so very much, Steven. Jesus! The way he used to hold me at night. His gentle words when I was sad. And those that set me straight when I needed it. I even miss his temper. Sometimes especially his temper"

"Do you remember when we first moved to Westcreek? I miss the piggyback rides he used to give you all over our yard. I never heard you laugh so hard, Steven. Never so hard. "'Round and 'round the shrubs and apple trees, you two went. Jesus!"

She approached the ladder in the small hallway, taking a shorter drag off her cigarette. "I know you don't approve of how I act. I can't say that I'm any too proud, either. I slosh myself for the company of men, I know. But I made a promise to your father. At his grave I promised to take care of both of us, anyway I could. And look." She swept her hand without rhythm through the air. "This place is falling apart. We're going broke. Your father didn't leave us a dime. His family's poorer than we are, and my family won't talk to me. We're desperate, Steven. We've got to get out of this town."

"So what if I trick a man into loving me, into thinking he's my world? We have to survive. We have to be taken care of. Love can be gotten later. Ya know what I mean? It's… the idea of being loved, anyway, right?"

"But who's really being tricked, eh? Who's really being fucked over, huh? I'm sorry. So sorry."

"Am I making any sense?" Gloria asked the trapdoor. "Do you understand that we can't make it on our own? We just can't." She batted a tear from her cheek. "I wish you'd talk to me. Your silence hurts. Call me a slut or tell me to go to hell, just say something! I don't wanna lose you, too, Steven."

Not a word or sound came from above.

Gloria became terribly uncomfortable. She became nervous, almost like a shy schoolgirl called on by her teacher for an answer, and torn between responding and crawling into her desk. She was powerless. She fidgeted. She rubbed her temples again and then whispered to Steven.

"Okay," she said. "Okay… I see. Nothing's any different between us… I'm sorry. I can understand. I embarrass you. God help me. I embarrass myself. But I'm going to get us out of this place. As soon as possible."

Gloria stepped away from the ladder, meekly, and toward her bedroom, her voice trailing off. "Good-bye, son. I won't be home until late. I'll bring you back somethin' to eat."

And the sort of Snow White got ready for work, early. Nursing aches and pains all over her body, she wandered into a space of few comforts and very few furnishings, a part of her seeming left behind. A long shift was ahead.

But maybe a new lumberjack or miner will stroll into town, naively looking for work, she thought. Maybe a man of truer intentions will sit at the counter, make eye contact, and give a smile. Maybe she'd finally find that sort of prince she so desired.

Just maybe.

Steven leaned against the little attic window. From his crow's nest view of the world, he heard every word uttered by his mother— he felt every breath exhaled, and as he watched her walk plainly out the front door, he wanted to scream—to run after her. It was hard remaining still. He loved his mother, dearly. It's just that the fire in his belly would not understand "the promise" nor tolerate any kind of reconciliation, and so he simply continued to watch, with longing. And in silence.

And he remembered a softer time—a picnic many years ago with his father and mother. It took place near the top of the valley, and after a long morning of forest hiking and exploring. The three spread out an Indian quilt upon the earth, pulling a bounty of breads, meats, and fruit from a wooden basket, and then ate as if starving. But it wasn't the food that the almost man remembered most. Nor the vibrant earthen tones of the quilt. No—nor the legendary tales of Indian heroics that his father told. Rather, it was the dancing—dancing between two.

Steven had visions of his father and mother. He had visions of his father standing suddenly, offering his hand in a sort of courtship, and his mother being hoisted upwards and into a pair of strong arms. Moving to only the beat of laughter and giggling—she in a white flowing dress-like pullover—the two turned in circles with the fervor of a couple just married. And their eyes—they never lost sight of each other. Blue eyes stared into brown, and it was as if the world suddenly stopped. Suddenly froze. Or maybe just suddenly didn't exist. They made love with just their spirits. Truly. Steven thought they resembled a music box winding down. The two moved slower and slower, and it seemed as if their bodies melded into each other, becoming one. They had one thought. One feeling. One heartbeat. Before long they had come to an absolute halt, laughter's beat dying off into love's stillness. The two just stood there, locked in each other's arms—locked in each other's gaze—brown and blue becoming gray. And Steven was there to witness it all. He had never seen his mother such a glow.

And, he would never see his mother such a glow again.

Back in the attic, Steven's eyes were closed. Such an array of images skipped his heart and pained his belly, and he was in need of comfort. He'd try to find it within the old black chest. Crawling on his hands and knees and to the center of the attic, he tossed back the lid and retrieved the top hat, cape, and cane. He wanted so badly to perform magic, even if only in his mind. It was all he felt he had.

Maybe I'll perform new tricks deep within the woods, he thought. During a picnic. Maybe I'll conjure up family and entertain them with love.

And a new dance unfolded.

But this particular show would not go unnoticed. It was as if the attic suddenly sprouted eyes and a mouth, and to the off-beats of Steven's movements.

"Steven," a whispering voice said from seemingly everywhere. "Steven, come to me."

The little Indian pivoted about, looking upwards and downwards, and soon after he heard what seemed to be twenty or so rodents scampering across the roof. Earily.

"Steven," the whispering voice said again. "Steven, bring your magic to me."

Was he going crazy, he wondered? Were the town elders playing tricks on him? Where did the words come from and what could make such a racket from above? There were many questions, only one with an immediate answer.

"Steven…"

The voice became more localized. It seemed to be coming from outside, and so Steven crawled back to the window and with both curiosity and fright. He looked about sporadically. First downtown. Then further west. Then somewhat south. And finally, north, his neck crimping a bit in an effort to see what he could see. And there by the tree line was an unusual sight: a human figure appeared to be standing—just standing all alone, staring back at Steven.

The storm front had finally reached the edge of Westcreek, and so the little Indian had trouble making out all the details. But it seemed like a man stood by a tall fir tree just a few yards up the valley. The man was tall, a bit stout, dressed in a robe of earthen tones and leaning on what looked like a wooden staff. But the face… the face was fuzzy.

"Steven," the voice whispered even softer. "Dance with me. Bring me your love."

A chill engulfed Steven's spine. His heart felt terribly warm, and he began to imagine the unimaginable. Was the crazy old Indian right, he wondered? Was his grandfather really alive and seeking him out? Or had all his dreaming and wishful thinking caused a sort of mirage?

"It can't be," he mumbled. "I thought I'd never see you again."

"Come to me..."

The man did not move... Steven continued to question, and finally, he trusted his heart. Almost leaving his skin behind— shaking even, he bolted from the window and descended the ladder, barely allowing a second to elapse while grabbing a light, gray jacket. He then flew out the kitchen door with no reserve. He had to get closer. He had to check his heart's honesty—his gut's pleasure.

"Grandfather?" he yelled. "Is that you?" He approached tentatively.

There was no answer. But Steven didn't need one. He hobbled toward the figure like a passenger about to miss the train ride of a lifetime, and behind was left the security of his little home. The kitchen door remained open and yet Steven could've cared less. He was hopefully on his way to a reunion.

"Grandfather!"

The closer he got the further back into The Great Forest the man seemed to drift. The little Indian was making very little headway. A few feet into the trees, he stopped and assessed the situation. Going on meant stumbling blindly through heavy brush, maybe getting lost, and encountering who knows what. But returning to his home of plywood colors and the little hollow above meant returning to an empty village where only the past provided warmth.

Steven was antsy for something in the present.

"Grandfather?" he called again.

Still no response.

Without much thought, he continued into the forest and up the valley, chasing a sort of specter that gradually disappeared altogether. Lightning stuttered gently on the horizon and a new wind blew from the southwest as if to push or carry Steven along. But toward what, one might ask? And toward who?

And Steven's journey would not be made alone. He had companions. Near the tops of the jack pine and birch, twenty or so sort of animals jumped about from limb to limb, just out of view, hissing occasionally and carrying on in gibberish. The little Indian had made his train, it seemed.

But the ride to the final stop—what he hoped was the final stop, would be anything but pleasurable. Indeed.

It would be down right Earie.

MOB RULE

Having completed a full day of police business related to the four murders, Sheriff Waters came back to his small office on Main Street, alone. The case was progressing not. Matter of fact, the mystery deepened. As he sat once again, solidly, in his squeaky chair—as he reflected on what he knew about the deaths and circumstances of the previous night, he began to perspire. His armpits began to drip, and some of the uncomfortable feeling was due to the warm office temperature; most, however, was due to anxiety. You see, Sheriff Waters felt that he was racing against a sort of town clock.

He rubbed his big nose and thought. The county coroner's office called earlier to confirm initial suspicions. Bernie was killed by a high-powered rifle, and they were ninety-five percent sure it was Bull's. The other three were killed by a .38 caliber handgun. Ballistics tests from the Twin Cities were still pending, but even if they pointed to an internal affair, even if they could prove who shot who and with what, the theory was still moot: a key murder weapon was unaccounted for. Where the hell was it, Sheriff Waters questioned? Where was the .38 caliber handgun?

Town interviews conducted during the day shed little light on the whereabouts of the weapon or on the case, as a whole. Nobody saw or heard anything. Everyone had a firm alibi. Most stayed indoors on account of the bad storms, and even more disheartening was the fact that no one could even venture a guess as to why four grown men would wander around in a forest late at night, heavily armed. No prior conversations were recalled. No suspicious behavior was witnessed, beforehand. And no notes or journals kept by the four, if any, were discovered by family or friends. It was like Bernie, Bull, and the twins were found dead in another country, and Westcreek was on the outside looking in. The good sheriff was at square one.

Maybe even a few steps back.

He peered out through a small window on the west wall. Staring at brighter and brighter flashes of light on the horizon, he wondered about the arrows, hatchets, and spears found at the crime scene. Was there truly an Indian hand in things? Or was there a conspiracy, like his illing gut told him, a sort of diversion away from what was simply a tragedy among friends? Questions…

Still more questions loomed.

And pressure. Sheriff Waters felt pressure from his conscience, pressure from Jake, pressure from the town, pressure from "the law book," and everything as a whole seemed to get hung up in that tumor of his. His stomach hurt something fierce. Maybe it was time to call in outside help, he said silently. Maybe it was time to call in a second opinion. Procedure was becoming less and less clear.

Just then, Amos came stumbling though the door. "Sheriff!" he yelled with slurred speech. "Sheriff, what ya doin' to bring justice to my peoples?"

"Get the hell out of here, Amos!" Sheriff Waters barked. "You're stinkin' drunk again!"

"Whisky calms the nerves. Helps, it does, during times like these. I's surprised yer not in similar shape." He wove his way to the lawman's desk. "Ya gonna throw me in jail?"

"I might."

"A pity. Just ones more distractions for ya. But it might be safer for me in here."

"What do you want?" Sheriff Waters barked again.

Amos leaned against the desk for support. Then he narrowed his eyes in seriousness. "Almost a hundred years ago our nations came to a table in this very valley. To signs a paper that would end all wars and spells out how life would be. For Indians. For Whites. Through the years, both sides would test that paper. A riot here… a riot there—a dispute every now and then, yes. But peace would hold. Hears me: peace would hold!"

"What are you getting at, Amos?" Sheriff Waters said, losing patience.

"The town. She's full of unrest, the likes I's never seen. Yer people are a buzz over Redskins coming back to the valley. To murder more than just four, they thinks! Crazy it all is! Gossip! But energy builds! It could threaten these years of tolerance! Nows what ya going to do to keep the peace for me's and my people?"

Sheriff Waters stood. He peered with wavering commitment deep into the dirty Indian's, glossy eyes. "As I told you earlier, an investigation is underway concerning four suspicious deaths. Any civil unrest that may arise as a result of this investigation shall be dealt with accordingly and by the law."

Amos danced around with mirth, his forehead wrinkled, his laughter hoarse. "Of course, of course—a great White solution to a great White problem! Yes, yes, a great White solution to a great White problem!" He became still, almost falling over. "Those suspicious deaths, Sheriff: Who's yer main suspect? Me?"

"At the time, you were passed out in front of the café."

"Dones yer homework, Sheriff. That you have." Amos leaned over the desk, cupping his mouth as if to pass along a secret. "Then who, maybe still of the Red kind? Decoreous? He's still here, eh? Still around?"

Sheriff Waters turned sheet white. He moved quickly around the desk and to confront Amos. "Who told you that?"

"No one."

"Tell me, dammit!"

Amos pointed at the good sheriff's chest. "No one. I felt him. Here…"

"What do you know about Decoreous?"

"That he's crazy—crazier than I and not above murdering. Here me, Sheriff: there can be no peace with him around. I's and my people demand justice. Run him out of this valley—this State, for all I care, like ya shoulda done before! Do your 'investigation,' but do it quickly. A near hundred years without war may come to an end." He smiled, slyly. "But then maybe our sheriff won't have an office left to hide in."

Sheriff Waters looked away with irritation. "Get the hell out of here, Amos. Go sober up!"

"Not in this town," he answered, an eye winking. "Surely not at this time." To the door, he wobbled. "Careful where you tread, Sheriff. If yous goes and talks to that Indian. The forest... she ain't always what she seems."

But Amos didn't leave.

Outside a disturbance was noticed of both sight and sound. In the middle of Main Street a crowd assembled, numbering nearly thirty light faces. The crowd was full of angry chatter and lit up by lanterns and torches. They came for Sheriff Waters.

Amos grinned. "Looks like I's aint the only one lookin' for answers. Now, how 'bout that great White solution?"

Sheriff Waters shook. His eyes and ears were hurting. He'd been there before, and once again he'd have to face a lot of sort of paranoid misgivings. He'd have to face a town's power in numbers. So with a hard swallow, a deep breath, and a slight wince from that sort of tumor within, he headed for the door plagued by indecision and sweating even more. The town clock had struck midnight. Time was up.

Amos watched Sheriff Waters. He seemed to enjoy the man's uneasiness. Matter of fact, and judging by his taller stance and brighter eyes, the scruffy old Indian appeared a bit more sober. Just a bit.

Just a bit more in control than before.

A sea of White, tense faces greeted Sheriff Waters as he stepped out and onto the boardwalk. Three generations of friends and neighbors were arranged in a tight half-circle in front of him, not a one saying a word and yet all asking a hundred harsh questions with their eyes. It was almost like a street-side inquisition, and Sheriff Waters was to be the focus.

He scanned the assembly. Trace was in the front row, his powder keg arms crossed and stiff. His younger brother, Daniel, was at his side, and like his older, he resembled Bull, but only in looks. Large muscles were absent, and at best Daniel's frame could be considered "normal." He just didn't have the family power, and maybe that's why he hung so closely to Trace. With his father gone, maybe he needed a new role model to gravitate toward—to watch over him, to guide him. Both men glared at Sheriff Waters.

Other young were present, including Benjamin, a man named Beckett, and Charles P. They were in the middle of the group, maybe more toward the east end of the half circle, and all three could be considered quite suggestible. Benjamin was the youngest, nineteen, an entrepreneur seeking opportunity and finding nothing in Westcreek. He was tall and blond, a handsome Norwegian eager to fit in with his new acquaintances. To the contrary, Beckett was anything but handsome, but still he aimed to please. If the price was right. Slouching most of the time and scowling, he had only a few teeth and an ever-increasing bald spot for which he hid under a mangy, Australian-style hunting cap. He looked dirty and disheveled, and was often a conduit for town gossip, especially if the gossip concerned Indians. He loved Bull like a second father and would do anything to avenge his loss. All he needed was a target.

That left Charles P. He was the town clown. A baby's face on a plump little body, he was always good for a joke or two, and usually at the expense of the nearby Reservation. He was loud and obnoxious but often scared of his own shadow, so he stuck close to the masses, entertaining, drinking, laughing, and then drinking some more. He had a part-time job working for the DNR, but it by no stretch of the imagination provided a living. Therefore, he had to borrow money. Usually from town elders. Indeed, he owed them a lot.

Benjamin, Beckett, and Charles P. —all three just stared.

Sheriff Waters swept across the remainder of those that gathered, and with unsteady eyes. He saw cold looks and grinding jaws, wrinkles on elders who saw many a fist fight between Red and White, and the lack of innocence among the very wee—some as young as ten or twelve—sort of hand-me-down attitudes through the years pretty much negated any sign of innocence, and now Sheriff

Waters had do deal with it all in the present.

He had to deal with everyone.

He tried to act official. "What can I do for you boys?"

"We want the truth, Nat!" a redheaded, red-bearded elder shouted from the back. Words goin' 'round that there's a murderer in the valley. An Indian off the Reservation lookin' for some kind of revenge."

"It's just a rumor. There is nothing to suggest that any of us are in any kind of danger."

"Then who killed Bernie and the others?" a voice yelled out. "The wind?"

Sheriff Waters became flushed. "An outside source may not have been involved at all. They may have killed each other."

"Bullshit!" somebody screamed.

"What about the spear stuck in the ground?" Beckett added. "Sends a pretty strong message to anyone White, I'd say. Or did the winds do that, too?"

Angry chatter again spread across the group, and Sheriff Waters tried to bring back order, his hands tentatively out and calling for quiet. "Please, please, everyone, calm down. Now all I can tell you is that we're in the midst of an investigation. Cautious steps need to be taken here before we jump to conclusions. I assure you, any threat to your safety will be dealt with, swiftly."

"You're givin' us just words!" another voice said. "Words don't protect our families! But a damn good shotgun will!"

"Please, listen to me," Sheriff Waters tried to interject. He was becoming dizzy, the barrage of questions and comments coming from every direction. "If you all just—"

"What about the pistol?" Trace yelled the loudest. "Where is it?"

Charles P. spoke up. "You've questioned everybody in town! When ya gonna talk to the Indians on the Reservation?"

"What are you keeping from us, Nat?" Trace asked.

Before long the crowd began pushing and shoving, getting closer to the boardwalk, and Sheriff Waters simply couldn't digest all the commotion. He literally felt like collapsing. "Please…"

"Where ya gonna go from here?" Charles P. yelled, cupping his hands over his mouth. "Tell us, dammit, we have a right to know!"

"BOOM!" and a pistol went off into the air, the men of Westcreek jumping. The blast came from the back of the group, and so everyone hastily turned to identify the source. It was Jake.

"Now that's enough," he said. "Everybody just relax, take a step back and give Nat some room. You're acting like a bunch of savages."

The crowd parted. As Jake walked casually toward his superior, they stood dumbfounded, a sudden lump of respect thrown on top of what was already there.

"Now it seems to me that Nat has made things pretty damn clear. You will be given information that you're entitled to. When you need to know. Nothing more. If there's a threat to this town's safety in any way, you'll know about it from us, immediately. Now let us do our job."

Each man retreated a full stride from the boardwalk, making more than enough room near the front. All were silent.

Jake stepped up to the boardwalk, his gun placed back in its holster, Sheriff Waters pushed to the side. Like a chief diplomat, he addressed the crowd. "You asked about where we go from here. I'll tell you. I called the tribal council and obtained permission to carry out our investigation on their land. I informed them of the situation. They've agreed to cooperate fully. Nat and I will leave for the Reservation at first light."

"And do what?" Charles P. asked.

Jake glanced briefly at Sheriff Waters. "First and foremost, to question, one, Decoreous Blackfoot."

The crowd became restless again, and Sheriff Waters felt like his heart was going to rupture.

It was like Jake had let him down.

"What the hell is he still doing around here?" someone yelled out.

"That Indian is a danger to us all!" Beckett added. "He uses black magic!"

"He torched a White family's home, for God's sakes!" Daniel chimed in. "He's capable of anything!"

An elder from the back raised his fist. "Where is he? We'll go with you tomorrow and help chase him out! For good, this time!"

The crowd's negative energy grew… pushing and shoving ensued, once more… Sheriff Waters lowered his head… and Jake took another shot at the sky, bringing back order.

"Your assistance is not needed," he said calmly. "Decoreous Blackfoot is wanted only for questioning. Nothing more. Any of you who think otherwise, and who interfere with the process of law—you will be arrested." He reholstered his gun for a second time, and then placed both hands comfortably on his big leather belt. "Is that clear?"

The crowd's uneasiness continued, but a sort of passive understanding emanated outward.

Jake nodded his head with authority. "Now you boys go on home to your families. There's nothing more to be said on these matters tonight. Nothing more you can do."

The men of Westcreek slowly disbanded. With reluctance. Still in busy chatter and maybe a bit disgruntled, they pulled apart and headed for almost every end of town. The show of force was over. Jake seemed in control.

"Go on," he urged, their pace not quick enough for his liking.

But not everyone was ready to call it a day.

Trace and Daniel remained. Like statues, they didn't move, their piercing eyes staring down both lawmen, and as if having been denied something.

Jake tilted his nose upwards. "That includes you two, as well."

"Where is Decoreous?" Trace asked, spitting through his teeth.

"I can't give you that information."

"Why not?"

"It could compromise the investigation."

Trace smiled oddly, trying desperately to stem the tide of overwhelming anger. "Tell me, do you know what it's like to lose a father?"

Jake could feel his intentions. "Hunting down an old Indian won't bring him back, son."

"No," Trace answered, balling his fists, "but it will even the score.

Nobody hated my father more than Decoreous. Just before he was chased out of Westcreek, he vowed revenge, specifically against my father. And if Decoreous is still around, if he's out there somewhere, I'd say it looks like he finally made good with his threat. I'll accept no other explanation for my father's death. Now I want justice."

"You better leave the justice to us," Jake responded, not backing down. "I do not want any more bloodshed in this valley. If there are any new developments that concern your family, we will let you know."

Both Trace and Daniel searched the deputy for the truth in his convictions. Looking deep within his eyes, they tried to find a glimmer of the man they knew—their neighbor, their friend. They found nothing. Only a deputy sheriff.

"You both better get on home," Jake said plainly.

And they would, however not right away. Bull's sons were in need of support. Not breaking eye contact until the last possible moment, they turned and headed toward the café for a few too many drinks, their minds awhirl over the many ways to kill an Indian, Trace leading Daniel. Jake had seemingly doused their fire. But the embers would remain.

Jake faced his superior. "The town had a right to know about Decoreous. Going 'by the book' allows for public disclosure of those sought for questioning."

"I know," Sheriff Waters mumbled, wanting to say more, but unable to.

"We don't know what we're getting into. We don't know how crazy or not crazy that old Indian really is. This puts the men on a state of alert against any more 'house burnings'… or worse."

Sheriff Waters simply stared at the boardwalk.

"I'll see you at first light." With a parting nod, the deputy left his sheriff's side to do nightly rounds and checkup on any pesky remnants from the unrest. He would start with the café.

And the good sheriff was thus left alone. In front of *his* office, he stood by himself, reflecting on how once again he was just a bystander in it all. He was literally pushed away from the power, and maybe he never really had it in the first place. He was pleasantly surprised by his deputy's handling of the situation, and yet overly concerned about his lack of candor regarding sensitive information. The mix of resulting emotions gave the sheriff an even sourer stomach, and such was the nature of dealing with Deputy Jake Flint. He was a hard man to figure out; a sort of fence rider, at best—an antagonist to sort of business as usual.

The wind began to gust more heavily, and Sheriff Waters thought back to when Jake first came to Westcreek. He was fresh out of the law enforcement academy—a big city boy. Terribly wet behind the ears, and yet bringing a lot of knowledge, high ideals, and motivation to police work, the good sheriff remembered how quickly Jake took to the routine of running a small town, with all its paperwork, minor squabbles, and tons of down time. Jake was respectful, thorough in problem solving, and dependable, and Sheriff Waters tried to nurture those characteristics and others throughout the years. It's just that something happened along the way. Jake had a change of heart. He became more distant. He started spending more and more time in the café. Jake began respecting his elders a bit too much. And he just simply became hardened—with alcohol—a bit at first, then greater concentrations and as his prowess grew around town. That Westcreek air, Sheriff Waters mumbled to himself. That damn Westcreek air. He sighed.

In the morning, two lawmen would visit the home of Decoreous Blackfoot and for questioning. They'd travel over many hills and step deep onto Ojibwe land. One would be armed and walk with a solid backbone; the other would be again gunless and still look for something—something to support a big frame.

THE
REUNION

Steven was having quite a time of it. Deep within The Great Forest, he was terribly lost, the male figure nowhere to be found. But he continued to search for what he hoped was his grandfather, and with both a renewed sense of life and eager eyes. He went up the valley, his footing awkward, his body bounced about like a metal sphere in a wilderness game of pinball—bumped hard into tree trunks and boulders encountered every so often. Tossed roughly to the right, he was—tossed roughly to the left, and the dense cover and weather did little in regards to aiding his journey. The broad tree limbs above allowed for minimal light to filter down, and for seeing by. The flickering lightning provided just brief glimpses of his surroundings. And the once prodding winds were now whipping with cold.

The little Indian was suddenly caught in a sort of war zone.

"Grandfather!" he yelled with urgency. "Help me, please!"

Near a cranberry bush his good leg became entangled in a pile of small logs and tall grass.

He fell almost immediately.

And descending from the treetops, seemingly in greater numbers, a sort of animal gang came closer. Near the bases of the jack pine, birch, and even amidst the lilac bushes, and while imbibing in Earie prattle, they seemed to play a game of tag with each other only a few feet from Steven's body; he was surrounded. Helpless. Unable to really see anything, Steven could've sworn he heard a few familiar words from the creatures. "You go, you go," he thought they said, "too slow, too slow."

The little Indian was beginning to wish he had never left the attic.

And he struggled to his feet. But still further up the valley and deeper into the forest, Steven went. The terrain traversed was much the same, save for the addition of a few mud holes found here and there. Steven ricocheted off of one Norway pine that had small broken limbs jutting out, and a couple caught his jacket, snagging the material. One even got him hung up. Literally running in place, he built a quick fire in his gut that fueled a violent jerk away from both the stub and the tree. He was free, but growing more and more frustrated with his lack of progress and uncertainty in regards to direction. He stumbled forward to the left, forward to the right, and at one point his bum left leg got hung up in a deep mud hole. Down again, he tumbled, and with a grimace, his sort of companions moving closer in. Steven feared he might be in danger.

"Save me from these things!" he wailed. "Somebody!"

From a prone position he got his first real peek at his worries. There, in the middle of another cranberry bush was a pudgy little, humanoid body about the size of a baby black bear. There, showing above the exposed roots of a maple tree was a pair of almost hush puppy-like ears. And there, suddenly, right in front of his face, was a pair of incredibly skinny, incredibly hairy little legs. What were these beasts, he wondered in shock? Upright dogs? Mutant badgers? Miniature black bears from hell? The portfolio of images just didn't add up, and yet the little Indian wasn't about to wait around for the complete picture. He had seen enough.

"Steven…" the whispering called out even more plainly, more loudly.

Steven bumbled his way to a stand, losing a shoe. His physical system became hyper as he slipped into the flight portion of the fight or flight response, and he wanted nothing more than to go home. But which way to travel? The storm intensified, now directly overhead. All directions looked the same—all trees, and the resulting panic caused even greater disorientation. Should I just run, he thought? Should I try and hide? He felt truly in peril.

The whispering was all around him. "Bring your magic to me…"

Steven stepped away. Then he stopped. The wind began to howl and the nearby tree limbs flipped and flopped in seemingly unnatural ways. With the help of the dismal lighting, it seemed almost like larger than life, bony skeletons did a horrifying dance in front of him.

So he turned away.

The little Indian headed in the opposite direction. Then stopped. The earth began to move under his feet like a herd of small Gophers borrowing about, haphazardly. He was pushed backwards and forwards, again and again, and at least to some degree he resembled a surfer catching a series of "bad waves." Disaster was imminent. He was bound to topple.

But the ground would seem to be the least of his problems.

A solid bolt of lightning… a heavy clap of thunder… a gust of swirling winds, and Steven caught a flapping tree limb squarely in the side of his head. He fell like a lifeless sack of potatoes to the cold earth below, a seeming mere helpless Fawn in the middle of a Great Forest. And he moved not.

Game over, it seemed.

And yet he awoke. With a startle. His head throbbing and amidst cobwebs, Steven sat up to discover that he was out of the woods. No dirt was felt beneath him. No wind or prickly pine limbs hassled his skin, and the little Indian slowly became aware of being within the confines of a warm, little cabin and atop an old brown couch. Someone or something had brought him here, and with a jolt of fear he scanned the place to try and make sense of it all. His eyes were met with softness.

The dwelling was no larger than a trailer home. Minus the succinct inner walls, it was made of solid oak logs and lined with fifty or so candles, the cabin's only lighting. These candles, rich with wax buildup, were placed on a variety of little wooden tables or within floor stands fashioned out of crude metal. The flames flickered almost rhythmically—hypnotically, and the total effect seemed to accent a shrine of sorts found on or near four walls. And Steven was in the middle.

His anxieties lessening and giving way to a little curiosity, he focused on the south wall. Four paintings in old wooden frames drew most of his attention. Done in rich colors, the paintings depicted the somber faces of four Indian Chiefs. Their heads were covered with lavish feathered dress, and each had deep red skin, a strong jaw, and brown, almost mysterious eyes, as if staring down some distant storm. Surrounding each painting was a veritable treasure trove of items from the distant past. Feathers of eagles and hawks placed in deerskin headbands were draped around upper corners. Fox and wolf hides were hung at angles between each chief, and as if showcasing the harvest of some long ago hunt. Ornate spears, bows, and hatchets could be found propped up against the wall or the many little wooden tables, and Steven began to wonder about the hunts and wars these weapons might've seen. Did they belong to the chiefs, he wondered? Were they all held at one time by great men? His heart became a bit warmer.

Steven studied the east wall, and still from the couch. More mementos were seen, and this time just one painting. Near a small wood-burning stove kicking out heat, three hide-covered drums lined the floor. They were large and meticulously painted, supporting big hairy mallets just waiting for someone to grab 'em and pound out a beat, or at least that's what the little Indian thought. More spears were spied. Topped by sharp quartz points, a good six or seven were set at various angles along the wall, a sort of crescendo effect that lead directly to perhaps the most magnificent of all the paintings. It was the portrait of a warrior. Atop a jet black steed, a deep red man of rippling muscles and loin cloth held a hatchet up high, screaming in defiance and amidst a circling of White men with rifles. It was as if the warrior possessed not an ounce of fear. It was as if he outnumbered his foes and was about to drop the hammer—to end, if you will, decisively, some long ago battle. Such a scene moved Steven, mellowing his initial concerns. Inspired him, it did, in such a way as to encourage further exploration of this wonderland he awoke within. He arose from his bed and walked to the west wall, a door, and a little window. And with still more questions.

Where was the curator of such treasures, he wondered? Where was the magician he so longed for?

Steven approached the third wall of the shrine. Starting by a wooden door, he hobbled from left to right like an eager buyer in an antique shop, going by ceramic vases, colorful weavings, and tobacco pipes placed carefully upon more of those wooden tables. Each item ranged in condition from shiny or almost new to tattered or old, and yet the values of all were extremely high. Especially for an Indian youth looking for something to hold onto and anticipate, and yet it was a simple picture on a little windowsill that was most valuable. Indeed, it was worth ten times its weight in gold, and Steven's heart beat faster just from the sight of it. Placed in a little silver frame, a black and white photograph showed a proud, middle-aged man of darker skin holding a wee little boy with crutches. Smiles were terribly radiant. Colors were absent. And yet there could be no mistake—it was him.

"Grandfather…" Steven whispered to no one.

"Dear me, dear me," a soft voice said from behind. "Is it really you?"

Steven jumped with alarm, turning toward the north wall, the shadows, and to see a very old man rise from a chair. Holding a dark wooden staff, the old man shuffled with arthritic pain across the dirt floor of the cabin and to get a closer look.

"After all these years. It is truly you. And no longer the boy I remember, but instead it is a man that stands before me. Welcome, my son."

Steven stared into the face of his grandfather. He saw a pair of very tired eyes, a quivering mouth, and skin that was terribly wrinkled, and yet such a face was the most beautiful he had ever seen. It was soothing. Still, Steven spoke with some reserve.

"I saw you out my window. In the woods. I tried to find you, but you just vanished."

"A man as reviled in Westcreek, as I, must be careful where to step. I couldn't chance being seen by anyone but you. I could only start you on your journey and watch your progress from afar. For safety. I… am sorry."

Steven tried to remember. "The forest was dark… there were

animals... the storm got bad... and then..."

Decoreous touched Steven's lumpy forehead with tenderness. "With a shiner like that, I can understand the fog you struggle to see through. Good thing you stumbled upon my home, when you did."

He seemed to speak in only partial truths.

The two just looked upon each other, Steven overwhelmed with emotion and stifled into inaction, his grandfather embracing the moment and smiling.

Finally, Steven broke the silence. With questions. "Why didn't you come for me sooner?"

"I couldn't risk the harm that might come to my family; you, your mother, and father, for to be associated with the devil—a man who partakes in 'black magic,' is a terrible thing. It could have brought you all years of scorn and pain from others. It was better that you all thought me dead or far away."

Fighting hurt, Steven tried to understand. "Then why have you come now?"

"I... am dying," his grandfather answered with a forced smile. "The winds—they have told me that I have very little time left upon this earth. I grow very old. I suppose it is selfish, but I had to see you just once more. My grandson, the one boy—the one *man* who showered me with his love. It was a last request."

The two exchanged a myriad of warm stares and until Steven's grandfather abruptly shifted gears.

"Dear me, dear me, where are my manners? Here we just stand. You must be weary from your trip and parched. Come." He shuffled to the north wall, a little metal stove, and a boiling kettle. "I'll fetch you some hot tea. Living deep within the forest offers me little opportunity to entertain. I'm afraid I'm a bit rusty." He hummed a cheery tune.

Steven hobbled back to the couch, watching his grandfather with interest and ignoring the former talk about dying. He only saw a man glowing with life—with contentment and pride. Wrapped in a heavy robe that dragged upon the floor, Steven couldn't help but stare at his skin—his deep red skin with all its wrinkles. It was like a badge of honor to the boy, a reminder of all that a forgotten culture was and maybe ever would be again. Indeed, the curator of the shrine was a treasure, himself. Steven had to know more about his existence.

"Do you live here alone?"

"Not entirely, my son. The forest—she has been known to offer a companion or two. Mostly of the four-legged kind. I'm rarely kept lonely." Having poured hot fluid into two little cups, he shuffled to Steven with almost giddiness. "Here, my son, to us, a celebration."

Cups were clinked.

Steven embraced the tea. "What do you do here?"

"I tend to a flock, one might say. A duty handed down to me by your great grandfathers and great, great grandfathers. It's a job very dear to me, but one that does not take a great deal of time. Therefore, I spend much of my day in the hills searching for herbs and relics from our past. The relics I try to preserve in my little home, as you can see." He sat slowly and with pain next to Steven. "But I always take a moment or two each day to watch over my family in Westcreek. From a distance." He giggled. "I've seen you grow, my son. I've seen your life unfold."

Steven turned away. Knifed by a memory always close at hand, he tried to gain at least some degree of comfort by gazing upon the black and white photograph. "Then you know about father's death?"

"Hmmm?"

The old Indian nervously dropped his tea. With startle. "Dear me, dear me, I've went and made quite a mess. I'll have to get a damp cloth and clean this up, immediately." He tried to get up, but as if knowing the futility in his effort to deviate from the question—the reality of it—he sank back into the couch. With closed eyes. "Yes. I felt a horrible pain in my heart that day, but refused to recognize it for what it was. The winds even told me, but I refused to listen. I guess I blamed myself too much. Had I not been such a burden on the town, I could have somehow been there to save him. Save him from himself. Even traded my life, gladly. It hurt that much. Dearly."

He turned to Steven. "How have you faired, my son? Too much about me."

Steven reestablished eye contact. "I cannot forget what happened.

Nor forgive."

His grandfather searched for wisdom. "Your father was a wonderful man. And he loved both you and your mother more than life itself. For most the time on this earth, he gave strength and dignity, a caring hand to anyone in need. Only toward the end of his life did he step off his path of honor. I'm afraid he became a victim of the sickness in this valley, long before he was killed. Tragic, his loss is, my son. But you must bury your hatred. Do so in memory of your father."

Steven didn't comment. He simply looked back to the photograph. And the old Indian felt his longing.

He switched gears, again. "Such a conversation is not fit for this night. We must celebrate our reunion. There will be plenty of time for grieving. Tomorrow, maybe. But not now—now we must find joy." He rose with even greater pain and then hobbled to the little photograph. "Tell me, my son, do you still fancy mystical ways?"

"Yes!" Steven answered, vaulting to a sort of cripple's stand.

"Then we must go. To see this flock that I speak of and practice magic just one last time. Just one last time, then I may truly rest in peace. When my time comes."

The two departed. Slowly. Making their way out the door and to the southwest, they walked side by side, like days gone by, stepping one, two, three and occasionally one, two... three. Behind, a wind gust funneled through the cabin door and window, extinguishing every candle within. The sort of museum was closed, it seemed, and left to watch over things, from a distance, were thirty or so little creatures carrying on in Earie gibberish.

Indeed.

The Seduction

There was a break in the clouds. Above the clearing and just after the midnight hour, the weather seemed to run out of steam, allowing both moonlight and a few hundred stars to shine down upon a boy and his grandfather. The two took to a sort of stage and from the northwest, stepping carefully over uneven ground and rock that plagued the openness. They were on their way to the middle and that huge boulder—that platform that fell below the dark mine and yet towered over the sleepy little town of Westcreek, below. One was eager for a magic show, the other to roundup his flock.

Steven passed the boulder. "What is your 'flock?' What kind of animals? Where are they, Grandfather?"

The old Indian stepped carefully up to and onto the boulder, The Great Rock, and like a conductor rising to a podium, his wooden staff firmly in hand. "Easy, child. Easy. One must not search terribly hard for what is already present. Behold."

"But I don't see anything."

His grandfather smiled. He looked to the stars. "Watch and wait… listen and wait. Shhhhhhh."

"I don't understand."

"You will, my son," the old Indian assured, nodding to the trees. "Just search within your heart. Just search. Look. Listen. Shhhhh."

Then a small breeze entered the clearing. It was pleasant and yet musty and amusing, tossing Steven's black hair about playfully and in cycles, as if a bus or two were moving by every so often.

In excitement, Steven began breathing heavier. He became more and more aware of a pulling sensation deep within his gut. It tickled and felt almost like a thousand little hands were tugging at his intestines and nearby muscles. And he gradually eyed the sources of such a feeling—the culprits, if you will. They were all around him… and yet they weren't. They were ethereal, and yet with definite form. He could see them—yet not. They were like bubbles, some big and some small, and yet each appeared in definite form, like that of an old face. A thousand or so such forms could be seen floating freely amidst the winds. They moved with almost fluid motions and near Steven and his grandfather. In and out, they soared—in… and out.

So suddenly the two were not alone.

"Is this your flock?" Steven asked.

"Yes."

"What are they?"

His grandfather smiled. "The very life force of our culture. Your ancestors going back over a thousand years. A flock of spirits. As a guardian, as the last chief of our people, it is my duty to watch over their existence, their treasures, and their land—to watch over my land and your land. Until I… too, join their ranks and return my duties to the forest."

With a shaking hand, Steven reached out to touch some of the spirits.

They felt cold, gelatin-like and yet comforting, and again their movements messed his hair. "Is this where you get your magic?"

Steven was falling in love.

"Yes, my son. The spirits affect everything. And I'm connected to them. My will becomes their will. My feelings become their feelings. The impossible becomes possible." Steven's grandfather gently raised his arms, staff included. He spread his fingers out wide. "One just has to know where to touch."

The spirits flew in more of a circular pattern, and closer to the treetops. A galaxy of shooting stars fell around the clearing like rain and with a twinkling quality. And it was all just a start. A brevity of sight, if you will.

"How did you get this power?" Steven asked with intense curiosity.

"For an Ojibwe Indian, you can't get what is already given to you," the old man answered with a chuckle. "It's in our blood. But for most, only to a small degree. Only a chief or guardian may command this magic to the fullest."

"Does the magic last forever?" Steven asked, reaching out to the stars.

"Only as long as one's strength remains strong. And only… only if the magic is not abused, like when emotions collide. Otherwise it fades."

Decoreous wore a look of concern.

The crippled boy wasn't paying attention, though. He was too busy playing, his own spirit overjoyed. Jumping about like a drunken ballerina, he touched a hundred or so of the big faces, watching each change form almost continuously. And the beings of long ago seemed to return to Steven a sort of positive regard. Circling him above and below and just generally all around, they pursed their lips, they smiled, and they opened up wide with surprise and as if to laugh, but any one look lasted only brief seconds before melding into another.

They were poofs of sort of smoke.

"Make them do more, Grandfather!" Steven shouted with gaiety.

The old Indian winked. He raised a pinkie into the whipped air. "Dear me, dear me, but of course."

And then the inanimate became animated.

Rocks in the clearing, those of all shapes and sizes, color and texture, took on a life of their own. They defied gravity as the spirits raced about and whispered amongst themselves. Rising into the air, one after another, the rocks rotated around the clearing, Steven and his grandfather, a sort of centerpiece. They moved slowly at first; then faster, with lighter rocks moving a bit quicker than heavier ones. 'Round and 'round, they went. 'Round and 'round. A great carnival ride had begun.

"Everything is connected," the great mystic said, admiring his work, "from the smallest pebble to the largest tree, from the smallest insect to the tallest man. And everything has life. The spirits, they tap into that life and control it. It's energy. It's just a matter of telling them what to do."

And his grandson still wasn't listening.

In awe, enthralled with it all, and giggling for reasons even he could not entirely discern, Steven felt those little hands pulling at his intestines and nearby muscles even more. So he pulled back. With his spirit. And suddenly another world sort of opened up. Shockingly, in a way. It was like a single strand of thread suddenly extended out from his gut and split into a brilliant spider's web, and all he had to do was gently pluck a string. He was literally "on-line" with the spirits, his will becoming their will. His feelings becoming their feelings. Under the watchful eye of his grandfather, a little Indian boy tried his own hand at real magic.

Indeed.

And the rocks lost their spacings. The rotating continued, a few rocks crashing into each other, breaking up. Some of the earth shrapnel dropped to the ground; some continued around in a circle; and still other pieces shot out over the treetops like a homerun ball in a wilderness game of stick—Steven, a sudden apprentice, at bat.

And Steven could hardly contain his excitement. Years of dreaming and pretending led up to this moment—a moment in which he was master. He had the power. As more souls swooped into the clearing, as forest life began appearing around the perimeter with shyness, yet curiosity, he stood a bit taller and stepped upon his crippled leg with a bit more weight—more decisively, even. He was falling deeper in love, you see.

"Look, Grandfather!" he yelled, pointing to the animals. "Do you see them? Can you see them all?"

"Yes," his grandfather answered with surprise and feeling like just a casual observer in the whole scheme of things. "You've become quite a man of the forest. Almost a guardian, yourself."

Deer, raccoon, martin, badger, and bear peeked over bushes and tall grasses to get a look. Sniffing the air and pacing about, they processed with little animal minds the hubbub before them. Cute, they acted, a bit standoffish, and even in the presence of mostly gentle creatures both in and around the clearing. They needed just a little encouragement to join in on the celebration between grandson and grandfather; or so the sudden magician thought. They needed just a little prodding. That's when Steven pulled them on stage.

He plucked another string. With more confidence and more strength. Feeling a rush of adrenaline, he facilitated a lifting effect, floating all beasts carefully up into the air and into the clearing. Slowly but sort of surely. He felt that passengers were needed on the carnival ride, and the process of loading went anything but smoothly. Raccoon and Martin pawed at nothing and in an attempt to get away. Deer occasionally tumbled end-over-end. And black bear—a pair, heavy and snarling, flew only a couple inches off the ground, their backsides bumping hard against the dry earth and every so often. But all the animals had a seat upon the sort of merry-go-round. And gradually earth and beast spun together as a whole and to the will of one little Indian, his sudden flock working hard at the chores set before them.

Near The Great Rock, Steven performed engineering duties. Like his grandfather at his eighth birthday party, he ran to all points within the ride, checking speed, distance between animal and animal, and animal and rock, and overall height of the circling. It was an arduous job, at best, one for which Steven performed sort of wonderfully. The bears became too heavy at one point to continue rotating, so they were allowed to scurry back into the bush, but for the most part the carnival ride was a huge success. 'Round and 'round, creature and stone went, 'round and 'round and at sometimes dizzying speeds.

"More!" Steven shrilled. "There must be more!"

He felt the merry-go-round lacked sound and light, so he danced about, plucking two strings upon the web at once. Special effects were the order, and they began without delay. Heat lightning flashed across the sky as if the valley was in the midst of a dry spell, and yet the temperatures were quite mild. And the light had rhythm. One, two, *rest*, it went. One, two, *rest*, and the whole effect resembled that of a strobe light. Thunder from far away accented the rhythm by booming on beat *three*.

And Steven's grandfather—he was becoming less and less impressed, and more and more concerned. Relationships, he thought, were being built much too fast. He looked to the spirits. "Taken quite a liking to my grandson, have you? Be careful. He is a boy with a heavy heart…"

And Steven was heading for a climax. Stepping to the south of The Great Rock, he raised his hands high into the air and to no reserve. Though becoming terribly tired and a bit stiff, he reached for one last string, his emotions high, his belly full of all that was good. All that was good.

Around the perimeter of the ride he called upon another galaxy of shooting stars to fall like a big curtain around the stones and critters, a sort of visual tremolo that started toward a grand finale. Thunder became off-beat and loud. That heat lightning flickered faster and more brightly. And the souls and wind whipped about at ever-increasing rates. Where was it all leading to, one might've asked? What high note would be hit to cap off such an extraordinary show of magic?

None. Steven lost his strength.

He wouldn't even see the ending. With his breaths becoming shorter, his eyes becoming heavier, the little Indian dropped to his knees. A sense of overwhelming peace washed over him, the magic so pleasing.

And too great was the need for sleep. The whole experience literally wore Steven out, and he could not fight the gradual slide downward and into a prone position. He was passing out. Struggling to keep an eye open, his head gently fell atop a rock.

Then he sighed. Then he smiled.

And within no time at all, the little Indian drifted into unconsciousness, his dreams comprising even greater feats of mysticism.

The wise Elder giggled.

He reached for the web and reestablished his connection to the spirits and in an effort to bring things back to a gentle hum. Musically. The shooting stars slowly lost their spark. The thunder and lightning simply dissipated, and that left just the mechanisms of the ride itself to be dealt with.

"*Bisânabiwin, nikâniss*," Decoreous whispered to the sky. "*Bisânabiwin.*"

The response seemed well disciplined.

The winds decelerated. The big faces became even more ethereal. The rocks, large and small, fell with a series of thuds. And deer, badger, raccoon, and martin were lowered gently back down to the earth as if they were all on little elevators, and then they scampered back into the forest cover, some more swiftly than others—some a bit more flustered. The carnival ride had ended. The show was over. It was time to make way for the exits.

Steven's grandfather stood straight and tall upon The Great Rock.

Above the valley, he surveyed all he could see with pride. His flock was accounted for and healthy. Indian grounds, especially the many, many hills, were lush and full of life. And Decoreous' grandson, a sudden guardian's apprentice, was back under Decoreous' wing and full of love to share, if only for the day. It was truly a night of celebration, Steven's grandfather thought.

Truly a night of... mystical happiness.

ON FINDING A PRINCE

Gloria went home. Her shift at the café was over. Walking in the middle of Main Street, alone, and listening to the off-beat chorus of a hundred crickets, she moved into and out of dim streetlight, her mind counting down the steps until she could soak in a nice hot bath. Behind was twelve full hours of serving up greasy hamburgers, mixing strong drinks, and listening to foolish talk about her ex-father-in-law's return to the valley and how he hid in the woods just waiting to take his next victim. Her eyes and ears were sore from it all. She was literally exhausted. Even so, and as a chill tickled her spine—as she crossed her arms in an effort to gain warmth, her perfectly round chest heaving, she still had enough mental energy to say a couple of silent prayers. Mostly to herself. She felt she had to. She needed help. One prayer was said in hopes of receiving Steven's forgiveness; the other in hopes of being granted a miracle and in regards to her and her son's living conditions.

On her left and near the little hardware store, Gloria suddenly heard a commotion. It sounded like a metal barrel that had been knocked over, near the front entrance, under the wooden awning, and atop the boardwalk. She couldn't see the source, however. It was too dark.

"Hello?" she said timidly. "Who's there?" Only the crickets answered. With discord.

Gloria walked faster. She stared stiffly ahead, and that's when the sound of someone or something running could be heard back near the general vicinity of the hardware store.

"Hello?" she said louder.

Still no response.

Was it Amos or some other town drunk rustling around, she wondered? Was it an animal or two looking for food scraps?

Gloria stopped. Afraid, and not wanting to be afraid, she mustered up enough courage to take a few steps toward the boardwalk—to investigate. And that's when Dex jumped from the shadows, holding a thorny rose.

"Hello, fair maiden!"

Grabbing her bosom, Gloria reeled back. "Jesus Christ, Dex, what the hell are ya doing?"

"You said you liked a man who was full of surprises."

"The key word was 'man.' Not teenager. I already have one of those at home." She caught her breath and then continued her walk—annoyed, her hips swaying robustly yet without rhythm.

Dex pursued. "I can't help it," he said with whimsy, "you make my heart feel twenty years younger!"

"It's called puberty, Dex. It will pass."

"Have you thought about my proposal?"

Gloria walked faster. "What proposal?"

"Of marriage. You, Steven, and I, living happily ever after..."

"I've tried not to."

Dex ran ahead, blocked her path, and then presented the rose on bended knee. "Would this help sweeten the offer?"

Gloria took the gift of affection, her smile insincere. "You'd have better luck with gravel. But watch the kiss goodnight. It could be a bit dry." She dropped the rose upon Main Street, and then walked around Dex like he was a pole, or something. "Good-bye."

"I give up," he said softly. "I've tried poetry, music, and flowers. You and I have been friends for years, and yet I get nothing but a cold shoulder in return." He turned and spoke to her back. "Why can't you love me?"

And indeed, the reasons were at least somewhat elusive. Dex was a handsome man. Though dressed simply in a pair of faded blue jeans and an insulated, black flannel shirt, he was tall and of fair complexion, his body well-sculpted from top to bottom, hulking at the top and slendering at the middle. And his face. His face was tight and long, dimpled on the chin, and accented most by a pair of hazel eyes that could reach out and capture the attention of most women in Westcreek. Most women, indeed. Just not Gloria.

She paused. Feeling a need to bring closure to the total history of Dex's come-ons, she spun around and explained herself. "You and I are from different worlds. That's why I can't love you. Your's exists no further than this valley. You keep telling me that you're going to 'weather the storm' and someday rebuild a lumber industry that has been dead for years. In this town. Regardless that so many are leaving. It isn't going to happen, Dex."

"Working the land was my father's and grandfather's profession," he said with a bit of defensiveness. "I grew up in the trade. It's all I know."

"They both went broke."

"They made enough to provide for their families! That's all I expect." He shook his head and thought about the future. "There is enough wood in this region to get any mill working at full capacity. It's just a matter of time before the State brings in new contracts. The U.S. economy is struggling. But hell, developing overseas markets alone could keep this town busy for decades. And the mines... this place is going to prosper, Gloria. All that's missing is time and two people to share that prosperity with."

Gloria crossed her arms, unrelenting.

"I want to build you that dream home," he continued, moving closer. "With my own hands. Right here in the valley, small, with a big yard and a white picket fence. All I need is your heart to get started."

"Dex, Dex, Dex," Gloria said with a condescending tone. "The little boy who never grew up. Never stopped dreaming. While you're struggling to put bread on the table in this God-forsaken town, Steven and I will be far away, somewhere we can have a real chance at life." She turned away. "So why don't you take your foolish hopes back to the bar and soak it up with the others. I'm not interested in your fantasy world."

"I'm surprised you don't join me—"

"What?" Gloria asked with hostility, whirling around with an annoyed look.

"Back at the café... for a couple of drinks. We can toast my fantasy world—the one about making Westcreek work... and yours about building a better life for your son."

She bullied up to him. "What the hell are you saying?"

"You keep giving me this song and dance about getting out of here for Steven's sake. Keeping a promise to his father. But all the while Steven sits at home, alone, without a mother. At least in my fantasy world, family would never be abandoned."

"You don't know anything about us, Dex!" Gloria screamed. "How dare you say this to me!" She balled one of her fists and raised it to his chest.

Dex stepped closer—touching his chest to her chest, even, his voice softening. "I know that a boy spends long hours in an attic looking through keepsakes. I see his light on until the wee hours of the morning. Day in and day out. When was the last time you talked to him, Gloria, I mean really talked to him? Felt his pain? Touched his person?"

"That's none of your concern."

"But it is," he said, gazing deeply into her eyes, "I'm in love with you. I care about you and I care about Steven. I can't stand seeing either one of you hurt."

"Stop trying to be some kind of hero, Dex," Gloria said with suddenly more bark than bite.

She was slowly, so very slowly being taken in by his look. His eyes.

"Lower the walls that keep me out. Let me be the bridge between mother and son, so you can get back to the relationship you used to have." He tilted his head as if preparing a kiss.

"Stop..." Gloria said without much conviction, her lower lip quivering.

Dex moaned, softly lubricating his oral area, and took a deep breath.

"I'm making enough money to support all three of us. You can quit your job and get back to the task of mothering. You can quit being...

the town whore."

"SLAP!" and Gloria connected her fist squarely with Dex's cheek, the words hitting a little too close to the mark. His face was red.

"Go to hell!" Gloria snapped.

Dex was mostly unharmed. Suddenly regretting his words, but still caught up in the emotion, he grabbed Gloria with firmness, yet gentleness, and then laid a kiss upon her semi-moist lips, passionately, twisting and turning, with eventual over-wetness.

And Gloria was left breathless. Wobbling in her stance, she felt angry, hurt, and yet overly warm—all at the same time. The moistness of Dex's lips were so attractable and soothing, and yet so anti-magnetic. Still locked in his arms, she struggled with these states.

"Surprise..." Dex whispered timidly.

"Let me... go," Gloria responded, the words hard to come by. "I... don't want you..."

Dex obliged. Berating himself internally for his actions, he let her go. "I'm sorry, Gloria. I just..."

"Don't do that again. Please..."

The two gazed upon each other like they had a million things to say... and yet nothing came out. But their eyes would communicate everything. Exchanged was a sense of disgust, a sense of need, a sense of grief, and a sense of repressed love, and that's when Gloria broke off the conversation. She couldn't bare to be bare again.

Running from Dex's side, her hand over her mouth as if holding in feelings that might leak out, she hurried the rest of the way home. In her little house she might get back a certain amount of composure that was lost. She could maybe refocus and get back to the task at hand—get back to her preparations for a grand escape from Westcreek, even without a man. Maybe... now, especially without a man.

Dex broke out of his silent shell, calling after her. "Gloria Johnson, I love you! I will never stop loving you! Just let me into your heart!"

His fair maiden disappeared into the night.

He had seemingly failed again.

Standing alone in the middle of downtown, Dex stared at the red rose laying in the gravel, his mind contemplating any and all ways to repair the damage, and, indeed, he'd of done just about anything to make things right. Maybe even abandon his dreams. Maybe even leave Westcreek; the woman was becoming an indispensable part of his soul, and as such, he just couldn't let go. Matter of fact, he wanted to hold on tighter. Touch her more deeply than any man ever had or ever could. Get to the very heart of who she was. But how?

And when?

A door flew open... a figure stumbled into darkness... the same door was thrown shut behind... a sink light was switched on, and just like that Gloria was back within her home. She was out of breath, her pink little waitresses' outfit uncharacteristically wrinkled and sweaty. Outside was an encounter she'd just as soon forget—a confrontation her prepared, orchestrated little world wasn't ready for. Dex had gotten to her. Again. But it wasn't his snide remarks or cheap come-ons or even his slippery kiss that most disturbed her. No. Rather, it was his piercing eyes—his soulful gape that looked so hard as to render her almost naked, against her will, and anyway Gloria wanted to leave it all downtown. She didn't have to deal with it anymore. She could relax. Get her thoughts on something else.

Gloria searched for a cigarette and a lighter within her apron, bringing both together with a flick. Many quick puffs were taken there in a corner of the kitchen, and in totality she resembled a sort of Snow White on coffee break and in the downstairs of a house with a sort of red light in the window, her makeup smudged and runny, and her black hair frazzled. But she wasn't thinking about the next trick or prince who might come along; she was instead taking inventory with her eyes and mulling over simple logistics in regards to a great move.

Gloria surveyed her sort of castle. Kicking off her faded pumps, she walked on painful corns and to the nearby living room, switching on a single bulb that dangled from a cracked ceiling. Shaped like a big bank vault, the living room was highlighted by dark green carpeting, a set of closed blinds, an old '75 TV, and a couch, chair, and ottoman of bland colors—each piece covered with plastic. The place of designated comfort wasn't much. It rarely got used, and that's what pleased Gloria the most: a potential buyer would surely be impressed with its preserved condition, and the crack above could be fixed with a bit of caulk and a lot of white paint. She walked back to the kitchen. With vigor.

The eating area would probably require a lot more work, she thought. A small wooden table without chairs sat upon cracked, off-white linoleum, and in each of the nearby corners could be found a plethora of dust bunnies. The west window wasn't much cleaner either, and Gloria knew she'd have to do a lot of scrubbing to get the area respectable. But what about the floor, she thought? How could she hide the recent years of neglect that left it marred and unsightly? She decided to let the new owner figure it out; to pray that a man with a fixer-upper mentality would come across this modest piece of real estate and be willing to put any and all effort in to making it right. She could tout the dwelling as a resort home—not far from the picturesque lakes and towering trees of North Central Minnesota.

Gloria walked to the two bedrooms at the south end of the house with reluctance. Taking a few more puffs off her cigarette and smiling to think such late-night treks across the cold floor may be numbered, she entered her bedroom on the right side. It wasn't much to look at. Just a lot of white walls with picture-frame outlines, boxes, and a queen-sized bed that could be disassembled in minutes, even without help. The room was just the way she wanted it: a vagabond's handling of things, and all she needed was a place to travel. She hoped her son's room was as "mover-friendly."

Gloria stepped across the hall. With reservation. Approaching her son's room slowly and wondering what mood he was in, she stood in front of his closed door. Though wanting to assess his readiness for departure, she got hung up on an ill feeling, and it was directly related to their last "interaction." She was worried that Steven might still be angry. That he might be chilly or even enraged if she violated his space, and such an unpredictable and inflammatory response to a mostly neutral interaction could be traced to his father...

It was both nature and nurture.

You see, Gloria mourned a very loving, but sometimes, very

hostile man. One moment he could be stroking her cheek with affection, late at night, and while cuddling in bed, and the next he could be throwing lamps and chairs against the wall, screaming at the top of his lungs. Things could change that quickly. He had a Jekyll and Hyde personality that was further complicated by the state of affairs in Westcreek. You see, he was supposed to be "just an Indian." He was supposed to move he and his family to the nearby Reservation, collect State reparations and casino profits, and live as if in another country. But Gloria's husband would have none of this: He wanted to be judged solely on his character and hard work ethic—to live and breathe where he chose and with whom he chose. It's just that the predominantly White town would not accept him. He was rebuffed time and time again when seeking out employment. No one would hire him. He even offered to volunteer his time in an effort to prove his worth in the area of lumber processing, and yet there were still no takers.

As a result, he became more and more abusive at home. He began drinking heavily. And one dark evening his social frustrations and naturally, hot blood came together, kicking off a crime spree that tragically ended in death.

Gloria remembered particulars in regards to their relationship.

Into her consciousness came visions. Of mostly innocuous interactions between her and her husband that flared into yelling, violence, or silence. She saw a disagreement about whether or not a wife should work outside the home turn into a barrage of four letter words and from one, male source. She saw a macaroni hot dish being hurled across the kitchen, a response to a discussion about where and when to build the new family home—a discussion one week old, even. And she also saw a series of long nights in which husband and wife slept far apart in the same bed, not a word exchanged and yet both awake, the trouble not easily identified.

But there were good visions as well. Like of a surprise picnic for three one afternoon following an intense argument about what school Steven should attend—public or Reservation. Gloria loved her man on this day—his best day, and his worst day, it's just that she never knew what to expect from him. She never knew what to expect from

Steven, either, and growing up he was a witness to his father's Jekyll and Hyde personality, first hand. Then add that blood thing.

Gloria wanted to knock upon her son's door, her hand raised. But she stalled, wondering: Would he invite her in? Would he respond with harsh words? Would he throw things? Or would he simply ignore her?

Suddenly, the floorboards in the ceiling creaked, and Gloria startled. She turned her attention to the attic. Afraid and not wanting to be afraid, and out to prove Dex wrong, she pushed a long-overdue physical meeting between mother and son.

"Steven?" she said cautiously. "We need to talk. We can't keep avoiding each other. Enough is enough. I've made a decision about our future and you need to know about it."

She began climbing the ladder, her words only partially thought through. "I want to be out of this town within a week. Use the little bit of money I've saved and get an apartment in the Twin Cities—live in a shelter, if we have to. Let's stop waiting for life to happen. Let's make it happen ourselves, okay? We'll get out of here."

She approached the attic, her movements slow. "I'm coming up, Steven. To talk about this. Okay? I think your father would want us to take a chance. I could find a job at a local restaurant. We could list our home from the apartment instead of waiting here for a buyer. Okay? Steven?"

Gloria reached for the trapdoor, with shakiness, and that's when some heavy stomping was heard.

"BOOM-BOOM-BOOM!" was how it sounded, and it was like a pair of big boots jumped solidly above her. In rage.

She shrieked. She dropped from the ladder in fright, and then cowered next to a nearby wall like a little girl lost.

"I'm sorry," she said in heavy whispers, the assertiveness gone, "I'm so sorry. So sorry. I didn't mean to anger you. We'll talk when you're ready." She trailed off with apologies, her eyes tearing and red. It was all like Deja Vu to her, and she and Steven seemed the farthest apart two people could be.

"We'll talk when you're ready… I'm so sorry."

Gloria would stay in her condition for most of the early morning. Adding occasional wallows of self-pity, she'd stumble about the lower level without intention, doing mindless chores and just waiting for her son to descend from above.

Then it would be a different moment—a different mood, maybe, and another chance to bond and prove Dex wrong. That was the plan, anyway. The best a seeming little girl could come up with.

THE QUESTIONING OF DECOREOUS BLACKFOOT

Steven awoke. With an anxious startle. He was back in the cabin and again atop the old brown couch, this time his body wrapped in a quilt of many earthen tones. All around him were lit fifty candles, and yet there was no sign of his grandfather. Indeed, the old man was gone, and Steven wondered in regards to his whereabouts. Was he fetching water for tea? Was he gathering wood for the stove, the flames growing dim? Or was he playing with the ancestors of ages past, in and about the hills of the valley? Steven had to know the answer.

Bouncing off the couch with elevated vigor, his adrenaline racing, he hobbled toward the cabin door. He had a deep need to embrace the reality that was his grandfather—to bask in the old Indian's love, and if given the chance, command, maybe, even greater feats of magic. The reunion between grandfather and grandson was all Steven had dreamed it would be. It had filled the little Indian's belly to the point of overflowing and with all that was good... all that was good.

Beginning his search, Steven left the cabin.

The clouds over Westcreek reconvened. Big and black and rolling into each other, they smothered the pressing sunlight and dominated the sky. The lull, so to speak, was over. Indeed, a new storm of unprecedented strength was forming over the town, a lightning bolt and rumble of thunder leaking out in the process and every so often. The air was moist and heavy, smelling of rotten peas, and it was as if something wasn't right—something wasn't pure in the valley.

And between Westcreek and the clearing, amidst tall but meager jack pine and waist-high rushes, a pair of humanoid figures with lanterns were met by another in a sort of early morning rendezvous. Two shook hands and were cordial. The third took a step back, his terribly white hands placed on his terribly little hips.

A conversation then ensued.

"Sheriff—Deputy!" Steven's grandfather cried with forced surprise. "Imagine meeting both of you out on my daily walk. What brings you so deep into the woods and at such an early hour?"

Sheriff Waters sighed. He spoke gently. "I'm sorry to disturb you, Decoreous, but there's been some trouble back in town. We need to talk to you about it."

"Oh?" the old Indian replied, kneading his wooden staff, roughly.

"Two nights back four men were found dead near the old Dawson Mine. Three were shot by a handgun. One by a rifle."

"Dear me, dear me, … anyone I may have known?"

"You knew all of them," Jake chimed in with both self-confidence and suspiciousness. "Particularly Bull and Bernie."

Decoreous acknowledged only Sheriff Waters. "What happened?"

The good sheriff removed his tan hat and wiped away sweat that accumulated over his brows. "We're not sure at this point. As part of our investigation we're talking with anyone and everyone who may have seen something. Heard something. It's just part of procedure."

"I understand, my son."

"We didn't find the bodies until almost four a.m. Figure the deaths occurred around two. Do you remember anything about that night? People being around? Shots being fired?" He waited patiently for an answer.

Decoreous looked to the earth in seriousness. "Two nights ago. I spent the day foraging for mushrooms further up the valley. Then I visited two old friends at the Reservation Community Center. I was back to my cabin by ten p.m. I was quite tired. I don't think I even awoke until dawn the next morning." He thought deeply. "I'm sorry. I can't recall anything that may be of use to you..."

Jake looked away with impatience.

"I dearly wish I could help you more," Decoreous added. "My thoughts will surely be with those who are grieving."

"Wait a minute," Jake snapped, raising his hand as if to cease any further condolences. "That's it? You mean to tell me that you just slept through it all? A short distance away from a crime scene, and you didn't hear a gunshot or some kind of scream? Nothing? You didn't see lanterns or maybe the blast of a shell coming out of a barrel?"

"Two nights back a bad storm gripped our area," Decoreous responded without making eye contact. "Anyone would have been hard pressed to see or hear anything. Then consider the senses of an old man."

Jake wasn't satisfied. His mind awhirl, the questioning reached a new level. "Where are these two 'old friends' you said you met with? Can they verify your story? More importantly, who can verify your whereabouts at the time of the deaths?"

"Jake!" Sheriff Waters yelled, not liking his partner's sudden tone.

But Decoreous would downplay the situation.

He forced a smile. "It's quite all right, Sheriff. Quite all right. Your deputy is simply doing his job." He looked at Jake. "I'm afraid I was alone. Like most days—like most these past years I've spent in the forest." He paused. "Does that trouble you?"

"Shouldn't it?" Jake replied more loudly. "Given the violent history you had with Bull and Bernie? You, being a short walk away from their dead bodies and unable to come up with a solid alibi? Shouldn't that trouble me? A man might say you'd be a prime suspect in their questionable deaths."

"Goddamn it, Jake!" Sheriff Waters yelled. "Stop this!"

But it was like he didn't exist.

Decoreous could smile no longer. "When I lived in Westcreek, I never hid my feelings about those two. This I freely admit. There were far—far more men I liked better. But to be capable of murder—"

"You act as if Bull and Bernie hurt your feelings, or something," Jake blasted back. "Both of them were responsible for running you out of town. They got liquored up, assembled a group of friends, dragged you out of your bed—in the middle of night—and then chased you into the forest." He became animated, pointing his finger and raising his voice even more. "Bull assaulted you with a 2"x4"! You were bludgeoned! You were left with nothing but the clothes on your back! Lord knows you'd have motive."

"But not the rage... not enough to take four lives!" Decoreous appeared tense. His face was reddening. "Anger in my heart, yes, but not the rage needed to murder."

It was as if the two were racing toward some higher boiling point.

Jake stepped closer, violating personal space. "How about revenge? Is there room for revenge in your heart?"

"No!" Decoreous screamed, planting an end of his staff firmly into the ground. "I have been, and always will be, a man of peace! Look elsewhere for your prime suspect!"

Jake couldn't let go of what he saw deep within the old Indian's eyes. "Then show me your home! Show me you don't have a .38 caliber handgun hidden away! Show me!"

"Enough, enough!" Sheriff Waters yelled his loudest, grabbing Jake by the collar. "You're out of control!"

Jake fought the hold. He kept on targeting Decoreous. "Do you wanna know what I think happened? I think Bernie, Bull, and the twins were out poaching animals. On Reservation land. I think they got caught in the storm and sought refuge in the old Dawson Mine. Somehow Bernie got separated from the others—maybe he was trying to escape! Maybe he was trying to run from some fifth party in that clearing!"

"Go easy, my son," Decoreous warned, feeling the words to come.

"I think it was you, old man! I think you finally got revenge against our town! Against Bernie and Bull! You stalked them! You shot 'em all up! And in the chaos Bull's rifle fired, a bullet deflected off a rock, and it killed Bernie—by accident! The bullet was in his throat sideways, for God's sakes! Bull would never intentionally hurt Bernie!"

Sheriff Waters bear-hugged Jake in an effort to contain the escalation. He even pulled him back a few steps. "I'm ordering you to stand down! Stand down and get control!"

"I think you shoved their deaths in our faces," Jake spat, not missing a beat and fighting Sheriff Waters with newfound muscle. "I think you littered the clearing with Indian shit just to add salt to an already open wound! I think you were laughing at us all!"

"Go easy, Deputy," Decoreous muttered with a terribly stiff jaw. "I'll ask you just this one last time."

Jake screamed. "Dammit, Indian, show me where that handgun is! Show me what you've done with it!"

"That will be all!" Decoreous screamed back.

And that's when the rushes all around began to move.

It was as if twenty or so small animals became spooked. It was as if they were scurrying about aimlessly near the ground, wiggling the tall weeds, violently. And then there was hissing.

"The forest," Decoreous said more calmly, "she seems to have grown tired of your words. I'm afraid you've outstayed your welcome."

"Watch it!" Jake cautioned, throwing his superior aside with a powerful shove, his eyes darting about from rustling to rustling. "What are those things?" He removed his pistol from its holster. "Sheriff…"

"No!" the good sheriff cried, tumbling to the ground and sensing the gravity of the moment. "Jake, put it away!"

But Jake was in his own little world. "What is all this, old man? More of your black magic? Your tricks? Tell me!" The gun barrel weaved to the left of Decoreous; then to the right of Decoreous. Then back to the left. "Tell me, dammit!"

Decoreous was still. "They are simply creatures of the forest who are concerned about your lack of respect. They demand that you depart in peace."

"Don't give me your bullshit!"

"Put the gun away, Deputy."

"Do it, Jake!" Sheriff Waters pleaded. "Please!" It was like he'd been there before.

Jake refused to relinquish the power. "Are they more of your wild dogs? Huh? Trained to attack us? Call them off!" He pivoted about. He pointed the gun to the south, to the west, and just any place the rushes moved. "I mean it!"

"Slow, my son, slow," Decoreous encouraged. "Lower your weapon. Maybe we can still get back to a more calm discussion." He suddenly felt ill. In his lower regions. It was like a flu and due to something—something sensed in the winds. "Please…" He looked as if he'd seen a ghost, eyeing the heavens.

"Dear me, dear me… you!" He suddenly become lethargically, emotionally acceptant. "I will still save one last trick… in honor of you…"

Jake returned to a front and center stance. And instead of weaving his gun to the left of Decoreous—instead of weaving his gun to the right of Decoreous—he split the difference and cocked the hammer. "Fuck your peace, Indian! Call them off! Now!"

Sheriff Waters reached for one of Jake's legs. Unable to stand, he shook it as if in some obscure way trying to dislodge the pistol. "No!"

"CLick-Click-click… BOOM!" and Jake's gun threw a hunk of lead directly into the heart of a near defenseless man. And yet a trigger was never pulled.

Sheriff Waters cried out with hoarseness… Jake turned pale white… the creatures yelped, and Decoreous fell first to one knee, then to both, then finally to a prone position beneath the rushes and atop the black earth he loved so dearly. A once proud chief was reduced to nothing more than a series of short, raspy breaths and occasional choking noises. Moved very little, he did, and yet quite suddenly there was a fourth party present to witness it all: Steven.

About fifty yards up the valley one little Indian watched with both horror and disbelief. He was near a thick balsam tree, his dark brown eyes quivering and replaying the trauma of the moment again and again within his head. Steven was lost. Colors were blurred. He was neither here nor there or really anywhere and everything around him was without animation. Like his grandfather, he, too, was short of breath. He, too, was choking. It was almost like his own body lay bleeding upon the ground.

"Grandfather, Grandfather!" he wailed. "What have *you* people done?"

A strong, second wind mobilized him. He hobbled quickly down and over the hills in and an effort to aid. But he wouldn't make it to his grandfather's side. No. He'd get only so close. For you see, an Earie obstacle came about. Above the rushes.

Like big balloons suddenly filling with helium, twenty or so miniature, troll-like creatures floated up—up into the air. They arose with intention, their hairy little bellies and hairy little cheeks bulging beyond capacity and looking as if to burst. And they were active, these beasts. Skinny little arms and skinny little legs clawed and kicked at the winds in circular patterns, providing propulsion for getting around. And their big, oversized ears flapped slowly and offered some additional assistance with lift, but generally served only to stabilize the creatures and exact directioning. Earies were out of the shadows and far away places, you see. That which often went bump in the night was in the middle of a skirmish and looking to defend—looking to serve a master and his grandson.

"Stay low, stay low," they said to their protectees, "no go, no go."

But Steven tried to ignore the jabberings. He had to reach his grandfather. Calling on all available power, he bounced off of inflated body after inflated body, sometimes hitting the ground and having to rise up again. He was frustrated—almost enraged, even, over his lack of progress, and his goal could not be subsequently met. The Earies countered his struggling by playing a sort of hog-pile game—a few exhaled and drifted onto Steven's back and shoulders. They covered his mouth and eyes with long black fingers, and gradually the mounting weight dragged the boy beneath the rushes and out of sight. There, he was allowed to move very little. There the creatures were hoping to hide him and just a few feet from his kin.

"Stay low, stay low," they reiterated, "no go, no go."

The little Indian was helpless.

Sheriff Waters and Jake wished they could have faired so good. They were being mugged. A majority of the beasts were assaulting both lawmen, drifting about like hellish plastic bags in a strong breeze and while scratching at faces, necks, hands, and just any old exposed skin. Small droplets of blood appeared where they clawed, and both Sheriff Waters and Jake knew they were in extreme danger. You see, instincts kicked in. They had to escape.

"What are these things?" Jake groaned in shock, holding his gun loosely and trying desperately to protect his person with swatting arms. "Sheriff?"

The good sheriff finally got to his feet. Nursing a twisted ankle, he, too, tried to keep the Earies at bay. "I don't know! But we have to get out of here! Run!"

And Jake followed the order. With the greatest of obedience. Dropping both his gun and lantern, he bolted down the valley side at a high rate of speed, grazing tree trunk after tree trunk, and occasionally tumbling end over end. Nothing would stop him, it would seem. And he never looked back. He never even noticed that his pair of silver shades and small pack of toothpicks jiggling out of his pocket along the way. Worse, he never even noticed that his superior was lagging far behind and in need of help. Jake truly acted like it was every man for himself.

And Sheriff Waters was, indeed, having trouble. He and his hefty frame tried, in earnest, to retreat, but the Earies were just too menacing. They were all over him like an angry swarm of hornets, cutting and piercing and drawing still more blood, and he was just about to give up—just about to give into the pain of his face and ankle, ultimately surrendering to the will of the creatures, when the assault was suddenly called off, as if instinctively. At a point where Reservation land ended and Westcreek city limits began, the Earies stopped and watched the good sheriff stumble about, some rising into the treetops for a better view. A barrier had been reached, one they wouldn't or couldn't cross, at least without proper guidance. So from branches high and bushes low they simply leered at a man lucky to be escaping with his life; a man anxious for once to get back to a town he never felt a part of.

The skirmish was over, it would seem. The situation was under forest control.

But the damage had already been done.

The Earies released Steven.

"Safe, no? Safe, no?" they uttered in deep voice, "can go, can go!"

The little Indian crawled to his grandfather. Full of fear and sadness, he frantically touched the old man's trembling face and spastic chest, as if unbelieving and needing to somehow verify. "Grandfather?" he whispered loudly. "Grandfather, speak to me. Please?"

"My son…" Decoreous answered in great pain. "I'm afraid I've misjudged my time on this earth. With you. Weeks have become days. Days have become… minutes. Minutes… seconds. The wind spirits… they come for me, on this morn." He choked.

"Save your strength. We have to get you back to the cabin. Get help from the Reservation doctor."

"No, my son… look at me. There is no hope." He pulled away his robe with little coordination. Revealed was a blood-soaked White T-shirt, especially near the sternum. "Hope dies with each droplet of life lost. Look, my son."

He gently pulled Steven's hand into the crimson flow.

"No…"

Decoreous' eyes became big. "Hear Me. Hear me, my son. My fate is certain. But yours, it is not. You must run from the forest and bury the hurt and anger of this tragedy. The forest… she is… no place for a boy all alone. Do so for me. Do so for your father."

"You mustn't talk. We're wasting time." He stroked the old man's forehead, trying to comfort.

"It is vital… that you leave this place! Promise you will, and don't look back! The forest will search for another… let it find no one. Let the valley just fall into a deep slumber. I beg of you… please. For I fear your strength. You… who shall be left. Your strength is need of a target. Your emotion an outlet. The forest must not know this, indeed. The forest can be quite … a sympathetic place, my son."

Steven clung to his grandfather, with full body. The almost man hugged his most beloved friend, trying to wish it all away.

Decoreous smiled. He choked slightly and then talked both softly and slowly. "The magic… you made it all worthwhile… Steven. You made life worthwhile. I'm sorry, my son. The wind spirits… they take me by the hand… "

And then the struggle was over. With one last, heavy breath, he simply slipped from one world into another, his flesh and bone left behind and to remain perfectly still. And the forest responded with a sort of quieting, you see. And the winds became lighter. The trees neither flipped nor flopped. And the Earies, and other nearby creatures of the forest, barely said "boo," and it was as if final respects were being paid.

And maybe they were. After all, a chieftain—the last of his kind— a guardian over the land, souls, and treasures of a mostly subdued people had died.

And no one or no thing would be more affected by such a passing than one little Indian.

Steven let go. He lifted his now bloody cheeks from his grandfather's bloody chest and stared upon the bloody face of death. His grandfather's big, brown eyes remained open and stared off into the distance, and Steven couldn't help but to remark silently on the total picture. It was like a shell laid before him, a mere carcass void of any inners and doomed to maybe just blow away, should the breezes pick up again; it numbed Steven. And he never felt… so alone.

And then Steven sat back and pushed away. Blood dribbled off his jawbone and down his neck, as he and his psyche tried to make sense of the senseless. And yet he couldn't. Part of his being wanted to hug, again, the body upon the ground; another to lash out at its vacancy. Emotions were mixing—colliding, as it were. But no action on the part of the boy would be taken upon the corpse. Instead, another emotion, much more powerful, would rush through his veins and cancel the others out, and it was like water broke through the Ottertail Dam and raced toward a reservoir too little and too weak to contain the fury. Something had to give, you see—within Steven's head. Something— and without fully being aware—he sort of stood, stepped over his grandfather, walked out of the waist-high rushes and like a zombie, and headed for a particular boulder in a particular clearing with something... in particular to say. Steven had no intention of leaving the forest, you see, and a brigade of Earies followed closely behind... with staff... and with robe.

"Must bring, must bring," the creatures whispered hoarsely and in unison, "to king, to king."

In the clearing rocky, ascending a boulder large and with steps so sure, Steven overlooked the town of Westcreek. And his heart began to pound. He became scornfully reflective, and surrounding him above and below were about a thousand big, ethereal faces, each flying terribly fast in a mostly elliptical pattern, his or her expression of uncertainty and fright, and then melding into grief and then back again. The state of their existence, collectively, was in question. Was this truly the end, they wondered? Was there anyone left to watch over them?

Visions came to the guardian's grandson: of a deputy's pistol going off in the morn... of fishbowl looks received from a White majority while walking down Main Street... of a long line of Indian friends and relatives forced to leave town on account of both the overt and covert behavior of others, particularly if the others saw ragged dress and sleepy-like looks... of faceless men out to defile a wanting mother... and of a plain funeral near a plain grave and for a much-loved father. Steven's breathing became terribly shallow.

He spoke to no one and yet everyone. "And then the thunderbird descended from above," he said forcefully. "With wings the size of small lakes and the head of an island, the beast brought within its claws a knife, a weapon to stab at the Great White Monster, who swallowed a village." He closed his eyes and shook. "Oh, little town. You've taken, and taken from this valley, gorged yourself, and now you lay helpless on the bank. Helpless. You must be paid back in kind. Made to feel ten times the pain you have inflicted."

And the clouds began to funnel slowly above, and Steven's rage reached out and grabbed at the web—the whole web, each and every strand. He was suddenly more than just connected to the souls. He was one with them and they with him, and their fluid expressions became much more decidedly angry. Indeed, they simply waited for a gate to open—some strings to be hammered upon, and to choose for them a course of agitated action.

Taking their own initiative, the Earies formed a circle around The Great Rock and the little Indian, a couple even scampering up to begin a sort of coronation. One scaled Steven like he was a standing tree— draping a bloody, earth-colored robe over his scant shoulders and twig-like arms. That sacred cloth hung awkwardly, like a thick bed sheet on a poorly stuffed scarecrow. But still it stayed around the boy, keeping him warm and hot. A second Earie with a noticeable limp, hissing and foaming at his little Earie mouth, delicately placed an old wooden staff within Steven's overly receptive grasp.

The look was complete, and the creatures of the forest, those both near and far, hummed or jabbered on together in a song that was void of the usual elements of music, but was a song, nonetheless. And it was of both evil and good. It was both joyous and sad. Lingering, it was the song of the forest and it glorified the risen and honored, yet possibly horrified, the fallen.

Throne ascension was both consciously and unconsciously accepted on behalf of Steven, and he continued in regards to physical emotion, getting an eyeful of Westcreek. With his belly full of all that was bad… all that was bad, he saw the entire valley in simply colors of red and white.

"Oh little town…"

"Get ready," he said even more forcefully. "Here it comes…"

Sirens began wailing within town limits. A storm warning was in effect, and indeed the skies were threatening. Hostile, even. But for one little Indian the weather was perfect—a sheer compliment to a magic show forthcoming, and the whole population below would seem destined to be a witness to its horror. Indeed.

"Here it comes… here it comes."
Steven descended the valley.

And two men were panting.
Sheriff Waters limped into his little office and shut the door quickly behind. Jake was seated at the metal desk, his head in his hands.

"What the hell just happened up there?" Jake whined. "I mean, we got our asses kicked. And by… what?"

"I don't know. The whole thing is just a blur." Sheriff Waters retrieved a white hanky from his pocket, and then proceeded to dab the many bloody openings upon his neck, face, and scalp. "It doesn't even seem real."

"Well it sure as hell feels real!" Jake yelled with terrified sarcasm, pulling Kleenex tissues from a drawer in the desk and attending to his own first aid. "The damn stinging won't go away!"

Jake looked at his superior with concern. "I didn't shoot that old Indian!"

"I know," Sheriff Waters replied, plainly.

"The gun just went off!"

"I know."

"You have to believe me!"

"I do."

Jake winced. "I mean, I was only trying to secure the area. My finger was no where near the trigger."

The words haunted the good sheriff—stabbed at his soul, they did. "I know." He thought about the stifled investigation, the increasing body count, and the growing animosity both within the forest and Westcreek. Moving to a black phone upon the desk, he made a decision, decisively. "We need help, Jake. I'm gonna call in State authorities."

Jake snatched away the phone. "The State? Are you crazy?"

"Things are getting out of control!"

"And what do you think they'll find, when they get here? Huh? If they start poking around into Decoreous' death?" The deputy shook his head, his tense blue eyes denoting a sort of paranoia. "You know how they are. How they might dig up more than just an accident. Put my credibility as a law officer into question. And what if they bring in the tribal council? Huh? My God, the inquiry will never end."

"So what do you suggest we do?" Sheriff Waters snapped.

Jake lowered his voice and made deep eye contact. "End the whole investigation. Let everything just die down."

"What?"

"We'll prepare a report and send it to Pine County. Tell them what we know. List all four deaths as probable homicide but with no solid leads and a missing murder weapon. We can classify the investigation as on-going. The actual report will just collect dust in the back of somebody's file cabinet—you know how they are, Nat. No questions will be asked. For years, even. Shit, we're not gonna solve this thing! We've questioned everybody and come up with nothing. We've had top professionals collect and analyze evidence that leads nowhere. We've come as close as we can to understanding what happened that night. So no one needs to be called in. State or otherwise…"

Sheriff Waters was flabbergasted. "You want me to be part of a cover up? To stop doing my job because a possible internal investigation might—might—depict you in a bad light? To basically save your ass, Jake? What about the man who lost his life, today?"

And there was an answer.

Jake plotted. "We never saw him. Never found him during our search, for questioning." He strolled slowly around the desk, so as to face his superior without a barrier. "Think about it: a man living for years… all alone is hard to miss, eh? We'll let people know that the reports about his existence turned out to be false. Tell a select few the truth. A select few who can keep our secret."

Sheriff Waters looked away. "And what do we do with his body?"

"Discard it," Jake answered, with swallowing. "Bury it. That's why we need to let somebody in on what really happened. Hell, Trace and Benjamin would jump at the chance to drop Decoreous in a hole. All we'd have to do is tell 'em where he lies." He ended with an odd little laugh.

The good sheriff felt like punching his deputy. No previous juncture in their relationship had ever elicited such a want, and he thought he could do more harm than a forest full of "wild dogs." And yet he fought the impulse. "Now you're asking me to turn a blind eye to corruption, Jake? Jesus! No! I won't do it. As sheriff of this town I have both legal and moral responsibilities. I expected the same of you. No, dammit, we're gonna do everything by the book!"

Jake guffawed. He walked to the office door, and then stopped. Then he took a forced breath. "By the book? Nat?" He bit his lip. "Were things done by the book five years ago? When that cripple's father was shot?"

Silence answered.

Jake continued. "As I remember, your gun went off accidentally, too. Just like mine. But things weren't exactly done 'by the book' back then either, were they? A sheriff got damn scared. He didn't call in the appropriate officials to investigate the situation. It became hush-hush. Hell, I don't recall a death certificate even being issued. The county never knew. Still doesn't know. It's like a damn Indian thief just faded away. Disappeared. Hell, we're far away from really anywhere, right?" Though still visibly shaken, he stood a bit taller. "So 'good sheriff,'... tell me about my legal and moral responsibility?"

Sheriff Waters felt gravely ill, sicker than he had ever felt in his life. With just a few verbal utterances Jake stabbed at the nucleus of his cancer—the very center point at which all that was known and unknown about that terrible encounter five years ago, and scrunched somewhere between was the reality of a sort of cover up. It shocked Sheriff Waters to be told what he already knew, and he reacted with a sort of conscious slumber. The demons were back. And this time they didn't bother knocking on the door to his sanity; they just barged right in: he was doomed to remember, deeply.

Jake felt for a toothpick in his sweat-drenched shirt, but was denied. "If it makes you feel better," he began with coldness, "I can fill out a form on the accidental discharge of a firearm, just like you. Place it behind yours in the file cabinet. That's where it still is, isn't it? Mostly incomplete? Even difficult to make out the hand writing?

Mine'll be another document that never quite made it out of town. We are the authority." He pondered. "Legal and moral responsibility... shit." Then he touched the door handle as if rubbing away a blemish on the metal. "You were a great mentor, Nat. You taught me everything I know about law enforcement. As an understudy, it's only right that I follow in your footsteps. I guess... my handling of this problem will be proof enough. That I'm walking right behind you."

Jake smiled, tensely. "Get rid of your conscience, Nat. With your past, it's not becoming."

To the east wall, and walking like he was naked and wanting to be clothed, Sheriff Waters stared out of a window and at the swirling black clouds. His seemingly good-hearted fight against wrong and for right was bulldozed, the remnants, of which, disappearing into that cancer.

His disease seemed to progress.

And Jake was about to leave. Opening the office door with a creak, he stepped out, and onto the boardwalk—but then withdrew such motions, as if suddenly in reverse. With his back to Sheriff Waters, he spoke softly. "That old Indian was lying. I could see it in his eyes. He murdered those four. At the very least, he knew where the gun was."

He glanced over his shoulder. "Do you remember my father, Nat? Huh? Do you remember how proud he was when I became deputized and assigned to this town?"

No response.

Jake reflected. "He was a cop, himself. But retired. Wanting to spend his golden years near his son, he moved he, mom, and my little sister to a plot of land just north of here. It was on Mille Lacs Lake— do you remember? He built a beautiful log cabin with his own hands— God! It was beautiful. All cedar with pine plum risings, do you remember? But at the time, there was a territory dispute goin' on between the Ojibwe and the government. Remember? The cabin turned out to be on Indian land, but a tribal elder assured my father that his property rights would be honored, no matter what the outcome of any following meetings. My father finished the cabin that next summer, despite tensions." Jake paused. "A couple weeks later... the elder and the whole damn tribal council came knocking with papers basically evicting my father from the land. They gave him two weeks to get out. No reparations were made—no money was given, by either the tribe or our government.

He and my family moved back to the Twin Cities and barely made ends meet. There was nothing anyone could do, legally. My father's dream home... my father's dream life, being near his son... I think the loss of it all sent him to an early grave. He was just never the same."

Jake sighed deeply, turned his head back around, and then he gazed upon a wind-wept Main Street. "The elder's eyes—Decoreous' eyes, they were the same. Full of lies. Just like most every Indian I've ever met. Not all. But most." He tried for a dramatic exit, but Sheriff Waters called after him.

"Jake," he murmured numbly, switching the focus. "There was a boy in that forest. He yelled out when Decoreous fell. Did you see him?"

"It's probably just some kid off the Reservation, Nat," Jake responded with a certain matter-of-factness. "Maybe he was lost. Those damn dogs probably got to him. It's the tribe's problem. Not ours." With that, he hurried away, his nerves still a bit ajar, his swagger all but absent.

He headed for the café and with a deep need to connect with those who might understand his situation. In a smoky corner out of the way and over whisky and beer, he'd whisper the details of a tragic morning to a select few who had a knack for turning fear into courage and painful wounds into the scars of a hero, and with a nod, a pat on the back, and the shake of a hand.

Jake was out to recapture his stature, it seemed.

And Sheriff Waters was left alone. Decimated in regards to character, he turned away from the cold outside, wandered listlessly to his desk chair, and focused on his cold insides. The cancer was crawling across his chest. It pained his heart so that each beat felt like it was going to burst through a rib or two and maybe shoot from his skin. Indeed. In a little dank and dirty office, a good sheriff had time to rehash the events of the day, the events of two nights back, and especially—and again—the events in a liquor store almost exactly five years ago.

But not all of his mental energy would be drained on the past. No. He also thought about cures for his disease. Like grabbing the black phone and making a call to the State; like leaving Westcreek in the middle of the night and never returning. And like opening his desk drawer, removing a seldom-used revolver, and taking but another life, one close at hand, and this time the pulling of a trigger would surely not be by accident.

But like most times, and with most decisions, he just couldn't decide what to do: to act or not to act, that was the question, and eventually he did nothing. The good Sheriff Waters was paralyzed into inaction.

THE
WAR

Prelude to War (Intro)

On the south side of town, sitting atop a broken old porch attached to a broken old home of chipped white paint, an old man of brown spots and a jittery lower lip sat rocking in a wooden chair. As if oblivious to the tumultuous skies above, he simply stared blankly at a dead maple tree in his yard, his mind on Indian folk. The old man was numb off slow gin, and in his lap he held a rusty rifle. If there was one crazy Indian running amuck in the forest, there was bound to be another, he thought. Maybe many, and he just hoped he could get a clean shot off before they crossed his property line.

He was sure *they* were coming; he hoped *they* were coming. By default.

Faintly heard, an old woman's voice from inside the home tried to call the old man out of the weather. But he wouldn't budge. He just rocked more slowly and held his gun even more tightly. Back and forth, he rocked. Back… and forth. Back… and… forth.

In a trailer home near the east end of town, and while a mummy and daddy were at the café, two little boys played an intense game of cowboys and Indians. Their cramped quarters served as a sort of battlefield. A ripped sofa and chair were set cockeyed in a little living room, so as to afford a brown-vested sheriff some cover. Nearby, in a messy kitchen of soiled pots and pans, a White Indian Brave with feathered headband of seagull's wing peaked out from underneath a card table smothered by a thick, red blanket—a teepee, as it were. A fierce exchange of missile fire between the two ensued, and the Indian

Brave scored first a victory, and then, ultimately, a terrible defeat. One suction-cupped arrow got launched from a flimsy bow. It struck the sheriff in the armpit, and the junior lawman dropped his wounded body over a portion of the sofa and in great theatrics. But with lasting strength, with gasping breaths and big eyes, the sheriff raised a silver capgun and let off a barrage of shots. More than one hit its mark. Popping noises caused the White Indian Brave to first jolt, then wobble, and then collapse upon a plywood floor so dingy. The Indian Brave would die. But the sheriff—he would live on to defend his town from other savages.

Later, the boys would change roles; the results, however, would be the same.

"Click... click... click..." was the faint and light rhythm heard.

Dex sat idle at a wooden desk. In a log cabin of his own fashioning and near the far, western edge of Westcreek, he stared at and not out of a tiny little window, watching the glass bulge and dimple to the wind's likening. His right hand diddled with a pen, and on his desk was a blank piece of paper meant to hold all the words he wanted to say. And to Gloria, but none would come to mind. You see, the words were all locked deep within a powerful emotion that had only recently been trampled upon. Dex seemed doomed to just feel and to not express.

But what was left to say that countless poems, songs, and letters hadn't said before, one might've ask? What could be told that his hazel eyes didn't already tell?

His pen's rhythm began to slow. "CLick... Click... click," it went.

Doc Baker ran desperately about town. He was a gray-haired little man with thick glasses and a bushy mustache, and he searched long and hard for a pair of golden labs that darted from his yard. It wasn't like them to disregard his calling, he thought. It wasn't like them to wander so far away. And where exactly had they gone?

Just off of Main Street he stopped to hone in on their distant barking. While hugging his own frame and a big blue parka in hopes of getting warm, he could've swore he heard them northwest of town, maybe where the valley sloped and the forest thickened, dreadfully. The barking was faint and yet full of fervor. Each dog hit a multitude of tones. It was as if they were yelling and screaming about something. Or at least at something.

Doc Baker wondered: Had they found a possum to harass? Or had the storm affected their senses and rendered them lost and scared? He tried whistling in an effort to call them home and with quick, deep breaths.

Then sirens came on. Interrupting his musical melody, five yellow horns on big wooden poles around Westcreek rose and fell with a shrill whimper and yet in a definite, sometimes ear-paining, scale. Total duration of their blasting was about five minutes, and afterwards a low hum trickled out of each. So Doc baker tried once more in regards to locating his dogs.

He listened. And heard nothing. Not a bark. Not a growl. Not even a yelp. It was as if the two had suddenly disappeared. He tried calling, whistling, and then calling yet another time.

Nothing.

An Earie feeling came over Doc Baker. He twitched his bushy mustache.

The café was packed with locals. A young, redheaded miner, new in town by Westcreek standards, tried to enter, but capacity had been reached hours ago. He had to settle for just peeking in. Thick tobacco smoke billowed out as he opened the door. Loud chatter greeted him, and seen was a virtual sea of solemn, if not agitated faces. The young miner would have to wait his turn, and maybe after the last ounce of booze was consumed. You see, an unseen sort of pecking order wafted his direction, and he existed somewhere near the bottom; he'd have to come back later.

Jake and his men were within that sea of faces. Trace, Daniel, Benjamin, Beckett, and Charles P. surrounded their town deputy and spoke words of drunken revelry. The tragedy of the day was nearly forgotten, and at the very least greatly suppressed. Power in numbers had heightened Jake's self-righteousness to new levels. Indeed, he was feeling comfortable again. He did his duty.

The young miner closed the café door with care. Shoving his cold fingers into the deep pockets of his jeans, he hurried down Main Street toward a little pickup camper parked near the northeast corner of town. This was home, at least temporarily. Such a small, scant accommodation was meant to suffice in the short-term and until he could find solid work and afford to buy a trailer near the still-inactive mines.

The plan was six months old.

Amos drank himself silly. Nursing from an almost empty bottle of Schnapps, cuddled up near an old wooden barrel in an alleyway downtown, the dirty-faced Indian conversed with some voices in his head.

"Have to wait..." he murmured. "Not your time. It is written... must wait. No... let the forest slumber." He suddenly slapped at the air with both of his hands. "Leave me be, you fools! All of you—be gone!"

Then he appeared lethargic, as if having trouble staying awake.

"Coat of flames," he whispered. "Blue... and orange... coat of flames. Die."

Slipping firmly into unconsciousness, Amos dreamed of an angry people without faces.

And they felt comforting.

From a bird's-eye view, the very heart of Westcreek resembled an old, western movie set, complete with tiny little spotlights that swayed to and fro and as if haphazardly searching for a star or two. You see, lighting was poor downtown, and mostly on account of previous, bad weather. Things were in disrepair. Tall, wooden poles on both sides of Main Street supported broken lamps or lamps without power, and so shopkeepers hung out lanterns on bent nails to supplement the loss of shine; especially that afternoon, for night prevailed upon the town. But the shopkeepers' efforts were in vain. At best, each lantern provided a big candle's worth of light, and anyhow there really wasn't that much to see. The streets were dead. Only the dust had life, and it sprung up all over within a series of miniature tornadoes.

To and fro, the lanterns swayed. To and fro, and a bit of low growling could be heard as a result of metal scraping metal.

To and fro, they swayed. To and fro.

In a dark general store, by a cash register ejected and holding a flashlight steady, a bald-headed merchant with bristly sideburns studied some inventory sheets. The electricity was out again. But being a stubborn man and a man of routine, he went ahead with his duties. His analysis would not be pleasant.

He rubbed his slippery scalp. Trying to prepare a mental list of items needed for ordering purposes, he ran down row after row of fully stocked product. Canned goods like corn, beans, and peas rose above his finger; so did boxes of mashed potatoes, rice, and pancake mixes. From household cleansers to multigrain breads, from heating oil and nails to mosquito spray and diapers, the whole place was packed to the hilt with potential sales. The only exceptions were in the areas of meat and milk.

Turning a page, the merchant eyed those items kept in a cooler near the back of the store. Here he had more than enough. Matter of fact, too much, and within two days hamburger, chicken, and many cheeses would be too rotten to sell and in need of discarding. Such was the case last week. And the week before that.

The merchant said a quick prayer and in regards to the power staying off; then he might at least be able to make an insurance claim.

Minutes later, the lights flickered on, and he snorted. Switching off his flashlight gruffly and allowing himself no more than a ten-minute break from his paperwork, he stared blankly into his empty cash register and reorganized his dismal thoughts.

Nothing would be in need of ordering.

Sheriff Waters was working, too. But not on inventory. Rather, he was trying to face more sins of the past. On his own.

Melancholy and slow in movements, he stood aside a metal file cabinet, the top drawer wide open. There he thumbed through old folder after old folder on his way to the very back and a pair of unmarked dividers stuffed with papers. At hand were a plethora of ignored police calls.

The good sheriff pursed his sweating lips. He reached for a stack of the mostly stained documents and like they were fragile glass, and indeed they had the potential for cutting; at his spirit, that is, and reciting to himself a sampling of the pen-scrawled information kept, he imbibed in a bit of bloodletting.

Sheriff Waters was determined to connect with the origins of his disease. Then maybe he could begin to find relief.

"J. White Eagle, April 5, 1990," he said quietly. "Man reports home burglary. Front door broken into with possible ax. Cassette radio and small television reported missing. Man requests police investigation." He moved to the underlying document. "J. White Eagle, April 6, 1990. Man reports second home burglary and property destruction. Reports one hundred dollars in cash missing. Reports windows broken and fabric on couch cut by possible knife. Man requests police investigation." He sifted through the stack and chose another, this one with a name first written and then crossed out. "May 25, 1992," he read. "Woman reports assault. States her husband, intoxicated, punched her in the jaw twice. Woman is calling from a neighbor's home. Requests police mediation."

Removing his hat as if annoyed with the fit and then tossing it atop the file cabinet, Sheriff Waters picked out one last document. Like the former, a name was first written and then crossed out. The date also appeared incomplete. "October, 1993," he said. "Man is calling from Reservation. States he was assaulted by two white males at the Westcreek Café. Man reports sustaining a black right eye and cuts on his face and left ear; is currently receiving care from Reservation doctor. States he can positively ID the two white males. Would like to file charges with the county." His mumbling lips trailed off.

The remaining police calls were more of the same content, usually hastily written, and sharing in one, overriding characteristic: no follow through—no action taken. And the good sheriff's big cheeks turned red with anger. Not just from the fact that Jake handled a majority of the intakes; not just from the fact that all the documents lacked in professionalism. No, also because of Sheriff Waters' own involvement; for his handwriting could be found here and there—he, too, put a low priority or no priority on some incoming calls. His decision-making was poor in some cases, and this is where he felt it all began.

This is when he could remember first experiencing symptoms. When he failed to question rightness over wrongness. When he simply did nothing. Truth, from reflection—it provided at least a smidgen of comfort deep inside the lawman. It allowed him to feel, wholly feel, long-suppressed emotion.

But where to go from here, he thought?

A few of Jake's words echoed in his head and in regards to police work. *"The reports will just collect dust in the back of somebody's file cabinet. You know how they are. No questions will be asked... so no one needs to be called in. State or otherwise."*

Sheriff Waters appeared even redder. His feet, his hands, and his mind were never closer to taking some kind of action, even a wrong one. He was closer to swallowing the most potent—yet bitter—of medicines, it would seem.

Was he still angry? Should she approach him? And if so, how? With what movements? Would he react violently? And why could she no longer hear his footsteps?

Gloria headed for the ladder. She pushed "another moment" and ascended rung by rung, her goal concerned with talking—really talking to Steven, for she dearly wanted to leave Westcreek the following day. Near the trap door she stopped, though. Wrapped in a flowery bathrobe of motherly softness, she hesitated, unsure of her reception, unsure of herself.

The storm. Its dark clouds hung over the valley like a thick shroud atop an open coffin, and at center was a sort of mischievous spinning. Twisting, turning, a wispy cone extended downward and then retracted—downward and then retracted, and it was as if the townspeople were being toyed with, mentally. Kept uncertain in regards to feeling. Jostled back and forth, they were, between heavy fear and relief and while staring out small windows or listening from cellars so cramped. Dirt comforts were pulled upwards and downwards... upwards and downwards. And the air. The air was terribly humid and cluttered with big faces. Ethereal forms flew into and out of the clouds, their mouths softly uttering as if conversing with each other or whatever was found within. And the storm seemed to respond. It fussed and with some sort of understanding. It lit up the sky with flashy emotion.

Sirens went off again within town limits.

Then came one little Indian.

Fire March

High noon and without sun.

And Steven entered Westcreek. With strength. Emerging from a heavy patch of thickets along the western edge of The Great Forest and stepping upon town soil, he walked precisely, slowly, and with motive, his shoulders looming over his deeply set head, his eyes straight forward and narrow, his staff and robe dragging first across weeds, then grass, then the strewn-about dirt atop Main Street. Behind, did scamper, about twenty Earies all in a line, and it was as if the creatures were enjoying a game of follow-the-leader. Or something. The Earies mimicked Steven with playfulness—a sheer glee, as it was, and the sort of march continued to town center and until their master scratched at the magical web with his gut, giving orders.

Action was the result.

The guardian's special pets disbanded. Running left and right and like perky little monkeys, their hairy little arms limp in front of their creature, they approached the old wooden buildings downtown with malicious intent. Some of the Earies simply skidded across the boardwalk. Others scaled roughly, the buildings, and their stain-worn sides and dumpy awning. A new playground was discovered, you see.

And Steven—he kept walking. He had a goal in mind, a sort of reckoning, and so the little beasts were left to drum up their own fun. They found some in the many lanterns that hung here and there. Snatching the light sources from their hooks, they scurried about, peeking through open doors and windows in search of human playmates. You see, the Earies were eager to play a one-sided game of catch, and a scant number of shopkeepers and general citizenry were destined to become receivers.

"To burn, to burn," they chortled quietly, "we yearn, we yearn."

Above the liquor store, in a small apartment with a slanted ceiling, the first "ball" was thrown. Loaded with kerosene, the lantern crashed through a chipped window, dropping to the slippered feet of an elderly waitress unaware and relaxing in an easy chair. The mixture of a hardwood floor, fuel, and flame created a splash of blue fire, and the woman jumped, danced about, and yelled—she wobbled to her apartment door and exited with hysterics. Many bookcases full of family albums with black and white photos were forgotten and certain to perish.

Downstairs and a couple of buildings over, in a soaped-up hardware store crammed with boxes, a grieving son finalized plans for going out of business. He was tired, reflective, and just about to call it a day when two fiery projectiles were lobbed through the store's open door. His response was one of brief pause—like it couldn't possibly be happening, and then he cowered in a nearby corner, the inferno growing, the heat uncomfortable, the roar getting louder. There existed no back door to the place, and so the grieving son's only chance at survival was to make a dash for it. Grabbing his father's overcoat, he stood timidly, jolted toward the blaze, but then backed down. Again—he jolted toward the blaze and then backed down, and finally he conjured up enough courage to escape—to vault certain death, protected by only a cloth shield. But success. He made it to the other side with a thud. And after quickly shedding his burning pseudoskin, he staggered out into the street, attempting to summon any and all.

"Help!" he cried, turning in circles. "Please… somebody. Fire! Bring the trucks around!"

Only one would hear, across the way. However, plagued with troubles of his own, this one could offer little assistance. Indeed.

The bald-headed merchant was chased from the general store. Forced through smoke and broken glass, he was relieved of his duties as a great many Earies took over the task of inventory control. In the middle of Main Street the man struggled with bewilderment and fright; back inside the establishment, the creatures jumped from shelf to shelf, clearing product. Cans of sauerkraut, string beans, and diced pears were kicked soccer-style and with almost little people's feet into walls, still intact windows, and other Earies. Toilet plungers, wooden trellises, and coat racks were disassembled and dropped like Tinker Toys upon the industrial, gray tile. And milk and orange juice jugs were squeezed roughly, subsequently showering the showroom with white and orange fluid. The site was chaotic and rambunctious: flames, smoke, wetness, long-eared critters, and property destruction—the whole lot of it.

And further devilish behavior was encouraged through busy, Earie chatter.

But not everything within the general store was to be treated meanly. On the contrary, one particular product was cherished. In the back corner, on a bottom shelf and in huge quantities, Steven's little companions found cans of candied yams.

"For yum, for yum," one of them shrieked above the almost deafening noise, "must come, must come!"

One by one they gathered 'round as if having reached a sort of lunch break in their day of games. Big ears raised slightly from mouth-watering interest, and seated Indian-style upon the floor, they shared very little, grabbing as many of the tin cylinders as possible, stabbing sharp, black claws through hard tops, repeatedly. Access to the soft vegetables within was slow and sometimes not at all, but for those that could pry the metal open—for those that wouldn't be left whimpering in almost human voice and with hunger, the payoff was a slippery, sweet treat. Piggishly, a few Earies gobbled down globs of candied yams, occasionally collecting small chunks and orange-colored slop on their almost, human faces. The feast seemed satisfying. It refurbished a lot of high-strung energy, and the beasts began wondering: Where more doggies? Where more friends? Where, where more fun? The lunch break ended. Quickly.

But the opportunity to finish their "work" would soon be in jeopardy.

In the middle of Main Street the elderly waitress, the grieving son, and the bald-headed merchant came together in a daze. Words were absent, faces were wrinkled in confusion, mouths gaped open, and slowly the three were joined by other folks from different points around Westcreek. All witnessed a number of flames that shot out of windows, doors, and crevices within the buildings' exterior. Damage was about one-fourth of the total area and growing, and no one in the group seemed to have enough gumption to do anything about it. They were in a sort of stupor. Not until Jake and his men emerged from the café did a plan even get organized for trying to save the town.

"What happened?" Jake yelled, almost stumbling over his perfectly shined boots, his eyes surveying downtown. "Who the hell did this?"

"More like what the hell did this!" the bald-headed merchant answered, angrily. "I saw bears! In my store!"

"And I saw an Indian boy!" an elder added, near the deputy. "East of here!"

Sheriff Waters arrived in a huff. Making his way through the crowd, and having heard the two men's answers, he sought out Jake's gaze. And he found it. Via concerned looks both lawmen shared a heightened sense of urgency, as if the situation had suddenly taken on greater meaning. Nothing was fully understood, but a chill raced down both of their spines, nonetheless.

"BOOM!" and a tall propane tank in the back of the hardware store blew. Men and women alike screamed and bumped into each other, roughly.

Jake attempted to bring order. "Stay calm!" he belted out with strained vocal chords, his arms raised for effect. "Dammit, listen to me! Everything'll be all right! Just stay calm!" He tried providing a focus, handing down crisis assignments to key figures present. He pointed. "Hank! William! Grab a couple of men and sweep the buildings! Make sure everybody's out!" He pointed again. "Jess! Get Jonathan and his sons! Bring around the fire trucks and start hosing down the worst blazes!" He pointed one last time. "Nat! Organize the rest of the men here into a bucket line! Have 'em wet down the wood that hasn't burned yet! Evacuate everybody else up the valley!"

With that said, the deputy and a few special others bolted away from the crowd. But Sheriff Waters delayed them all, wanting to know more.

"Where the hell are you going?"

"To the office!" Jake snapped as if having been asked a dumb question. "For rifles and shells! We need to secure the area! Find that 'Indian boy' and whatever the hell else is around!" He nodded. "All by the book!"

The good sheriff stutter-stepped. He acted as if wanting to join the group, moving forward slightly, and deep inside he felt a strong sense of duty to be present during all police business. It's just that he held back, tripping on his spirit.

Jake clarified any role discrepancy. "You're needed here, Nat! With the people! We'll handle everything else! Just keep your radio on!"

Sheriff Waters didn't feel too assured. He was suddenly overwhelmed by a haunting of how things had gotten grossly out of hand, and this time the feeling was even worse than before. And it was almost like an observable aura extended out from his being in regards to a likely response, for Jake read him perfectly.

"Don't call the State, Nat! We don't need assistance! This is a Westcreek matter!" His tone left little room for discussion.

Jake, Trace, Daniel, Benjamin, Beckett, and Charles P. ran off to a stockpile of arms. Along the way they grabbed a beleaguered Doc Baker, inquiring about the use of his dogs, and although the reply was negative, although their subsequent effort would be minus a set of highly-tuned sniffers, the morale of each man rose with each stride taken.

The townspeople looked to Sheriff Waters. With Jake and his men gone, he was counted on as a leader; all eyes asked wistfully for his guidance. The good sheriff answered with a racing heart and sweaty palms.

Could he keep them all safe, he wondered? Could he provide needed direction and organization during a tragedy? And most of all, could he be the sheriff he once was?

"BOOM!" and a second propane tank exploded.

Meanwhile, Steven conferred with the dead. East of the old, white church and amidst the wee cemetery, he explained his assault graveside and to his father. Calm, yet numb, he acted as if the backdrop of fire and chaos did not exist; it was just a talk between two.

He knelt. "Grandfather always spoke of peace. He said it was the way of the true Ojibwe. To pursue harmony and understanding with others and to never, ever place a spear, hatchet, or edged word in place of a handshake. Peace at all costs, he used to say. But Grandfather spoke of a peace between equals. It does not apply to this valley." He paused.

"The story of Bear and Badger, father," he continued, bowing his head and rubbing his blood-marred cheeks. "Do you remember? Day after day Bear chased Badger through the forest in a show of power. Bear slapped at Badger's head again and again, until one day Badger became cornered near a rocky cliff. Then Badger fought back. He snarled, clawed, and bit Bear. Bear ran off. And from that day forth the two shared the forest as equals."

Steven looked with forlorn to the darkened clouds above, the thunder rumbling. "Forgive me. I do not wish to dishonor you or Grandfather. But I must seek peace through power and terror. Only then can all men of the valley come together as equals. Only then can there be a handshake." He dropped his eyes down upon the simple headstone of black and white flecks.

A vision came: One of a handsome young Indian with dark, dark brows, tossing a crippled child high into the air. Deep in woods of mostly white pine and oak, a father and son spent a lazy afternoon together, teachings of the earth, wind, and sky behind them. The young father emitted a pride warmer than the summer day. And though his face and clothes were dirty and ragged, respectively, his heart and eyes were transcended toward something greater—it was just he and his son, after all. Up and down, the child went. Up and down and until the vision faded.

Steven reached for the headstone with shaky fingers and as if wanting somehow to be nearer to his father. "Until we meet again," he murmured.

But just before he made contact—just before he touched the coldness, the rock sparked. It twanged loudly, and before both phenomena came a high-pitched, echoing slap.

Steven had been found.

He stood abruptly. Scanning quickly back over his shoulder, he found a hulking, male figure standing near the northeast corner of the church, a shiny new rifle held stiffly in his hands.

It was Trace. And his face muscles were quivering.

Sudden predator and prey locked eyes. Terribly. And though both of their bodies appeared as if frozen, from one to the other was drifted an emotional heat containing a mixture of anger, hurt, and blame. Neither could see clearly. Both felt spiritually blunt or jabbed at, and at the very least predator and prey were made to feel uncomfortable. Such a heavy, perverse atmosphere hung about until a cry unexpectedly cut their connection.

"Do you see him, Trace?" Daniel called from still downtown. "Trace!"

Steven sensed an opening. With the swiftness of a deer, he bolted from his father's grave, hurdled the small white fence, and scrambled for the cover of the forest.

Trace got off two quick shots. "Slap!" and one missed Steven's back, left heel; "SLAP!" and the second whizzed over his head. Trace grumbled.

"He's heading north!" he hollered to his brother and any and all within hearing range. "Stop him!"

But it wouldn't happen. Not in Westcreek, anyway. The renegade Indian had made it to the treeline and was well on his way up the valley, leading his pursuers into and onto a more—one could say—even playing field.

The boy had a plan, you see.

And Trace, Daniel, and Jake fell into it. Converging near the town water supply, guns shaking and flashlights bright, the three barked at each other briefly about what procedure should be from that moment onward. They then conveyed their agreements to the others and via walkie-talkies. A few synchronized nods and the men went after Steven, their boots stomping firmly into Indian earth. Doc Baker followed slowly behind, his bushy mustache twitching nervously. He hoped all the commotion might scare up his missing canines.

Benjamin, Charles P., and Beckett heard Jake's radio transmission. They would eventually join the pursuit, but first the general store needed to be cleansed of its unwanted workers. The three men stepped up to the burning sidewalk in front as if approaching the counter of a shooting gallery at a fair. With clips jammed full of hard metal, they took potshots at virtually anything that moved. Earie shrieking resonated.

"BAM!" and a bullet nicked a knobby little elbow, spraying out light, red fluid and as one beast jumped from shelf to shelf.

"BAM-BAM!" and a couple more took it in the temple and neck. Both dropped. Fun, it would seem, was to be had, no more.

Pandemonium ensued, each beast bolting to any place hidden and free of fire and bullets. Lack of space, however, brought either a melting, gooey death or a slow fade-away, like that similar to a pellet through a watermelon, oozing internal fluid, the derivative. Few could survive.

Four Earies, in particular, tried to stem the emerging massacre. Spread eagle, they inflated, throwing up their bodies in sort of altruism. A slight wind from the flames pushed them toward their foes. Claws were out and flailing like windmills. And the human reaction became one of startle and spastic firing.

"Jesus Christ!" Beckett yelled, pulling the trigger of his weapon repeatedly and knocking off his big hat. Two Earie splatters—one in midair and the other atop the cash register, but both with dark-colored lungs and intestines emerging—were the result.

Charles P. accidentally shot three beasts of his own. "I thought these were 'sposed to be bears—what the hell is this?"

"Hold your ground!" Benjamin ordered, appointing himself leader and trying to draw a good bead. "Don't let 'em out of there! Take 'em to die or let 'em fry!"

But the three men had instinctively backed away from the bedlam, opening up a corridor of escape through a broken, far east window. One by one, those Earies that hadn't been blasted—those little creatures that hadn't been scorched black by the bright orange flames, scurried out, shimmied up the awning, ran across the rooftops, and made way for the forest safe. No more than ten would be left to make such a trek, however.

"Will rise, will rise," they babbled with almost annoying redundancy, "to die, to die!"

Benjamin, Charles P., and Beckett jogged away from the general store and around to the rear like a disciplined fighting squad, their guns swaying from side to side and ready to fire. They intended to cutoff the creatures. But upon arriving the area was found to be Earie-free.

"Damn!" Benjamin spat under his breath, searching intensely. "Where did they go?" He switched on his flashlight, shining it in several directions. Barely an insect moved. Barely an insect was seen. He felt like he let Jake down.

Panting loudly, the deputy came over his radio. *"Benjamin! Benjamin! Copy?"*

"Yeah," the fair-haired Norwegian answered, dejectedly.

"What's your position?"

"In the back of hell's kitchen, for Christ's sake!"

"Take your men and head north of town! Toward the ol' Dawson Mine! Spread out in case the Indian tries to double-back!"

Benjamin sighed, feeling cheated. "You got it."

Then he yelled at Charles P. and Beckett. "You heard the man, let's go! Move!" They took to the valley slope. The final three components in an all-White offensive were set into motion.

From a bird's-eye view the scene looked buggy. It was as if seven tiny fireflies flew away from a great bonfire, jittering about and penetrating deeper and deeper into darker and darker places. Buzzy chatter occasionally lifted above the otherwise constant racket from downtown, but for the most part the spread out mob embarked on a silent mission. Up and over the many hills, they went. Up and over the many hills, and only when their prime objective was met would volumes change. Drastically. Then buzzy chatter would turn to pressured pleading.

Then screams would rattle trees.

Then offensives would be squashed like...

Drums of War

Heavy, heavy breathing... some rousing battle cries... the calamity of twigs snapping, and Steven tried to stay ahead of it all. Wired, he was—calculating. In almost total blackness he zigzagged, on solid foot, his way through dense bush, trying to add to the good 100 yards that already existed between he and his would-be captors. However, no further ground could be gained. A lot would be lost, even, and for Trace was on fire. Terribly.

The strong man went berserk. Using only small shifts in the shadows forward as a guide, and as if suddenly channeling all of his brawn down and into his legs, he charged past a wary Jake like a soldier storming an enemy fortress, mowing over small popular trees and honeysuckle plants in the process. A low-pitched wail—full-bellied, mind you—accompanied his actions, and his overall goal became one of annihilating his chosen target. Terribly.

Random gunfire was let loose and to underscore such a sentiment.

And Steven wasn't prepared to counter, either Trace's weaponry or his speed. He didn't anticipate such a forceful objection to his imposed magic show, and so his inward plan became garbled, his steps became tentative, and his strength began to waver. And the forest didn't help matters much, either. Spiny tree limbs, most without leaves or needles, kept snagging the fine material in his robe, throwing off his pace. Soon anxiety would take over Steven's system, Trace coming on like a freight train—he could just feel him behind.

One of those random gunshots nicked the little Indian's shoulder, adding to his troubles. Though amounting to just a flesh wound, the stinging pain was so pronounced—so overwhelming that he was reduced to a cripple again, hobbling around and clutching his arm—still moving forward, as it were—but left to be greatly hindered.

And Trace would capitalize. Pouring on the steam and sensing a hit, he raised his rifle up high for a close-quarters bash. Dropping his light source, waiting for the perfect moment to strike, waiting for shadows to appear more solid, he pounded the wooden stock straight into Steven's skull. Another hit, and Steven took a tumble, looking like a squirming lump of flesh upon the forest floor.

"Damn you, Redskin!" Trace groaned, raising his rifle again for another blow. "This one's for my father!"

And he brought it down.

The second assault, like the initial gunshot wound, only grazed Steven's skin, connecting mostly with dirt and roots. But in slight contrast to the first, the second bash had ripped a small gash into the very center of Steven's head, drawing up warm blood and causing fits of slight nausea and blurred vision.

The almost man was suddenly quite vulnerable.

Trace towered over his foe. Twirling around, he let loose with a few more shots into the air and as if not rightly knowing what else to do with both his immediate displeasure and vent-up angst.

"Get up!" he demanded. "Get up, you!"

Cowering, Steven remained low. The full reality of his doings came rushing home and in the form of an aching noggin. He was at once regretful and yet proud, triumphant and yet defeated, and rolling about near Trace's huge, brown boots allowed him neither the option to escape or to overcome: he seemed trapped.

But mind you—the Indian still had strength. He still had fuel for combat. And he still had an unsatisfied, overwhelming rage. It's just that all three elements were stored deep in his gut, boiling together in a new sort of brew that required maybe just a bit more spark—maybe a bit more fire before it would surface. Currently any additional energy needs were to be ignored by the body. The little Indian's faculties were much too taxed by survival and pain reduction needs.

Jake arrived at the drama playing out. He was gruff with one of his own. Preceding Daniel and Doc, he stepped between Trace and Steven and with a sort of bigger man's chest.

"Take no action without me!" he said to Trace, pointing to the hulk's bulbous pectorals. "I told you I wanted the boy alive and unharmed! Now stand down! Stand down!" He shoved him.

And Trace—he shoved back. "Get out of my way! This is my fight, not yours! I could lose my home—my business, because of 'him!' Lord knows I've lost enough already... because of Indians!"

"We might all lose something! You saw downtown! But the fact remains: your place is not deciding punishment!"

Trace responded with sarcasm. "No. That's your job! Part of 'Jake's law,' right? When the sheriff's not around?"

"That's right," the deputy said boldly, his nose lifting. "The law and my interpretation of the law. I decide innocence and guilt, in the sheriff's absence. Punishment and acquittal. You simply respect my authority and follow orders. That's the way it's always been. That's the way it always will be. Don't make me out to be some rogue faction! Understood? I'm here for the benefit of Westcreek."

Their physical display of manliness—their pushing and shoving—continued, but Trace backed off suddenly. He was reminded of the truth in "Jake's law" and how it was always there. As a child of no more than 13, he could picture Jake patrolling the town streets by foot and like clockwork, night in and night out, answering calls without fail and with quick, satisfying resolutions and being greatly respected and even overly praised, especially by the elder men and women of Westcreek. So to deny Jake of his position in the present seemed like erasing a good chunk of his upbringing—it was all that Trace knew. And such memories were most times comforting. Thus, intentions became soft.

"Your father would want you to respect me," Jake whispered, going in for a sort of psyche kill.

Then Daniel approached his brother, placing a gentle hand on his

MARK-JOHN SCHMITZ

strained shoulder. "Give him room, Trace. We'll get our justice. We always have."

Benjamin and the others approached from the southwest, attracted by the loud voices and jumpy lights. Gradually a circle was formed, with Trace and Jake and a fallen Steven taking center stage. A feeling of overall discomfort permeated the air.

Then the strong man shoved Jake a final time and as if expelling a last bit of frustration, ultimately yielding to the deputy's way of thinking; he finished off with a reluctant nod of understanding.

Jake returned the expression. "Good, good," he quipped with a definite hint of satisfaction. "Now let's get on with it."

Steven became the primary focus.

Turning slowly, Jake hunkered down into a kneeling stance. He removed his hat, messed with his own greasy, brown hair, and shoved his tongue into a corner of his mouth, as if trying to displace a stubborn piece of corn. "Gimmee something to see by," he snapped at Charles P. And it was done.

The little Indian was moaning spastically and grabbing at his head. His features were somewhat masked, but his identity was certain.

"You…" Jake muttered with only a moderate amount of surprise. "Jesus. And you were there in the forest earlier, weren't ya? Grandson of Decoreous. Out to settle the score, I suppose."

Jake shook his head. "Did you start those fires?"

"Yes," Steven coughed.

"Did you lead those 'things' into our shops and homes?"

"Yes."

Still speaking to the boy, Jake inspected his men and with a defined amount of comfort. "Then you're like your grandfather. A criminal… that's troubling. Very troubling." He toyed. "Now, if you were in my shoes, what would you do in a situation like this? Huh?"

"Slit my own throat. Pray for a quick death."

A delayed, nervous laughter grew amidst the circle. Charles P., his beer belly jiggling, eventually produced the most noise.

But Jake wasn't amused. Turning red, he scorned Steven. "Watch yourself, boy! I'm calling a special court, right here, right now. And

128

everything you say can and will be used against you. Call it 'Valley Justice.' No lawyers. No tribal representatives. No paperwork. And sentencing will begin immediately. Your plead is guilty."

"String 'em up!" Beckett cried, his foul teeth showing.

"No, shoot 'em right here!" Benjamin demanded. "We'll bury him next to his grandfather!"

Jake was curt. "Shut up, shut up!" he shouted, not taking his eyes away from Steven. He tried to break the boy. "Do you understand your lack of rights here? Huh?"

The sort of designated criminal wasn't listening. He was becoming psychotic in his pain. First he touched the blood that began to trickle over his brows. Then he rubbed his soiled cheeks. Then he kneaded the black, black earth as if making bread dough. Over and over again he repeated these steps, chanting some sort of mantra and becoming less and less aware of the outside world and more and more aware of the inside; he was desperate for help.

"*Pasigwi, wejitod nandôbaniwin,*" he said, as if in confidence. "*Pasigwi, nin migadimin.*"

Jake was still waiting for a response to his question. "Are you aware that you lost what little rights you had? When you lit that first match? Huh? Answer me!"

"*Pasigwi, wejitod nandôbaniwin,*" Steven kept saying, his repetitive behavior continuing.

He was drifting further and further away.

"What the hell's he doing?" Benjamin remarked, leaning on his rifle and studying the little Indian. Indeed, it all seemed so odd.

The winds began to pick up and unexpectedly from the south. They blew straight through the trees and with a throbbing forcefulness, a legion of spirits riding along and remaining mostly unseen by the untrained eye.

But *they* were there. Suddenly everywhere.

Jake seemed totally blind and depleted of all patience. He stood and yelled his loudest, attempting one last time to gain a sort of submission. "God dammit it, Indian! I demand your respect! Do you understand these charges?"

"Perfectly…"

Steven made very dirty, very bloody eye contact with Jake. It was like that brew down below finally received enough heat to boil over, his pupils dilating and registering a sort of "maximum pressure reached." He looked as if he wanted to gnaw upon Jake and maybe spit him out. Steven's body was rigid. Movements appeared exact and in slow motion as he laid an ear to the earth, listening for something. Something. Pain and injury became secondary, and that magical web that extended out from his tummy—that communication board that was connected to all things great and small, became farther reaching and more vivid. And Steven didn't plan on just plucking a string this time; he wasn't going to hammer upon a couple, two, or three strands. No. He intended on grabbing the whole damn web, and twisting.

"Here they come," he mumbled swiftly as if catching a greater bout of psychosis. "Here they come, here they come, here they come…"

The White posse became ghostly still. Each looked to another as if the other had a good explanation for why Steven behaved so, for why the atmosphere changed so, and for maybe why it seemed like the whole group was no longer alone. A presence, or many presences were felt, and even Jake became flustered, checking out the nearby trees and bushes as if rational answers might be spied. But… nothing. And more questions would be added.

"Here they come, here they come, here they come…" Steven said again.

New audibles tested hearing. First, some light Earie giggling came from a ways outside the perimeter and from many different points. It was rather ridiculing and lasting just long enough to bend a head or two forward in puzzlement, begging for clarification. But none would be given. Then came soul-chilling war cries. From overhead, constantly shifting in position, a great many voices drowned out the former and seemed to sing a horrid scale of screams.

It was more than Jake and his men could stand.

"We need to get out of here!" Doc stated fervently. "This, this ain't right!"

"Who are they?" Charles P. barely spoke. "Where are they? And why do they sound pissed?" Flashlight sweeps would reveal little.

Jake made a hasty decision, trying to seem still in charge, and yet he nearly wet himself. "Start moving back to town. Over the hills. Now go, everybody."

"What about the Indian?" Trace asked.

"Leave 'em. He can fend for himself. Now c'mon, let's get out of here. Keep your guns ready."

The deputy and his men at arms vacated the area one by one and like a group responsible for breaking a pricey vase in a glass shop— nobody heard or saw anything. Jake lead the retreat, mind you. But none of the seven would get far.

You see, a sort of security team had been summoned, destined to surround, their organizing factor, instead of a whistle, a resonating kettledrum from... somewhere.

"Bum... bum... bum," it beat with solid rhythm. "Bum... bum... bum." And the earth vibrated as if its topsoil was a drumhead.

"Welcome my defense," Steven mouthed plainly. "Dearly, welcome my defense."

Law was in the middle of it all.

Downtown, the battle was a losing one, and Sheriff Waters knew it. The ravenous flames had devoured two-thirds of the simple wooden buildings, heroic efforts falling short. It was time for a full-scale evacuation. So hot off of sending workers this way and that and with buckets spilling over with water, his orders eagerly anticipated—hot off of loading an old orange school bus with the area's elderly, their praise and thank yous endless—and hot off of rounding up a frazzled black cat for a terrified, orange freckled boy huddled in an idling old car, the good sheriff made some tough decisions, his ego burgeoning.

Harping, he pointed at four grimy fire fighters. "Hey, roll up those hoses and pack'em away! It's too late! Get both of those trucks to the western edge of town and await further instructions!" They apparently did not move fast enough. "C'mon, now, go!" And it was done.

He swiveled to the west and searched afar. "Buzz, Buzz!" he called out, his hands cupped and for a megaphone-like effect. A middle-aged man of pudgy cheeks and an arthritic walk waved back. "I'm sendin' anything with wheels your direction! Get things organized! We're gonna sweep the valley for anyone still around! People first! Valuables second! Got it?" The response was muffled, but judging by Sheriff Waters' pleased expression, it was one of understanding.

Suddenly a group of four, young lumberjacks in oversized coats sprinted by. He grabbed one. "Whoa, whoa, son, where ya goin'?"

"To the tool shed, to save our equipment!" one of them answered.

"No, no! Forget it! It's too dangerous! That place is packed with fuel! I want you boys to head to the east end of the valley and start lettin' everybody know transportation is on the way! Hit every home!"

"But, Sheriff—" another chimed up.

"Don't argue with me, son! Just do it! The forestry service is on the way with an aerial dump! We gotta get moving! Now go!" He gave all four a gentle nudge, and although each flapped a lip or two in hushed protest, orders were followed. Sheriff Waters was in control.

Alone now, in the middle of Main Street, he took a much deserved break, dropping his hands to his knees and in an effort to replenish sorely missed oxygen. It was then that he reflected on the big picture: Westcreek would be no more. And yet as he watched, as he circled about, he wasn't saddened.

The town may have been lost years ago.

He thought about fate and how it might've been altered. Questions arose. The work contracts with Boise Cascade—what would have happened to the stale, economic conditions, had they materialized? Would the town have prospered? Grown? And what about the new families that may have settled as a result—could they have diffused the mostly old attitudes in the valley? The good sheriff even thought about his own responsibility in things. If he would have fought being pushed aside as leader in town, more forcefully, could later racial conflicts, home loss, and property destruction been averted? It all came down to simple speculation. But Sheriff Waters felt deeply, in his heart, the true answers, and it was at about that time that a scared, tearful voice from behind surprised him.

"Where the hell is my son?"

He spun around. His head felt woozy from past lackings as he saw a frail-looking Gloria standing just a few feet away and still in a bathrobe. "What?"

Her voice rattled. "Steven. I thought he was in the attic, with his memories. But no. I looked everywhere. We have to get out of here. Have you seen him?"

"Maybe."

It suddenly hit the lawman—Steven—the boy at the scene of Decoreous' death, the boy spotted at the east end of town—all possibly the same. Sheriff Waters felt foolish. He wasn't even aware that Steven was still living in the valley, for he hadn't seen the young Indian in some time. He assumed that the boy lived with relatives on the Reservation, after his father's death, and to maybe avoid mob rule insanity, like that launched upon his grandfather. He apparently assumed wrong.

"What do you mean, 'maybe'?" Gloria asked with a shaky kind of suspicion.

"Jake and a few others are searching for an arson suspect. The one who started these fires. I think it's your son."

"What?" the lost mother said, words coming out slowly and fumbled. "How? You're lying…"

"I'm afraid not."

"For what reason would he…"

"Maybe revenge."

"You sure you're not just looking for a certain skin color? And he happens to fit?"

"I promise you, his rights will be protected. I'll see to it myself." The good sheriff took a step forward.

"Then you're telling me he doesn't stand a chance," Gloria said crassly. "Sheriff, your promises mean little to me. Tell me, will I need another black dress? Will another accidental bullet take another part of my family? I'm surprised you and your 'misfiring gun' aren't searching for him. Save me any concern. You've done enough. Really." She looked as if about to break down.

"I'm sorry," Sheriff Waters replied, unable to come up with

anything more substantial to say. The self-esteem he had worked hard to raise dropped a peg or two.

"Just tell me where Jake is so I can save my son."

She was dead serious.

But the answer would come from an unexpected source.

An old yellow pickup came skidding alongside Gloria and Sheriff Waters. It raised a huge plume of dust, and inside Dex was behind the wheel. "Gloria, get in!" he demanded with care. "I know what's been happening. I know where Steven is! I heard from a few wood cutters coming out of the bush. He's up near the ol' Dawson Mine! There's a logging road that can take us back there! C'mon!"

Gloria hesitated. Unsure of what to believe anymore, she simply stared at Dex.

"Please, trust me," Dex said with soft, yet focused eyes. "I want to help. Steven is in great danger." He held out his hand. His voice and demeanor denoted a man unconcerned with any possible secondary gains, and as such Gloria became humbly attracted.

As if an invisible entity was leading her forward, she moved to the passenger side of the pickup. But before climbing in, and just as the heavy metal door creaked open with a shove from Dex, she glanced back. "Gather up some sticks and marshmallows, Sheriff. I'll return with my innocent son. And together we'll toast this town a proper farewell."

Gloria, Dex, and the old yellow pickup sped away toward the northwest, heading for a road that would demand all a 4X4 had to offer. Maybe even more.

And Sheriff Waters—he was left to imagine. About being there for Gloria. You see, he would have done anything to assist, even carried her by foot up the valley and to where Steven was, if he had to. He would have done anything to try and right the past and save the future. Indeed.

Amos had been watching from in front of the law office. With both straps on his grimy bib overalls dangling and clanking, he staggered his way to the good sheriff's side. "Still winning popularities contests, I see!"

"We're evacuating the area, Amos!" Sheriff Waters said roughly. "I want you off the street and into a vehicle, immediately!"

"Ins due time, ins due time. But first I must give ya a warning. 'Bout those seven lives in The Great Forest. Lookin' for the Johnson boy."

Sheriff Waters wasn't listening. "I didn't make a request. I gave an order. If you'd care to be handcuffed and dragged out of here, I can arrange that. Either way you're leaving, now." He started power walking toward the west, anxious to get the rescue caravan moving.

"Hears me!" the stout Indian yelled ahead, trying to keep up with uncoordinated steps. "The Johnson boy—he's crazy! Crazy likes his grandfather and in commands of powers too terrible to even mention!" He sniffed the air. "Smells, smells the winds and knows what I says is true!"

"Keep away from the flames, Amos. You might explode. Now get out of here before I arrest you!" He was unconcerned and contemplating human shelter needs for the upcoming night.

"Thinks it's the booze talkin', eh? That I'm drunks in what I says? Possibilities brought me to this! Possibilities! Those men could be killed tens times over! Made to suffers horrible deaths! Now what ya gonna do?" Amos was falling far behind.

"We're in a state of emergency here! I don't have time for your games!" The lawman increased his pace.

Amos finally had to stop, panting loudly. "What about the radio message?"

"What, what the hell are you talking about?" Sheriff Waters spat with annoyance, whirling around.

"This one…"

The walkie-talkie on the lawman's belt came alive with static and horror-struck mumbling. *"Sheriff… something's wrong up here. The ground… under… it's moving. Can you, can you hear it? It's coming from all over! There's… something under us! Sheriff?"* The voice dissipated.

Sheriff Waters grabbed for his communication box, eyeing Amos. "Jake? Jake, is that you? What the hell is going on? Answer!"

There was a long pause.

"Jesus, oh Jesus… Mother of God!" then came back, Jake's words crackling the airway. *"Jesus… they're everywhere! No… no, how? Sheriff?"* Background screaming, almost child-like, reverberated. *"Jesus, Mother of God!"*

"Where are you, what's your position?" Sheriff Waters shouted with alarm.

"North of the spruce grove… the north forty acres… on the hills… Sheriff?"

Static won over the reception.

"Jake? Jake?"

Nothing.

Amos crept closer, a slight grin leaking out. "They'd be in Guardian Hills, Sheriff. 'Cept those hills ain't hills at all. They'd be burial mounds. Full of death and looking for life. Listen. Listen!"

Sheriff Waters tried to heighten his hearing and there, above the wood crackling, above the fires' constant hum, and above the distant conversations related to evacuation, he could hear drumming.

"Bum… bum… bum," it went. So faint, it was, but deep, bass-like. "Bum… bum… bum."

Amos nodded his head. "Now what be yer great White solution?"

Sheriff Waters calculated his next move. He reviewed the status of his leadership efforts, the peculiar words of Amos, and the disturbing, very disturbing call from Jake, and all within a couple of seconds. Then he sprinted back to his office.

"That's my sheriff!" Amos commended. "Go get 'em 'Lone Ranger,' save the day! But remembers: the forest, she ain't always what she seems! She ain't always what she seems, Sheriff!"

Waving a callused fist in mock revelry, Amos gradually began to snicker. He let out a little giggle at first, like a controlled hiccup, and then it built into an all-out, riotous, knee-slapping orgy of laughs. Such a festive, internal mood was created that he felt he just had to share it with someone or some ones, and a man and woman scurrying by and toward the fire trucks became victims in his sort of fun. Locking arms, he do-si-doed the two, humming a sampling of lively melodies as if the

New Year were approaching. His knees were bucked up high, and on more than one occasion he almost fell over.

"Celebrate, celebrate!" he exclaimed to his unwilling partners. "The fireworks is alls around us! Chaos—she's better than any whisky, eh? Dance! Dance!"

'Round and 'round, the three circled about. 'Round and 'round and with Amos leading the woman, and yet the woman trying to escape.

Sheriff Waters flew through his office door and raced to his desk. He had just given the order to begin "operation sweep" without his presence and via walkie-talkie. Two critical tasks were left to be completed: one involved calling the State of Minnesota; the other, retrieving a seldom-used pistol and a handful of shells. Desperate times called for desperate measures, he thought.

Indeed, desperate times may call for desperate measures. Again.

Help was sort of on the way.

Dance of the Skeletons
The earth was giving birth.

Under and all around Jake and his men, tiny, bony fingers pushed through the ground and as if reaching for the air. Dark in color, grasping, wiggling, they were connected to bony palms—which were connected to bony wrists—and which were connected to bony arms. The whole process of emergence for these parts was slow but constant, and at one point a good hundred or so "sprouts" could be seen. It all looked very much like growth within a cornfield and under time-lapse photography. Only difference: here the growth was fluid and anything but fruitful.

The seven pursuers of valley justice were tripped up on their way out. Except for Doc, they just couldn't get away. A virtual free-for-all existed as each man tried steadfastly to escape from the hills, bony hands and fingers gradually catching boot straps and pant legs.

"I can't move!" Daniel screamed, able to shuffle his feet only a couple of inches in any one direction. "They've got me good!"

"Jake, help me!" Benjamin pleaded, three or four sets of digits working up toward his knees. "Please, get 'em off me! Get 'em off me!" But Jake could not. He was having similar troubles of his own.

Trace suggested a practical solution. "Beat 'em off with your guns!"

And each hacked at the calcified limbs like a crew of lumberjacks chopping at seasoned timber. Some benefits were derived. A few bones were snapped in two or even crushed. Unfortunately, however, for every one grip that was lost, two or three more were added.

"It's not working!" Charles P. shrilled, dropping to one knee yet continuing to hack. The beings were pulling him down. "Now what?"

Skulls and shoulders began to emerge. Dirt chunks popped up as greater bone masses made their way into the world, and most notably were chattering jaws that seemed to hanker for the taste of skin, fat, or maybe even blood. You see, rotten teeth were biting at pretty much anything live. Thrusted forward by bobbing heads, they chomped left, right, and center. And when they made contact, when they latched on to human tissue, muscle jerks and wailing followed.

"Get rid of these things!" Beckett commanded Steven, struggling to maintain control of his rifle. "We give up, we give up! No more!" But the little Indian would not hear of surrender.

Taking his ear from the earth and relying heavily upon the wooden staff for support, he brought his sore body upright. Then he surveyed his sudden army like a proud general just rolling into camp near the front lines, his eyes, though, appearing glossy, as if in a trance. "*Nishiwe, nin pâpijindan,*" he mouthed, "*anwebia gigi-oôssima dash nimishomiss.*"

His wishes would be honored. The bony beings got organized.

Many of the skeletons pulled their torsos, hips, and wobbly legs above ground, initiating a sort of "operation burial." They took newborn steps, branching off into smaller units and to assault Jake and his men with palsy-like, forearm slaps and kicks. Droopy ceremonial robes and simple loincloths dribbled from their frames with each attack. To be sure, some of the skeletons remained low or even half submerged, preparing new graves or searching deep within the mounds for weapons to use. But for the most part, a vast majority of the undead had risen up for hand-to-hand combat.

"Shoot 'em, shoot 'em!" Trace shrieked in growing desperation, fumbling to ready his rifle. "It's our only hope!"

A symphony of gunfire transpired. It was composed of both high and low-pitched tones, and major damage was suffered on behalf of Steven's soldiers. Femurs and tibias went flying. Skull plates, ribs, and kneecaps shattered. Close to fifty rounds were unloaded upon the aggressors and yet they kept coming. Sometimes upper bodies or arms alone would crawl inch by inch to the living and then simply pile on. The weight became increasingly heavy—constricting, and for two men in particular it was all just too overwhelming; one was Benjamin.

The tall blond fell hard against the churned earth. There he thrashed about violently in a last-ditch effort to escape. But to no avail. You see, nine skeletons, most intact, were working him over. Four from within one of the mounds yanked at his lips, neck, waist, and boots, drawing him slowly into an egg-shaped hole about thirty feet in diameter. The other five were above ground, either pushing on his back or covering the entire group effort with clawfuls of turf and dirt. Benjamin seemed helpless.

Soon most of his body became entombed. Toward the end he tried desperately to keep his head above plum, particularly his nose and mouth, but earthen material was flung about in such a way as to plug pretty much every orifice. Benjamin strained his neck for air. He lurched his back again and again. He coughed with dryness as dirt particles settled at the bottom of his lungs, causing intense pain. But it would only last a few moments, a few climactic seconds. Then his entire body would relax, terribly. Gradually only his blond hair was left to be seen, his spent rifle laying just a few feet away.

And it wasn't supposed to be like this for the young entrepreneur. He was supposed to be breathing in money, not death. You see, he often dreamt of opening a fly-in lodge on Turtle Lake, which was about thirty miles north of the valley. Saving every penny earned doing odd jobs in Westcreek, he dreamed of someday building a huge log cabin with big picture windows looking out over the water. And docks. He wanted to cover the shoreline with docks holding scads of fishing boats and float planes that brought guests in from the Twin Cities, Duluth, Fargo, or just any old place in the Midwest, maybe beyond. And one day, after the lodge was fully operational, after a certain point came in which he had to turn customers away, he dreamt of sipping an expensive champagne on a nearby, rocky beach—a sort of victory drink, and while watching an orange sunset. Indeed, he hoped someday of reflecting on his mega success.

In the present, however, hopes and simply wakefulness were lost. Benjamin faded to black.

Daniel was the second man to become overwhelmed, but unlike his friend, he didn't put up a fight. He couldn't. Shock had muddled both his physical and mental state, leaving him in a basic sitting position against a small oak tree, quiet, his arms folded and his eyes and mouth closed tightly, as if meditating. How odd, he appeared—almost like an uprooted tree stump just waiting for disposal. And six skeletons— landscape workers, if you will—were all too willing to take on the job. They tugged at Daniel's fine hair, wimpy arms, and brown pants, but in opposite directions, as if maybe unsure of which grave to settle the man in. Back and forth, the seesawing went. Back and forth and with the young man supplying no resistance.

His brother, about twenty yards away and having better luck at survival, attempted to rally his younger's cause.

"Get up, Daniel!" Trace demanded, slapping another clip into his rifle and firing upon anything that touched his own person. "God dammit! Stand up and defend yourself!"

The words weren't received. And team north of the fiend tug-of-war dominated, toppling Daniel end over end and into a sort of final resting pit. There he curled up like an infant, shaking, the skeletal troop either swatting dirt over him or brandishing rusty daggers to poke at his neck or scrape at his scalp. These latter acts of cruelty proved to finally be his undoing. Blood gurgled up from at least two points along his jugular vein and sponged to the surface of his forehead. Though skin penetration did cause several body jolts, he remained true to his vegetative condition and to the very point of death, manic passivity giving way to tired eyes, shallow breathing, and a slowing heart.

And what would Bull have thought, his son succumbing to Indian folk, one might've thought? Would he have turned his back in shame? Would he have hollered in protest? Or would he have organized a lynch mob against the undead to right a great White wrong? You see, Bull had always taught his boys through father-son lectures and countless behaviors that there existed a natural hierarchy among people, to assure peace and order, and that one must be diligent in regards to making certain—by any and all means necessary—that lines between ranks never become blurred. Given current circumstances, however, not only were lines becoming blurred, but the hierarchy itself was being turned upside down.

In the afterlife, father and son could maybe discuss the merits or lack of merits associated with such a straightforward philosophy. It seemed there'd be plenty of time.

Trace wasn't ready to let his brother pass on, though.

Witness to Daniel's inhumane treatment and forced internment, the big man became sick with heroism, his adrenaline racing. "Daniel, no!" he cried. "Hold on, hold on, I'm comin' for ya!"

Literally dragging a few skeletons, he cleared a path by swinging his gun like an oversized machete. Side to side, he swung it, and with both hands. Bone was knocked back or out of the way. Little steps followed. Little steps that brought him closer to his brother. Then closer yet. A one-man force, he resembled, and Steven's soldiers, particularly those pummeling Jake, Beckett, and Charles P., reacted with alarm and counteraction.

Most stopped in midpunch or midkick to gravitate toward Trace like magnets to their unequals. A silent order to squash the uprising was understood, and in the transition a few of the slower skeletons or those simply not whole in form were trampled by the faster. Nonetheless, Trace soon found himself in the center of a massive crowd. It was anarchy.

But it was also a golden opportunity for three.

Jake and the other two men found the odds of escaping to be greatly enhanced. Left to face at most three skeletons each, they fought back with renewed determination. Jake became the first to break totally free. Dropping his rifle, he pulled a shiny new pistol from his holster. At close range and as if holding a smelly can of bug spray to rid his person of pesky flies, the deputy proceeded to nervously shoot at skeletal palms and elbows. As luck would have it, he ended up hitting more than he missed, getting loose and rising to a stand. Then he was able to hightail it out of there with some fancy footwork, peeling off residual fingers and arms. But the journey away from the mounds and down the general slope would not be without peril. It would not be without alterations in course, for wind spirits swooped at his head from both the south and west. So Jake headed east. Faltering, running blindly, he made it almost one hundred yards before encountering more wind spirits, these thrusting hard into his sternum again and again, knocking him back. So he headed north-northeast. Away from the "vial air" and "clattering madness," he jittered about with one specific mindset: find safety, find a good place to hide, and dead ahead, about a quarter of a mile, stood an old, abandoned mill and homestead.

"Jake, wait!" Charles P. wailed during his friend's departure and like a little boy lost. "God, almighty, don't leave us here!"

But the deputy's concern for his men seemed to be an afterthought. He just kept going.

Beckett took a lesson from Trace in getting free. Manhandling his rifle, he swung at the undead, albeit more like a homerun hitter than a trailblazer. Still, damage was done. Tight vertebrae and necks were severed, allowing the outback hunter some much needed breathing room. He used it to crawl over to Charles P.

"Get up, get up! This might be our only chance!"

"I can't! Look!"

Though doing a miraculous job of defending his life with a burnt-out lantern and a long flashlight, his rifle long since stolen, Charles P. was stuck, his left leg almost entirely below ground. A fiend was taking him under, the hard way.

"Try harder!" Beckett commanded with stressed exasperation. And two skeletons must have been too close for comfort, for he rose up and took another sort of turn at bat. Flailing leftly and rightly and groaning like a banshee, he connected with mostly ribs and arms. But a desired effect was had: the beings reeled.

"C'mon!" he commanded again and of Charles P. "Get your fat ass up!"

The stout jester pulled at his limb. He wiggled his bulky weight from side to side and for leverage, but with little headway made. "I can't, I swear!" he whined. "I need help!"

Beckett kneeled reluctantly and grabbed a big arm, tossing it around his neck. With weariness, he exhaled and counted. "One, two, pull!" An inch or two was gained. "Again, one, two, pull!" Another inch or two.

Meanwhile, a few skeletons, those not precisely atop Trace, were making use of old bows and arrows found within several mounds. They were bringing together flimsy string and crumbling wooden notches to fling about missiles, most, however, dropping straight to the ground without piercing any recognizable target. But still they tried.

"One, two, pull!" Beckett strained. Charles P. finally came loose, like a stubborn weed, his leg free.

And both men clamored away from the hills, Beckett steadying Charles P. Tumbling occasionally, they encountered the same airy hazards as Jake, eventually being routed in the same general direction. A quiver or so of arrows escorted them.

"Phew-phew-phew-phew," was the sound heard behind and past their ears. "Phew-phew… phew."

One rotten bolt, only slightly sharp, punctured Charles P.'s shoulder blade. Another shot squarely into his left thigh. The immediate pain was stinging and of hindrance to the overall, dual locomotion. Still, the two mob members were able to move—to escape, feeling lucky to be leaving in one piece. And it was all due to Trace.

Bull's oldest son dug frantically with his bare hands. And for Daniel. Huddled over by punching and kicking enemies, he unearthed a pale face, a chin, and then he slowed when coming across mushy dirt near the neck area. The tactile stimulation alone was somber-making, and a terrible aching spread throughout his body. Stopping his efforts, Trace realized that Daniel wasn't coming back. It was too late. He could only stare at his younger's, half-open eyes.

"No," he first said. Then, "no! No!! NO!!!"

Jumping up, becoming incensed, the big man grappled all available skeletons, slugging at their heads and tearing at their pelvises. He pivoted in all directions, giving equal attention. Though terribly outmatched, Trace held his own, taking out flank after flank.

"You'll die for this!" he yelled with futility. "I'll kill ya, I'll kill every one of ya!"

Then a reinforcement arrived. For Steven's soldiers. And of the grossly macabre.

The whiny of a horse rode the air. It echoed off the trees, and such a sound prevailed that Trace turned with distraction to the west. He stood frozen from what his eyes saw, like a rodent caught in the headlights of a big truck.

How could such a sight be, he wondered? Was it an illusion? A trick?

A bony steed walked with rhythm through the tall grass and dangling pine limbs. Standing almost six foot at the shoulder, the animal snorted and whinnied some more. On its back sat a demon of sorts—a calcified militant with absent eyes. Covered by dingy white feathers, adorned by colorful beads and holding a long, wooden spear, the being appeared annoyed with Traces mere existence, its jaw quaking, its focus serious and true. And with a stomp of the steed's heavy hoof—first once, then twice—and a race toward gallop, the demon initiated a hunt for life. Trace's.

And Trace—he remained very still. The skeletons were scraping at his body but he was too petrified to fight back, let alone dodge the coming bullet. Seemed indecisive and weak, he did, alone, and he took to praying silently for some grand intervention.

But it would never come.

"Uhhhhhh!" he groaned flatly, his eyes bulging and his muscles flexing for impact. A collision was certain. Soon horse and rider were upon him, a great many skeletons stampeded in the process and unwittingly. The spear tip entered his chest like a toothpick through butter and with a "Schloop!" Tissue and crimson drops squirted lightly outward, from both his front and back. The big man let out a gasp, a gurgle, and then he fell to his knees, supported forward by the spear's stiffness. Somehow he mustered the fortitude to look upon the hardened face of the demon, conveying a sort of sadness and maybe hoping for pity in return. None was granted, however. And slowly Trace slumped without peace. He died not fifty yards from where his father met his own demise. And in a culvert of spinning, gray clouds and a bright, shimmering light, leaving his flesh behind, he was met by the embraces of lost family, friends... and even Indians. The path taken, thereafter, was unknown. His neurons went flat, you see, closing the window into that world. Slowly. So very, very slowly.

Later that day a soft, young woman of rosy cheeks and a quiet disposition would wonder regarding Trace's whereabouts. A long distance love living in Hinckley, she'd wait by the phone, picking at her skin, wondering why he hadn't called. She'd question their last meeting: Was I too pushy? Should I have really brought up my dream of marriage and family? Was it wrong to talk of living together in Westcreek? She could never understand his reluctance to talk about his home.

And she would miss his hugs, all the while, waiting. She would long for his warm talk, playful tickling around the ribs, and often shy-like smile. Indeed.

Grabbing the phone, shook by negative scenarios playing out in her mind, she would eventually dial Trace's number again and again, yielding each time a dull ring that sputtered her heart. Not until weeks later would she discover the true nature of her lover's ambivalence. And via simple letter.

In direct contrast, Steven got to witness Trace's death, firsthand. He ordered it. He got to feel it all in the here-and-now, and suddenly the dominant emotion within was not without challenge. Rage had enemies.

Steven released the web. He relaxed his posture, his brown eyes pulled back into focus. Brushing his gaze back and forth across the carnage before him, slightly unbelieving and grappling with responsibility, he felt like a conqueror and yet a villain, proud and yet somehow terribly ashamed. Things were not clear, and it took distant chatter from Jake to realign his convictions and ultimately beat the war drums once more.

"Help, help, Sheriff?" Jake cried into his walkie-talkie. "Can you hear me? I'm lost, you've got to help me!"

Charles P. let out a wallow or two from somewhere and even further away, like he was answering Jake. But that's as far as any conversation went.

Breathing deeply and nodding to the spirits that amassed overhead, as if an important moment were approaching, Steven poked at the web, falling all skeletons great and small and into sprawling piles of bone. Their immediate usefulness had been exceeded. Other battles would be called for in other areas of The Great Forest and with other soldiers. After all, the Great White Monster was still alive—wounded—but still alive, and as such the little Indian felt that there was much to be done.

And he was delighted with Jake's bearing. It revived a once dead plan. It rolled again, if you will, a once stalled, prime objective, and Steven couldn't wait to hold his own sort of court and based on his own ideas of valley justice. Jake was destined to play the role of lead defendant, and all he had to do was enter a makeshift courthouse deeper within the woods in order to get things underway. And that's exactly what he did.

Steven ran toward the north-northeast, his left arm pulled against his body, his left leg dragging slightly, a platoon of spirits following but with reserve.

Gloria and Dex
"Bump! Bump! Bam-Bam!"

The old yellow pickup crawled over the logging road, encountering mud holes, downed timber, and an assortment of tree stumps. Inside Gloria and Dex bounced around, trying to brace themselves against the roof, doors, and dashboard.

"Steven could be anywhere by now," Gloria said, staring blankly at a dented glovebox. "How will we find him?"

"We may not. Just so Jake and the others don't find him either. I'm afraid of what they could do."

Gloria thought. Then she smiled with reserve. "If he's in danger, he'll hide. I know it. He always did when he was little. If his father was out of control at home or maybe a bad storm was moving through the area, he'd practically disappear. I swear. I'd find him in a closet beneath a pile of clothes or behind the couch. Sometimes even crammed between loose floorboards in the attic." She swallowed hard. "I remember once, when he was six, playing alone outside, a black bear wandered into our yard. I was in the kitchen. Watching. Before I could get out there, he ran, like lightning, into the forest. It scared the hell out of me. I searched, but couldn't find him. I had to call Sheriff Waters for help. Hours later we found him curled up in an old, hollowed-out log. He was sleeping. Sleeping, Dex. I remember how peaceful he looked. How quiet he was. I reached down to touch his face and he didn't even stir. I carried him home." She closed her eyes. "I'd give anything to go back to that time. Start over."

Gloria glanced sheepishly at Dex, fiddling with her black locks.

"You were right about me. Acting like a whore."

"I was out of line, Gloria," Dex said sympathetically, trying to lessen his former words. "Please, don't."

"No, no. Sometimes it's hard to hear what you already know. After my husband died, I guess I didn't know what to do or how to act. Where to turn. I mean, my God, I lost the only way of life I ever knew. Steven, the only way of life he knew. I was scared. There was no way we could have survived on our own, money-wise. Definitely not emotionally. We had to depend on others in this town for support, even if all we got was a smile, walking down the street. But it's hard when you're not respected. Thought of as nothing more than a 'dirty Indian squaw.' That's what they used to call me. Men and women in this town, both. I used to overhear their little conversations."

"Westcreek can be damn prejudice. You know that, Gloria."

"Yes. But what's worse: Being prejudice... or accepting it? I played their role."

Three small logs were driven over with a "Bam-Bam! Bam!"

"The men at the café were the only ones who offered me any kindness," Gloria continued, pushing against the glovebox for support. "For a price, anyway. I mean, I let them use me. For a chance at security. A little hope. Maybe even a chance at new love. Just a chance." She squinted her eyes, as if experiencing pain. "I knew, I knew the way I carried on, staying out late, moving from man to man, would drive a wedge between Steven and me. I knew it. It's just that we were desperate. Still are. I was willing to give a little love for a new life. If I could have given Steven a new home in a new place, I thought all would be forgiven. Steven can be very understanding. It just never worked out. I've acted so stupidly."

"You were eager to trust, Gloria," Dex spoke up, wrestling with the wheel. "No one can fault you for that. Not unless they were in your position. I'm sorry for snapping at you earlier."

Gloria looked to Dex, vulnerably. She traced, with her eyes, his strong jawbone and serious lips.

"I killed his father..."

"What?"

"When my husband was especially enraged, one night. When he had drank all that could possibly be drunk. I set him up."

"Gloria, no, stop..."

"No, he hit me, Dex" she continued." Across the mouth. I don't even remember why. But he hit me and then ran out of the house. I knew he wanted more booze. I knew he was scared. Angry. And Sad. And the liquor store was closed. I knew... he'd break in, to get a little something. And some money."

Dex remained steady in his handling of the wheel.

Gloria shook her head. "I called the store owner. Told him of foul play on that night... and then hung up. Quick-like. It felt good. I was powerful. Though I felt scared, angry—pissed, I... could have a 'say.'" She squinted her face. "Jesus, Dex, I wished my husband ill will—I wanted him arrested—but not dead. Fuck, I didn't want

Sheriff Waters to kill him. I mean it. Just arrested. Maybe it would've sobered him up. Maybe he would've gotten his act together, ya know?" She ended with silent cathartic jabbering, evident only in her sort of mouthings and wallowing."

Dex tried to placate, his biceps bulging. "We need to think about Steven, Gloria. He could be in real danger."

Gloria looked with longing eyes to Dex. "You were the only one true to me, Dex. I mean, Lord knows I pushed you away enough times, but you always treated me fairly. With respect. You were a true friend. You said what was on your mind, even if I didn't like it. There was nothing hidden about you. You were... real."

She shook her head. "But I couldn't let myself fall in love. You were so damn stubborn! Hell bent on staying in this town no matter what! You wouldn't hear of leaving. And why? Because of family pride? You wanted to continue the family business so that you could suffer, too? Jesus, Dex!" She lashed out at his arm with a closed fist and with Nerf-ball effect, more to vent than to injure. "You were so stubborn about making things work! You chose a foolish dream over me!"

"BAM! BAM!"

The old yellow pickup came to a rough and sudden halt. The front axle got hung up on an especially large tree stump, both rear wheels sinking slowly into mud. Going forward, reversing, and then going forward again did little to help.

Gloria rambled, undeterred. "We could've been living far away from here by now, Dex! In the Twin Cities, Florida, Alaska for all I care! You could've built a dream home anywhere! Out of cardboard boxes, for all I care! Anywhere but here, can you understand that?"

"Yes, yes!" Dex said calmly, yet forcefully, grabbing Gloria's soft, supple shoulders with care. "I do understand. But I need you to listen to me, okay? Focus on what I have to say, okay? Can you do that?"

Gloria nodded, her body spasming with tears.

"We're stuck. I can't get the truck loose. I'm gonna have to walk the rest of the way in to find Steven. I need you to wait here until I get back, okay?"

"No!" Gloria groaned. "I want to go with you! He's my son!"

"It's too dangerous. Jake and the boys no doubt have guns. Just wait here, I don't no what the hell to expect."

"No, I have to see him, touch him." Gloria wiped her eyes and nose. "If you leave without me, I'll just follow you in, I swear. I have to be there."

"Now who's being stubborn?" Dex said a bit more lightly. He considered her words.

"Who better to know his hiding places? Who better to touch his face when he's sleeping? Carry him home?" She ended with brows raised, her tears falling even more.

The woodsman reluctantly nodded. He released his hold and then reached for the driver's side, door latch. "Okay. Let's go."

"Dex?" Gloria whispered, stopping him momentarily. "Do you really think he started those fires?"

"I don't know. You know what your son's capable of."

Gloria bowed her head. "I hate to imagine."

"When we find Steven we'll head directly to the county defense attorney. Somehow. Hike out on foot, maybe. If he's got a warrant out for his arrest, the authorities there will give him a fairer chance. Legally. Not here."

Gloria's senses perked up. "You said we? You'd go with us?"

Dex stared ahead to a few scattered logs caught in the pickup's headlights. "Yeah. There's nothing left for me here, anymore. Besides, what would people say about me helping a 'dirty Indian squaw?'" He ended with a two-part smirk: one small part humorous; the other quite serious.

Gloria smiled back as best she could, and for a few seconds the two locked eyes, exchanging deep-set emotion, strength, and a whole lot of hope in regards to the mission to be embarked upon.

Then two doors flew open with a simultaneous creak, and Dex made the quickest motions, thereafter. Retrieving a big light source that appeared much like a train engineer's lantern and from the scratched-up bed of his pickup, he ran around to take the hand of Gloria, gently. The darkest part of The Great Forest laid ahead for both, fraught with heavy brush, bogs, and Earie chattering from above that seemed to delight in their journey, the beasts talking feverishly when a few yards were traversed successfully and almost whining when either Dex or Gloria or both fell to the ground. The creatures seemed to be a sort of cheering section, you might say.

"Steven?" Gloria would occasionally call. "Steven, please, where are you?"

And the creatures would try to answer. "In house, in house," they would babble softly, "with mouse, with mouse."

Gloria didn't hear, though.

And a single siren lamented downtown. It was scratchy, so very, very scratchy, as if maybe losing its vocal might.

Indeed.

Frolic of the Spruce Trees

Sheriff Waters was well into his attempt at rescuing Jake and the other six. He was nearly halfway up the valley, running sort of comically, and in dire need of a breather, the physical demands of his search severe. Huffing and puffing, reeling about to both the left and right, and sweating profusely, he gradually came to a halt, leaning against a ragged birch tree for support. Disorientation was becoming a problem. He knew that north was uphill. He knew that the clearing was not too terribly far away, and from there he could find the spruce grove. It's just that his juxtaposition to the clearing was in question. Should I keep going forward, he wondered? Should I veer east or west, and if so, by how much? He looked to the skies for help.

Blackness was eyed. Boughs on the jack pine were so tightly dovetailed that he couldn't catch a glimpse of the sun's position, and anyway the clouds were thick enough that the strongest of rays would have been absorbed immediately. The good sheriff would have to make an educated guess in regards to which way to head, his lantern's glow constricted to a four-foot radius. So he went.

"Jake? Trace?" he yelled out. "Anyone, can you hear me?"

A few steps into his chosen direction and he encountered, quite suddenly, a membrane-like barrier of slime and foul odor, and at the torso-on-up level. Bouncing back and with a gasp, the lawman examined the impasse. Seen was not one but two canine carcasses stretched from paw to tree like wild game hung out to dry. Inners were mysteriously absent, carefully scraped out by something sharp, and deposited who knew where or in who knew what. Sheriff Waters convulsed as if holding back vomit.

"Boys! Boys!" he wheezed urgently. "Where are you? Answer me!" Glued sight-wise upon the horror, he retreated.

"Sheriff?" a wee voice said. "Help. I can't… move." The voice came from beyond the carcasses.

And Sheriff Waters responded. Giving the dead animals a wide berth, he side-stepped his way a bit further up the valley, his pistol drawn and shaky. "Say again, say again! Keep talking so I can find you!"

"Is it safe? Those creatures gone? They tied me down, it happened so fast."

"Doc?" Sheriff Waters exclaimed, making a tentative ID. "I hear ya! I'm almost there! Keep talkin'!" Carefully searching, he swept his lantern from side to side and soon The Great Forest gave way to a tiny, experimental plot of four-foot spruces. Packed tightly together, they comprised a sort of Christmas tree field, and bundled somewhere within seemed to be a lost friend.

The voice worried. "Have you seen the others, Sheriff? Anybody make it back to town? I heard screaming. Awful screaming. Running in the woods. Then quiet. Are they all dead?"

Feeling like he was almost on top of the voice, Sheriff Waters got down on all fours, pushing aside prickly branches and tall weeds. He uncovered an abundance of gray hair, a pair of cockeyed spectacles, and a twitching mustache. Doc was prone and held firmly to the earth.

"What's got you?" the good sheriff asked. "Why can't you get up?"

"They dug in the ground, Sheriff. Those things. Got ropes and put 'em all over me. More I struggle, the more they tighten."

Upon closer inspection, the lawman saw tiny tree roots extending across Doc's throat, chest, waist, thighs, and ankles. Resembled

Gulliver in the land of Lilliput, he did, and freeing him from such restraints would be more difficult than first imagined.

Sheriff Waters tugged on a root. It tightened. He picked at a different one, putting more of his back into it. The result was the same.

"See, see?" Doc chirped, wincing slightly.

"Hold still, now."

Retrieving a small pocketknife from his jacket, Sheriff Waters carefully tried cutting at a root. It was an arduous task, but one with an eventual, desired payoff. With a flat "pop!" the root let loose, each of its halves slithering back underground and with quickness. The other roots were then handled in a similar manner.

Once able to move, Doc clung with fear to his rescuer. "Jake and some others ran right by me, Sheriff! I wanted to call for help, but I was too scared! The creatures were after them, too!" He intensified his hold. "And they speak! Words! From animals? How, Sheriff?"

"Just calm down. Tell me more."

"They said things like, 'will end, will end... where began.' What the hell does that mean? How's that possible, animals talking, Sheriff?"

Sheriff Waters tried to remain objective. "Have you seen the Johnson boy?"

"Oh yes," Doc whispered, his bushy brows raised. "Near the clearing. He did all this, I think. Skeletons from the ground. Wind. Creatures... how? Why?"

Sheriff Waters looked about as if privately formulating his own answers. Then he continued his inquiry. "Which direction did Jake and the others go?"

Doc pointed. "Up that way. Toward the ol' Krebs place. But it's no use goin' after 'em. I haven't heard a sound from anyone for the longest time. They're probably all dead. We might be, too, if we don't get out of here!" He pulled at the lawman in an attempt to go home.

"No," Sheriff Waters replied decisively, not budging. He shoved his lantern at the little man. "Follow the deer path down the valley. Cut over to the west end of town and wait for someone to pick you up. Help should be arriving shortly. I need to find those men."

"You can't go up there alone!" Doc insisted. "You have no idea, the terrible things I've seen!"

"It's not open for discussion," Sheriff Waters said coldly. "I am ordering you to leave. Now go."

Doc studied his longtime friend. He peered deep into his eyes, and both seen and felt was a seriousness that could not be downplayed. Doc felt powerless. He just stared.

And Sheriff Waters shoved the lantern at him again. "Tell the officials down there what's happening. Now c'mon, go!"

Doc nodded, although failing to fully understand. Becoming too overwhelmed by his own need for safety, he grabbed the light and scurried away, his mustache twitching at ever-increasing rates. He would have given anything for company, and if not Sheriff Waters, than at least his beloved dogs. If only they were here with me now, he thought. If only they could lead the way home.

Sheriff Waters watched Doc's departure and to the point of disappearance. Then he sighed, trying desperately to internalize the strength just exhibited. Smack-dab in the middle of the spruce grove, and patting about his black belt for a small, metal flashlight, he turned his attention to the area still to be explored. The Great Forest waited for reentry. It was heavy with bush, possibly darker than before, and quiet—so ghostly quiet.

The good sheriff wiped his forehead and took a few steps.

A rustling sound came from his right and amidst the spruce trees. "Hello?" he shouted. "Who's there, Jake?"

With no response, and dismissing the occurrence as that due to a rabbit or some other varmint, he took a few more steps. His boot caught a root, sending him tumbling to the ground. Immediately more rustling noises were heard, this time from his left. With a bit more concern, he jumped back up to his feet, pointing the pistol about haphazardly.

"Goddamn it now, I'll shoot! Who's there?"

The growing ruckus spread behind and across, involving the right side again, and pretty soon Sheriff Waters felt nearly surrounded. By something or some things. He turned 180 degrees, walked backwards, and scoured visually for some kind of target. The tips of the spruce trees were shaking terribly, and although he took great care in placing his feet, he tripped again, this time falling ass first. That's when a sort of flogging machine started.

Pine limbs flailed up and down as if in a violent storm. They bounced vigorously, connecting with the lawman's face, arms, chest, and legs. His exposed skin suffered the most, incurring either whip marks or light rashes from pine needle contact. Trying to squirm away, Sheriff Waters walked upon his elbows and heels in a crab-like position. It was the best he could do.

"Slap!" and an especially large, lower branch cuffed him in the head, throwing his hat. "Slap-slap!" and two more raked across his nose and mouth.

Were those creatures wiggling the trees, he nervously wondered? Was the forest truly alive, as Amos hinted? Or was it simply straight-line winds reeking havoc?

The battery continued, and Sheriff Waters had a devil of a time getting a handle on the situation. Inches were being gained by crawling, but it seemed as if his path to safety was becoming cluttered with more and more trees. It was like some of the little spruces were pulling up root and planting themselves further along, as if to maybe assure a more solid line of flailing. The good sheriff had to jib and jive several times just to continue his way toward The Great Forest. He was straining. In pain, he was.

Letting off three gunshots, randomly, he hoped to hit the culprit or culprits responsible. But no substantial impact was made. The trees continued to flog.

At the grove's northern boundary, Sheriff Waters put all of his weight into escaping. Holstering his gun and tossing his flashlight ahead, he flipped onto his belly. He grabbed forcefully for two of the skinny spruce trunks, pulling himself upright and to his knees. And then to a stand. From there, he reached higher, for the nubs and limbs of the nearby jack pine and in an effort to gain leverage. Once secure, and with both strength and cataclysmic frustration, he swung his body mostly over and slightly into the last few, prickly barriers, dropping atop a moss bed on the other side and with a thump! Immediate danger had been averted. The Great Forest seemed a much kinder place.

It took him a while to get back up, rolling around a bit. His body was numb. And though frazzled and out of breath again, he scuttled for his flashlight, still determined to spot the reasons behind his maltreatment—anything. Creeping right up to the little trees, he threw his thin beam about to all points observable. Spruce tops barely moved. Limbs barely waved, and both at ground level and between the trees could be seen nothing out of the ordinary. It was like the trauma never happened.

In disbelief, Sheriff Waters felt for his raspberry, red face and with his raspberry, red hand.

Then he refocused, attempting to reestablish communication via walkie-talkie. "Jake? Boys? Anybody copy?"

Static.

He repeated the words. Static again.

Pivoting carefully to the north, his eyes peeling with difficulty away from the spruce grove, and feeling fearful and worried and yet determined to locate his friends, he set off on a trail he'd have to blaze himself, the Krebs place hopefully—hopefully dead ahead. And behind, the little spruce trees seemed to wave a bit, as if maybe bidding him a fond farewell. Indeed.

An Earie and Deerie Duet

A hoot from an owl… some mushy footing… a twig snapping, and Beckett and Charles P. continued their three-legged race away from places undead and hopefully toward places safe and real.

Charles P. was hurting. He was drifting into and out of consciousness. Going limp periodically, he was losing blood from his shoulder and thigh, and at one point he gave up moving altogether, crashing stomach first to the ground and next to a tall, tall, fir tree.

"I can't go on," he murmured, "I'm so tired."

"You have to!" Beckett snapped, pulled down to one knee. "Those things could be right behind us." He scanned the area, cautiously.

"I don't care. Just leave me here. Let 'em eat me. The pain is too damn much." Charles P. felt lethargically for his ailing leg.

"How bad is it?" Beckett asked.

"Bad. Real Bad."

Using his shaking hands, Beckett verified, tracing his friend's large limb and drooping shoulder. "Shit! It is bad. We can't wait. Those arrows have to come out now. Gotta bind your wounds." He propped his rifle against the fir tree, whipped off his heavy vest, and proceeded to tear small strips from his faded, flannel shirt. "Lie still."

"Oh, Jesus!" Charles P. trumpeted. "Jesus, Jesus!" He whined a bit and then wondered. "Where the hell is Jake, Beckett? Why isn't he here to help? Do you think he's in trouble, too? Do you think those bone beasts got him? Huh?" He lifted his head in preparation for a call, his jowls jiggling. "Jake! Jake!" he said.

"Shhhhh!" Beckett scolded, scanning the area a second time. "Do you wanna die, too? Jake's not gonna help us! He's a damn coward! Took off to save his own skin! It's just you and me. Now dammit, lie still!"

"My eyes are gettin' blurry. I feel so cold."

"You're goin' into shock. We gotta move fast. Get ready, I'm gonna pull one of the arrows out!" The outback hunter slowly and stiffly removed one hunk of wood jammed into Charles P.'s thigh.

"God, God, God!" Charles P. chanted and in tears, clawing for the fir tree. The arrow's absence left a small, pencil-sized hole. "Just let me die, I tell you! God!"

"I'm not gonna be here in this hell alone! You're stayin' with me!" Like an experienced EMT, Beckett wrapped the leg with several strips of cloth, each pulled snugly. "We're gonna fight our way out of here, together. Whichever way out is."

"Now I feel warm. Really warm. Just all of a sudden, Beckett."

"Your body is going into shock—I told you before! Now hold still so I can get at your shoulder!"

"No, no, I really feel warm. It's like a little heater is blowing on my face." Charles P. looked upwards. He saw a fury little snout, a black little nose, and two big, furry ears. "It's a deer, Beckett! I felt his breath! Look! He just came right up to us!"

Beckett was too busy tending to the other wound, dismissing his friend's verbalizations as delirium. He pulled on the second, much larger arrow.

"Geez! Geez! God!" Charles P. spat, grinding his teeth and banging his head upon the ground.

And the deer did not spook.

Charles P. smiled. He reached out with a tentative hand, to pet the animal. "It's like a little friend to watch over us," he said with whimsy. "To let us know that the forest will be gentle now. That we'll be okay. See, see, Beckett?" The deer licked his hand.

Sensing another presence, the near three hundred pound man gazed further up. "Hey, there's somethin' on its back. There's somethin' lookin' at me." Squinting an eye, he attempted to get a better picture. Brought into focus was an almost human face: a pair of beady eyes, a big, troll-like nose, a mumbling jaw, and some dark, wrinkled skin. "It's a little old man creature," he proclaimed with fanciful surprise. "A little old man creature on a deer, can you believe that? And he's lookin' at me funny. Beckett?"

His medic took sudden notice. Stopping first aid procedures, he saw for himself the reason for Charles P.'s curiosity. His mouth gaped open. A chill struck his lower back hard. Seen, and attached to the "little old man creature's" head was a set of big, floppy ears. "It's one of those things from downtown! Damn demon!" Beckett reached for his rifle. It was gone.

Prancing from around the other side of the fir tree, a second deer and rider approached the two men. "Fly above, fly above," could be faintly heard, "like a dove, like a dove."

The forest became a sort of work zone, Beckett a sort of cargo.

Preparing for flight, both deer jumped to the outback hunter. They nipped at his bony neck, shoulders, and remaining shirt until a good hold was gotten, Beckett yelling with contempt and striking out with closed fists. Such a defense had very little impact, though. He was destined to go up, up, up. Little Earie legs locked tightly beneath each deer. Then the guardian's special pets inflated their tummies and cheeks with suddenness, ears rhythmically beginning to flap. And with a rough jerk upon the nape of each mount's neck—first once, then twice—cranes and load started to rise.

Charles P. became incensed, the delirium more pronounced. "Beckett, get down from there!" he ordered. "Damn you, you can't fly! Let those animals be!"

Beckett hollered. He squirmed fiercely and punched, all in an effort to force a release. None would come, however. Quite the contrary, as it were. With Deerie forelegs and hind legs kicking in almost outward, circular motions, the mass joining rose higher and higher, spinning slightly and ruffling pine boughs unaccustomed to vertical intrusion. A one-story height was reached.

"I'm serious, Beckett!" Charles P asserted. "Get down from there and let 'em go... or I'll tell the DNR! They'll be pissed!" He whimpered, sanity making a brief appearance. "Please come back, Beckett. We have to get out of the forest together, remember?"

The two Earies were sucking in even more air. Frustrated and grumbling, some of the tree limbs impeding lift and setting their mounts at forty-five degree angles, the load bulky, the creatures tried adding to their upwards thrust by straining tummy muscles. And it worked. A second-story height was reached.

"Let me go, you damn things!" Beckett demanded, feeling desperate. "Let me go now." Almost crying, he clawed at the rib cages of both deer and kicked for all he was worth.

And his sort of wish would be honored.

Near the top of the fir tree, above most of the jack pine and valley in general, the two busy workers jerked back on their mounts a final time. "No more, no more," one of them said, "you soar, you soar."

Deerie mouths opened. Beckett was unloaded like a wrecking ball from its hoist, and down he went to the distant ground below. He fell with harshness through the trees and pinecones, his neck breaking his fall. Upon the hardened dirt, he lay, quivering uncontrollably.

Silence... then spoke Charles P.

"Beckett?" he muttered with stifled fright. "You okay? Come here, please. You have to finish my shoulder. You don't want me to bleed to death, do you? Beckett?" His eyes opened and closed, repeatedly. "I told ya, you should've just let those things be."

He dragged his big body closer to his still friend. "What about the game ranch we were gonna build. When money gets good. Who's gonna help me build it? Stock it with bear and moose? Huh? I can't do it on my own, so you better not die. Just a few more years and we'll buy the land from the Indians. That was the plan, right? Get it cheap from the Indians? Don't die on me, Beckett. Please. Help me build the ranch?"

The outback hunter did not stir.

And Charles P. collapsed. His face plopped atop soft moss and his eyes shut solidly. A picture of Wild Game Unlimited, the finished product and its broad acreage—a snapshot, if you will, was the last thing visualized. Charles P. walked after his friend, without feet.

A taunting breeze danced about each man's exposed skin, cooling redness and the warm blood within.

Above, Earies and Deeries circled. Silent witnesses to the passing beneath, they seemed somewhat like vultures ready to descend for a meal. But a distant calling—inaudible to those not indigenous to the woods—would alter their plans. It would draw them away from the work zone. You see, an order to assemble was given and Earie and Deerie alike were to fly north-northeast and participate in a very horrid court of law. Indeed.

"With grudge, with grudge," the Earies cackled, "to judge, to judge."

Thunder boomed. Lightning flickered.

The Trial of Deputy Jake Flint (Coda)

Jake crashed through a half broken, half-burned-out door. Alone, he sought immediate refuge from the sort of chaos of the hills. Where to hide, he thought—here, maybe—there, maybe. Indecisive, he was.

The Krebs place sat like a boxy skeleton in the very heart of The Great Forest. Former home to Adolphus Krebs and three generations of children, the fifties-style structure served as a base for lumbering operations. Adolphus and sons used to harvest precious timber, cut and process the wood, and then ship the final product to various locations across Northern Minnesota. Work was often back-bending and long, but ultimately leading to huge profits. It afforded the ten or twelve living under one roof comfort, security, and the perennial Autumn Feast, Adolphus and his lengthy, gray beard always seated at the head of a long table and before turkey, ham, and colorful vegetables of every size and shape. Seemed a happy and quaint existence, it did. It was man working the earth, providing for family, and celebrating good fortune, and all beneath the eyes of a nourishing God, or so Adolphus believed. Amen. Unfortunately, one night those eyes seemed to stray. At the hands of an arsonist, the Krebs were chased from their simple, white-blanketed beds, their home, and eventually from the only life they ever knew.

Jake stumbled about in the ashy aftermath of that night. Floorboards were scorched or even missing. Windows were shattered and cloth drapes—mere threads, mind you, were dangling. There was nothing to provide the frightened lawman cover, it was all vastly open, and so he made haste to a set of rickety stairs on the eastern wall. Maybe there was something upstairs to get behind, he thought. Maybe there was something to get underneath. He took two quick steps.

"Crash!" and his leg fell through to the basement. He howled and grabbed for a partially intact banister.

"Crack-Crash!" and the banister gave way. Jake floundered atop the rotten wood, trying desperately to rise up and escape.

Are those dead things gonna find me, he worried? Are those dogs close behind? And where was the Johnson boy? Only the frantic sounds of his behavior could be heard. Only a shadowy radius out from his person of thirty feet could be seen.

Jake finally broke free. He clawed forward like a mountain climber grasping for the very tip of a great summit, his teeth chattering. Pulling, reaching, pulling again, he made it to the top of the stairs, his lungs wheezing.

And the second level would offer just one hiding place. The deputy crawled to a far corner, skirting an enormous, singed hole in the very middle. A dark, wood dresser sat perpendicular to the north wall, and Jake grabbed an end, roughly confining himself to a wee area, hoping for anonymity. Then he waited. And waited some more, his sporadic breaths somehow kept in check. He would've stayed in that position for days, if he had to.

A short, creaking noise echoed from downstairs.

Jake startled.

Several more creaks followed, becoming progressively louder, and he could hardly contain his now cataclysmic anxiety. He peeked around the dresser, hoping to catch a glimpse of whoever or whatever was responsible. Nothing located.

Jake coward back into the corner, pulling his arms and legs tight, and maybe hoping he could become a part of the home's framework. Wait, he did. Wait for hopefully nothing to happen. He closed his eyes, tightly.

Then light breezes were felt. Blowing with an "Ooohhh!" through the west and north windows and through the little holes in the upper level, the wind funneled and circled about. Further, scratching, on the outside wall, began. It was like little varmints ran up and down the side of the house. Quickly. Loudly. And Jake bit his lip, questioning reality. He felt encircled.

Then came whispering from everywhere and Steven's soft voice.

"Order, order," he said. "All are present. Let the trial begin."

"Do you remember this place, lawman?" the little Indian asked. "Do you remember that horrible night a family almost burned to death? Think back. Think back, lawman."

Jake courageously, albeit timidly, peeked around the other end of the dresser, still wanting to see any and all of his opposition. Once again, he'd be left disappointed. Steven continued with his sort of opening statement.

"It happened years ago. On a dark but moonlit night. It was cold. Very cold. At two a.m. a fire started at the base of this very home. Someone soaked the wood with gasoline, lit a match, and no doubt watched from nearby. Flames shot up to the roof almost immediately. Imagine the heat in here. Imagine the screaming as the family woke. A father and two sons jumped from one of these very windows. The father broke his leg. One of the sons was burned badly, but would survive. You and Sheriff Waters were the first help to arrive. Then townspeople and fire fighters from outside the valley came running. Help even came from the Reservation. It must have been horrible, with people trying to save the home—people trying to save lives—people trying to understand how such a thing could happen. Do you remember? Lawman, does that night ever haunt you in your dreams?"

Not wanting to listen, Jake buried his head in his knees. But still the words penetrated.

Steven's now louder voice seemed to be coming from directly above. "In the family's yard and near their sawmill, hatchets, knives, and feathered spears were found. Reports about my grandfather being in the area, false reports, were mysteriously spread by someone. Some ones. It didn't take long for the 'Westcreek mob' to seek punishment on an innocent man." He whispered. "You know the rest of the story, lawman. Don't you? All too well."

"All too well," Steven repeated.

"Creak!" and Steven seemed to be directly in front of the dresser. "Now you've shot that innocent man!"

"That's a lie!" Jake yelled with exasperation, standing suddenly and in brat-like defiance. "The gun just went off! I didn't do it, I swear! It just went off! My finger wasn't even touching the trigger!"

"Another Westcreek accident?"

"Goddamn it, I'm telling you the truth!"

The interrogation intensified.

The little Indian's bloody face came into Jake's view, its supporting frame leaning forward. "Who set that fire, Deputy? Many moons ago. Tell me more 'truths.' Who framed my grandfather? Put my people's belongings all around the house for the mob to find?"

"I don't know!"

"Think, think from your heart!"

"I tell you, I don't know!"

A growling sound was heard.

"You, you were the arsonist, lawman!" Steven roared.

"You're mad!"

Steven sighed with trouble. "The home was built on Indian land. It rightfully belonged to my people. Krebs gave up both the land and the home, willingly, without a fight. He made plans to live and work in another part of the valley, using the little money my people could give him. But you couldn't honor Krebs' decision, could you? You couldn't respect my people's rights. Only your own. You risked a family's life to make a statement, to frame my grandfather, dishonor him, glorify yourself as a leader. You gave your people what they wanted most: a scapegoat, a cause to make their miserable lives better. You feared my grandfather's magic and love for children. How did that power feel, Deputy, chasing him away? How does that power feel today—killing him?"

"You have no proof!"

"I need no proof! I see your soul and it speaks! You were here with gas and matches, long before the fire started! Now look at me and tell me differently!"

Jake refused the request. He altered the conversation, his face tense. "Are you gonna kill me? Huh? Do it, if you are! Do it! Get this over with!"

And Steven obliged. Pivoting gracefully, he walked about his court. "My friends, tell me you verdict," he said and to the air. "To the charges of arson and murder."

"Guilty," answered a big face, floating in through the west window.

"Guilty, guilty," answered a couple more, rising up from the first floor and via the large hole between, their images terribly fluid. Nine others echoed the same.

"Then carry out the sentence," Steven ordered.

A commotion was heard, above Jake, in some of the rafters charred in color. Two Earies were busy tossing a heavy and taut vine over one of the beams, while a third dropped onto Jake's back, holding an end, a big noose dangling. Jake squirmed and attempted to dash. He yelled and batted about with both hands as if chasing away a swarm of bugs. But his actions were for not. The noose tightened around his neck, and in the rafters the Earies jumped with glee upon the vine, dangling in midair like old-world bell ringers, Jake brought to a quick stand and forced to tiptoes. The deputy's fingers tried desperately to loosen the hold. Unsuccessful, they were. Quite dearly unsuccessful.

And the executioners needed more ballast. Again from the rafters, more Earies piled on, some inflating and then deflating to exact positioning atop a brother's back or shoulder. Gradually, ever so gradually, Jake rose, gasping, struggling violently.

"Help, please, no!" he tried to say.

"Never rest in peace," Steven whispered.

The spirits funneled about the second level, calling out... the rafters creaked terribly under the great stress... the Earies giggled, and Steven closed his eyes, enjoying—capturing the moment.

"BOOM! BOOM!" went a pistol, one pellet of lead hitting a rafter, the other an inflated Earie.

"BOOM!" and a third snapped the vine in two, Jake dropping like an invalid across the dresser, his body even flipping end over end and to the floor. He struggled for air.

Sheriff Waters stood tall. He stared up from the first level, his gun pointed at Steven. "No more, son," he said calmly. "It's all over. Now move away from him. Slowly."

Steven approached the hole. "Sheriff... you, too, must face charges. Of murder. How do you plead?"

"Jake?" the good sheriff shouted, his focus still on Steven. "You all right? Talk to me."

"It's... my ribs," he answered with a harsh cough. "I think one is broke."

"Lie still." Sheriff Waters looked at Steven more intensely. "I'm not gonna tell you again, son. Move away from him. Your revenge is over."

Folding his hands gently in front of his waist, his staff planted, the little Indian sneered. "Not quite, my friend. It ends with you. Now listen to *your* verdict..."

"Guilty," a few spirits murmured or hummed.

And the hammer on Sheriff Waters' gun clicked forward a notch.

"Guilty, guilty," a few more murmured, mouths opening large.

The hammer clicked forward again.

"All are in agreement," Steven declared with seriousness. "Bring 'em to the feet of my father and grandfather."

"BOOM!" and Sheriff Waters' gun went off a fourth time, this time his finger not touching the trigger. Steven was hit.

He convulsed backwards, kept his footing, but dropped the wooden staff. His pectorals, directly above the heart, stung terribly, felt warm, and became wet. Immediately, the web he held tightly began to tear, its strands ineffective or just simply out of reach. Powers did not seem close at hand... or suddenly even real.

And the spirits flew haphazardly. They collided with each other, melded briefly, and then scattered in a multitude of directions, their mouths screaming with deep anger and yet not apparently at any one entity. The connection to Steven was lost. Without shepherd, the flock seemed. And they searched for something. For someone.

And the Earies. They appeared confused as well. They cried real human tears and whimpered like puppy dogs, each scrambling to a close window and by way of floor or air and like little children forgot by a parent or teacher in a suddenly scary, scary mortuary. Indeed, it was like a field trip gone bad, and each and every little critter yearned terribly for the safety of a tunnel under a rock or the highest limb on a fir tree, dropping from the window or rising upwards and to the ground or the trees, respectively. Deep into the forest dark, they went. Deep into hiding, without fun, with no candied yams, and at least until another master might call them out.

Deeries followed.

Steven was on his own, a last Earie whimper heard in the distance, the spirits beginning to fade. The little Indian wavered. He felt light-headed and faint, searching for something nearby to lean against, and yet finding nothing. He wished suddenly to be back in the confines of his little attic. To just close the door and keep everyone away, and without coordination he hobbled to a window, leaned feebly over the broken sill, and fell with a thud to the hard, black soil below. Movements were slight and slow, thereafter. His dance seemed over.

Inside the Krebs place, and with the immediate vicinity at least somewhat secure, Sheriff Waters tended to his injured partner.

Stepping carefully up the stairs and kneeling down, he felt Jake's body for other possible breaks.

"Busted rib or not," he said firmly, "you're gonna have to move. He could come back for us."

"It hurts like hell, Sheriff," Jake winced, his breaths still troubled.

"Just get up. C'mon." Forcing his arms under his deputy's pits, he hoisted the skinny man up and to a stand. Then he pushed him toward the stairs. "We'll head for the clearing. Find the others and meet up with the National Guard, they're on the way."

"The others are all dead."

"What?"

"Not until I say they're dead," Sheriff Waters snarled. "Now c'mon, go!" Prodding his lesser along, the good sheriff made way for the first level and the half broken, half-burned-out door.

And all the while, Sheriff Waters replayed the anxiety-provoking events of a fiery, fiery night many years ago, in his head, and with anger. He saw flames engulfing a home... he saw a family huddling by a sawmill... he saw Jake, the first on the scene, rounding a corner of the home, a toothpick in his mouth, his hands resting comfortably upon a gunbelt.

Sheriff Waters' heart felt its heaviest, yet its strongest.

He exited the Krebs place. He scanned the mill area with a shaky pistol. And then the two went.

REFLECTIONS OF WAR

Steven fought his way through The Great Forest. Desperately wanting to find home, he tripped backwards and forwards and from side to side along a sort of deer path, lower branches of the evergreen and birch stalling his progress like turnstiles unwilling to allow passage. He was physically drained of all but maybe a smidgen of strength. Emotionally numb, he was—disconnected, spiritually, and an overpowering need to nap existed.

The deer path eventually led to a wee clearing of droopy ash trees and a calm little pond. Near one of the pond's banks, Steven collapsed, his bloody hand splashing into the cool water. Above, the clouds, though still bulky, black, and full of storm, parted every so often, allowing moonlight to wash downward. Just briefly, mind you. Just a few moments until darkness would reign again.

The boy, almost a man, spoke psychotically, calling on the dead. "Father," he said with a rasp. "Dear father, hear me. The war is over and our village is nowhere to be found. The Great White Monster has defeated us. I have failed you and those who have went before. There is no justice in the valley. I am sorry, Father." He took his wet hand and touched the features of his face, daintily, as if his skin might be smarting. "I must know, will the young ones tell stories of me? Years from now, around a campfire, will I be remembered as a hero? Speak to me, father. Tell me of my fate. I must hear you."

The wee clearing became still. An image upon the water appeared, first faint and then quite distinct, and it was of a young Indian with dark, dark hair, a defined jaw line, soft eyes, and skinny lips.

"My dear son," a haunting voice said from the water. "You come to me with hands dirty, yet you seek purity. You have destroyed and brought death, yet you seek glory. There can be none of these. The war has been over for many years, my son. Its braves and soldiers all but gone, taking to their graves no medals, no honors, no true victories. Only pain. Only pain. My son, only pain."

With shaky fingers, Steven brushed at the translucent image, his heart aching and beginning to empty.

"The war you fight," the voice continued, "is for only one. For you, alone, and for what has been taken from you or never existed before. It's your heart alone that you battle with. The magic, your spear. Our people, your army. And the enemy you seek has no real face. Only a body to stab at. Hear me, my son. Hear me and know what I say is true."

The clouds devoured the moonlight.

"No, father," Steven protested. "No, I fight for us all. For you. For Grandfather. For the Ojibwe Nation. For all who have been hurt by the White man."

"And for what gain? For what profit? A trampled earth? A forest of burnt trees? A wagon load of bodies needing to be buried? Your war is hallow, my son. Its meaning lost within blood. The only pride left for you now is in ending your rampage. As guardian, you must dance one last time and bring your people to rest. The souls are troubled. Go to The Great Rock and call all together. Make all eyes heavy and voices quiet. This you must do—it is your duty. Go, now. Go. Before it is too late. I will wait… for you in light."

The clouds parted again, and Steven saw his father's image begin to fade. "No, come back," he groaned. "Please, don't leave me. I don't know the way. Why?"

"Go," the voice on the water said, becoming less audible. "Go…"

Steven's bloody face replaced his father's. A mere boy's reflection stared back, a harsher shade of red. Steven toyed with the image, feeling suddenly ashamed. He tapped at its features again and again, and all the while a myriad of little birds began to circle overhead.

"I have disgraced you, father," he mumbled to the pond. "And the memory of Grandfather. His magic was of peace. Mine is of horror.

My strength is dying and with it the power to command. I shall never be a great chief." He looked up to the birds. "But who will watch over us? After I am gone? After I have no physical presence? Who is left to protect our culture? Our past? Our treasures?"

Steven rested his head upon the muddy bank, closing his eyes. With feeble-like movements, he wet both hands in coolness—then attempting to remove the crimson coloring from his face and forehead. "I am so weary. I fear I may not make it to The Great Rock. Our people may never find peace, after all. Because of... me. Because of my rage."

The little Indian wanted to dream it all away, awaken near his chest of memories and other fancies in his warm home. And to see his mother. To look upon her face, nuzzle childishly in her bosom, and feel the softness of her fingers stroking his unwashed hair. In his fading reality, Steven could hear his mother's comforting words, used in times of strife, and only recently muzzled by his own stubborn pride and maybe selfishness. But there the words were—rhythmic, true, and surrounding. "Sleep, my baby," was sort of heard. "Sleep through the night. All will be well. All will be right." He was nearly home. He was moving through a white picket fence, walking up a white stone path, and nearing the open door to a little gray house.

That's when the birds slammed the door closed, ending his dream.

Robins, black birds, and sparrows dive-bombed him. They took turns pelting his person with sharp beaks and little claws. A "whoosh!" near his left ear—a "whoosh!" near his right, and a foggy Steven was brought to his feet in a slow-motion hurry.

"*Béka!*" he cried in the Ojibwe tongue. "*Béka nongom! Mâdja!*" The ailing chieftain jumped about as if trying to shake loose a clinging lot of ants. The winged terrors, however, would not be deterred. They were persistent in their violence, even toward each other, battling over Steven's skin and hair as if valuable nesting materials had been found. The flock eventually numbered thirty, and such an opposing force was created that the little Indian was driven away from the pond and toward the southeast treeline, the birds squawking and carrying on. Steven pleaded for help.

"*Bimibata igew awâss!*" he shouted to the again, dark heavens. "*Nin manitos, ondâss!*" And yet the situation worsened.

More birds joined the assault. Through his robe, new skin was taken from his sides and shoulders, and even tight quarters couldn't lessen the badgering. Steven squeezed between skinny tree trunks, trying to shave the things off like a logging truck crawling between towers. Claws held, wings flapped in angry protest, and if Steven wandered aimlessly too far to the left, they'd heighten their work; if he wandered too far to the right, they'd pick at his eyes, brows, and lips. Forward seemed to be the only tolerable direction. Little minds were dictating a proper course.

And where were his Earies, to assist, one might've asked? Where were the animals of the forest to champion his cause? And the spirits—why did they seem so far away?

From a bird's-eye view the whole scene resembled a performer, in spotlight, dancing awfully on a naturalistic stage and while being heckled. Moonlight reappeared, you see. It shone upon Steven and followed his struggling. The birds bounced into and out of the light as if maybe oranges, dirt chunks, or gray rocks were being thrown offstage by some unhappy patrons. Again and again, Steven was struck, his heart emptying even more.

And with pain, he was ushered toward a final falling.

THE FINAL FALLING OF STEVEN

An audience assembled. In The Great Clearing, around The Great Rock, and beneath a foreboding mine, a meeting of people occurred, mostly by chance. And the atmosphere of The Great Forest had turned decidedly cold and constricting, voices were hushed, and both lantern and flashlight danced with each other in a sort of triangular mambo. No one had a seat for the performance to come and yet all were silently invited. All were contributors in some way. All would be witnesses, you see.

A stoic, State militia, from the south, was the first to step foot upon the clearing. Numbering thirty, they were a rainbow of colors in plain, gray uniforms, sweeping the forest floor in a "V" formation and in a combined effort to complete a series of prime directives handed down by the State Department. These directives were: 1) assist with the evacuation of Westcreek; 2) search the north forty acres of the Minnesota Valley for both survivors and dead involved in a law enforcement skirmish; and 3) search the north forty acres for a young Indian boy, 5'7", approx. 125lbs, medium skin tone, suspected of grand arson and murder. In meeting their objectives, the militia appeared expressionless, focused, and synchronized in regards to gun movements, their semiautomatic rifles swaying from side to side... side to side... and side to side. Gloria and Dex were much less regimented.

They came from the west, stumbling, Dex ever-supporting

172

Gloria's falling body as she crossed uneven ground. The lost mother appeared flushed in the face, disoriented, and wanting. She would yell out, aimlessly.

"Steven? Please! Answer me! We have to leave here!"

And the final two audience members approached from the north. They were Sheriff Waters and Jake. Shimmying down the loose rock and just to the side of the mine entrance, Sheriff Waters dragged along his even now more dependent deputy. Jake wanted to stop badly and rest several times, but he was denied, his superior eyeing the State militia and walking faster. Only when Steven took to the stage from the east did the good sheriff pause, hunkering down over Jake, fumbling for his pistol. A fugitive was suddenly present, you see.

And the winds blew from the earth upwards... a thousand spirits cried out from somewhere near... the tips of the trees shook, and the flock of birds infatuated with Steven suddenly flew off into multiple directions simultaneously, as if shooting stars ordered to find their rightful place back up in the heavens. The little Indian was now on his own, uncoerced.

His vision was glossy. Colors were becoming plain and gray, and though he was aware of bodies and faces in the peripheral, he gravitated toward The Great Rock, undaunted, his gait much like that of a two year old learning to walk, tentative and wobbly. And his disease. It became terribly pronounced. His leg twisted and bent. His arm curled under his breast. He never appeared more handicapped.

Step one, slide, he went. Step one, ... slide. He made it to the rock, touching it timidly.

"Steven!" Gloria wailed, her eyes large and flooding with tears. "Steven, I'm here, baby! Come to me! Please!" Sprinting recklessly for her son, she fell twice, the second time held down by Dex's strong arms. He would not permit her to advance further. The militia was getting itchy.

Taking scattered positions around the southern part of the clearing and dropping to one knee, the thirty men and women squinted an eye intensely, searching for a part of Steven's body in their gun sights.

"It's him!" one of them yelled.

A Black sergeant, his lips big and strained, called out to the little Indian. "Get down on the ground, now! Put your hands behind your head!"

Steven wasn't listening, though. A sort of second wind carried him past the rock and into the general vicinity of his mother and her sobbing. He stopped just a few yards away from her, finally sensing the immediate danger. Stuttered, he did. "Mother? Is that really you? I cannot see."

"Get down!" Gloria begged. "They'll kill you! Please!" Dex kept a tight grip on her.

Steven's lower lip quivered. "Can you take me away from this? Bring me home? Maybe father is waiting. Maybe he and Grandfather are talking on the front stoop. Maybe we can all find a sunny spot in the forest. Somewhere on a hill. Have a picnic and share stories." He laughed with reserve. "Silly, huh? Thinking about a picnic? Now? But I can still see you and father dancing. So clearly. Like it was yesterday."

"I think the world stopped," Steven continued, somewhat slurred in speech. "I think it had to. You were so happy. I'd give anything to see you like that again. Anything to see us that happy again. I wish... I could just see your face once more and see that smile. That same smile from that day. Maybe I could be... real again."

Above Steven, the souls began to gather. He could sort of see their transparent faces, their angry faces, each stretching across the sky and melding into greater shapes of rage. Some even swooped down upon the little Indian as if to gobble him up with wide, open mouths.

"Magic, mother," he said, staring at the skies. "Grandfather's magic, the power I always wanted, the power I have... I had. It's leaving me. That which I loved so dearly... now consumes me. It's as if another voice is whispering to them. Telling them what to do." Steven tried visually to locate his mother. "I would have loved to have seen that dream house of yours. The one in the suburbs. In the Twin Cities. Far, far away from here. But I'll never make it. I can't turn back now. I can only be there ... in spirit." He forced a smirk. "Something between us again. Always something between us. And not just an attic, either. I'm sorry, mother." He staggered back to The Great Rock and in a terrible daze.

"Steven, come back!" Gloria shrilled, becoming hoarse. "Don't! We can still leave! Together! Please!" She trailed off into an inaudible wail, not fully understood. But she knew enough—she sensed enough to realize that her chance at touching her son, stroking his cheeks, had passed.

"Get down!" the Black sergeant said again. "We have you surrounded! We will shoot!"

Sheriff Waters cocked his weapon... more, enraged souls entered the clearing... the winds became wet, and Steven climbed atop The Great Rock, with difficulty.

He stood meekly, like a naked boy in the middle of a huge crowd. Reaching up ever so gently, his fingers stretching and shaking, he touched the ghostly ancestors he once fell so in love with, and they returned to him a sort of disgust, their faces knotted and their jaws ever-trying to bite.

"*Bisânabiwin, nikâniss,*" he said softly, ever so softly. "*Anwebiwin pindig ki tchibêgamig. Bisânabiwin. Ka minawa nishkadisiwin.*"

The spirits flew about faster, and so Steven tried one last dance in order to meet his father's wishes—to serve his duty. He led with his left leg, stumbled with his right, and then caught himself with his left. One, two, three, he stepped. One, two... three. Never before had he resembled such a drunken ballerina, and with each rotation he came closer to taking a tumble. He reached higher for the spirits; they screamed at him. He closed his eyes their tightest and sang a somber song; they spit at him.

One, two, three, Steven stepped. One... two... three, and pretty soon his last spark of strength was extinguished. He stood catatonic-like on The Great Rock, unsure of what really else to do. His heart was drained. He could see light and a figure. He wanted to fall.

"I'm sorry," he said to really no one. "My strength is gone."

Gloria screeched with anger and sadness combined, hitting the ground with her fists... Sheriff Waters hovered even more over a fallen Jake... the militia held their positions, and the spirits funneled around Steven, hazing his appearance.

Then guns went off.

Every rifle and every pistol in the clearing fired at the same time, no pressure applied to any one trigger. A shower of metal flew at, and into, Steven's body, jolting him, souring his still bloody face. He fell like an invalid atop The Great Rock, back first, his arms and legs sprawled with peculiarity. And his face was turned to the west, his eyes half opened, and maybe he tried one last time, just one last time, to see his mother. But he couldn't. He just lay there. Not moving. Drifting fastly to sleep.

And almost in a dissociative state, Gloria became silent, plain looking, and numb... Dex dropped his head against hers... Jake coward, hiding his face, and both the State militia and Sheriff Waters were facially shocked by the shooting. Each checked his or her weapon.

And the spirits. They rotated at ever-increasing speeds. As if generating energy amongst themselves, and to a crescendo-like rhythm of lightning and thunder, the beings whipped around Steven, gradually pulling bits of hair, skin, tissue, blood, and bone away from his center. It was like the ancestors of ages past wanted a keepsake of their guardian, taking what they could, leaving bloody clothing and then scattering into the trees and to the brightest flash of lightning and the loudest clap of thunder. They were gone.

Violently over, the show seemed.

And the winds—they died down... the air became much warmer... a hush entombed the clearing, and moonlight squeezed through the suddenly thinning clouds. The overall shine was like that of some mellow house lights coming up in a theater, and a stunned audience was slow to react.

What just happened, at least one thought? Why did it happen? Was there still more to come? And what did it all mean?

A short, Korean man with very thin eyes crept cautiously toward The Great Rock. He carefully examined all four sides, and as if misplacing something. "He's gone!" he yelled back to his superior. "Vanished in thin air! There's just a robe! Sergeant?"

The Black sergeant returned a puzzled look. Then he yelled out to the whole platoon. "Spread out, people! Search behind every tree and within every bush! He's gotta be here somewhere! Move!" And the men and women responded.

With concern, the Black sergeant stared beyond The Great Rock, to Sheriff Waters and Jake. And he stared at length. Then he set off to meet them.

The good sheriff was gingerly lifting Jake to a stand. More patient than before, and seeming somewhat melancholy and deep in thought, he led his emotionally drained friend slowly down the rest of the clearing. Along the way, another pack of toothpicks dribbled out of Jake's pocket; they went unnoticed.

"Sheriff!" the Black sergeant shouted. "Sheriff, can you explain to me just what the hell went on in this valley? Am I to believe that a boy burned your town, killed some men, and dug up a burial site?"

Sheriff Waters and Jake limped past the sergeant. A few paces south, the two paused, Sheriff Waters eyeing a smoldering Westcreek. "No, the boy didn't do any of this. We all did this. We all let it happen. Every last one of us. You and I alike."

There was a sort of corny silence.

And though appearing noticeably confused by the answer, the Black sergeant passed along a vital message. "The governor expects a full report on his desk within forty-eight hours. Is that clear?"

Sheriff Waters spoke plainly. "Yes. He'll have it. I'll tell him everything that's happened. Everything." He and Jake continued their descent.

The Black sergeant turned his attention to the platoon. "C'mon, people! Get a move on! Do your sweeps, find the body, and let's head for home!" He mumbled to himself, examining the clouds. "Strange storms you have in these parts. Strange damn storms."

Dex was having a hard time getting Gloria to her feet. She was rubbery in the legs, ghostly white, and seeming generally unaware. He held her like a father, in fun, supporting the weight of a little girl and on the tops of his feet. He literally had to push Gloria along, her eyes transfixed upon The Great Rock.

"We have to go," he said with care. "No one could have survived that. You don't wanna be here when they find him. I'm sure it's bad."

At the southern most part of the clearing, at a point where the jack pine shot up, two sets of paths came together, that of Sheriff Waters and that of Gloria. Each yielded to the other, their partners following suit. It was like a sort of uncontrolled, wilderness intersection with no clear laws regarding who should proceed. Both locked eyes, no words exchanged. Emitted from one to the other was a murky sense of betrayal, disgust, and deep hurt; from the other to the first was emitted a clearer sense of dishonor, responsibility, and sorrow. Such a metaphysical interaction continued beyond a comfortable amount of time, and finally Gloria turned her eyes to the earth. Taking the right of way, she allowed Dex to guide her down through the rest of the forest. Sheriff Waters and Jake followed, but at a great distance behind. The good sheriff's cancer was acting up again, you see.

From a bird's-eye view, it was as if a great exodus was taking place. Gradually, with Steven's body never being fully recovered except in bloody, sometimes globular tissue form, and with only a handful of National Guard members staying back, White, Red, Yellow, and Black descended the valley, and like a lost group of little, illuminated souls searching for home. Quiet, they were, introspective, slow in overall movements and maybe processing previous events internally or praying for some sort of future understanding. Near the valley floor they headed straight west, skirting a town once considered a heaven, but now resembling a hell. At one point the little lights moved closer together—ever so close, maybe to fortify their overall shine, and soon the only gravel road leading out came into view. Atop the road sat three, large school bus transports, their red lights flashing, and one by one, ever so slowly, the little souls climbed aboard, disappearing from sight. They were all exhausted, and yet their journey had just begun. It would be a long, long drive away from Westcreek. Indeed.

And Gloria—a sort of Snow White muddied by footsteps, was about to realize her dream. In the arms of a prince she was headed for the suburbs, a new home, a new life. But without her son. Indeed, without her son. Gloria closed her eyes, emotionally passing out. Her struggle to leave was over. Sort of happily.

"Sleep, my baby," she whispered with a smile, "sleep through the night… all will be well… all will be right."

Two huge helicopters with big metal buckets dumped water atop small fires still burning downtown… an eerie cry pierced the silence of the forest… thinning clouds became light and transparent, showing bright stars, and the bus transports disappeared over the valley top.

OF TREAJURE AND MIJFIRING GUNJ

Several days later the sun shone brightly over the valley. Its rays of light, glimmering and warm, streaked down to the earth, drying a morning rain from the boughs of the tallest pine trees, the leaves of the smallest lady slipper, and the boardwalk of the most gutted buildings downtown. Vibrant, the valley looked, so nurturing and green. And yet, so black and dead.

Life within The Great Forest was making a comeback, the conflict over. Chipmunk, rabbit, and skunk, bounding out of their nooks and making all kinds of racket, played games of follow-the-leader and tag. Feathered creatures, from the smallest hummingbird to the largest whisky jack, hopped down from their perches, scrounging for food near or upon the forest floor or simply from tree to tree. Deer was equally active. Practicing survival skills, doe pranced and leaped about as if being chased by a predator, while buck jabbed at a sturdy ash tree with his rack of horns and in a sort of mock territory dispute. And bear—with his furry butt seated smack-dab in the middle of a blueberry bush, he pawed and gnawed at the fruit, swallowing many mouthfuls beyond his capacity. Indeed, life was returning to normal within the forest—it was flourishing, and only one living soul, one human, would be witness to it all: Sheriff Waters. He came over a valley wall.

Alone, in a plain, tan windbreaker and baseball cap, and seated behind the wheel of an old, dented, white pickup, he drove sluggishly, his eyes rarely deviating from the remains of his former town ahead and below. Winding down the slope, kicking up minimal dust, he failed to notice the bounty of daisies on each side of the road and blowing gently in the wind, or the fire bush beginning to turn color, or the chicken hawk flying beside the truck in hopes a mouse might be squashed, spooked by a loud engine and crunching tires. Nope. Sheriff Waters noticed nothing. He resembled a man in a trance. Something had brought him back to Westcreek. Something called to him. Something haunted his being.

He parked in front of the old white church, the only building in town unharmed by the rapacious fires. Climbing like an old man from the cab, he took notice of the church's boarded-up windows and front double doors, trying to remember the last service he attended. And he couldn't. Maybe it was just too long ago or the service was unmoving, he thought; they often could be in Westcreek. The little attached cemetery also drew the lawman's attention. He inspected the small area and remarked silently on the growth of weeds and how you could no longer see the headstones unless you focused very, very hard. He sighed, turned slowly as if finishing up on a deep thought, and then walked tentatively down the middle of Main Street. It was time for a sort of homecoming.

And there wasn't much to look at but partial structure and black ash. A musty, almost pungent odor rode the air, and pretty soon Sheriff Waters unzipped his wind breaker, as if maybe becoming uncomfortable in temperature. From the left to the right, his eyes swayed. From the left to the right, and in front of the café, he paused, heading for the boardwalk out front. Standing with slumped shoulders, he stared at a big circle pressed into the wood. The impression was distinct and deep. Many summers ago a Norwegian known as "Barber Bob," a bald retiree from the army, used to give haircuts here for a buck and to visitors as well as locals. More than just a mini-tourist attraction, the big chair that sat on the boardwalk was a daily meeting place for young and old, men and women alike, and Sheriff Waters could almost see the people gather 'round, their steps light, their faces beaming, their hands extended to each other without reserve. And he could almost hear their conversations: of good fishing holes and hunting spots; of neighborly potlucks to come; of general news and life happenings outside of the valley. One particular scene was pictured so clearly within the good sheriff's mind: of Barber Bob snipping here and there on a head of hair, his audience razzing him in good fun about technique and form. Laughter was contagious. And Barber Bob—he just chuckled with heartiness, finished his work, took a buck, and with menacing eyes, called for his next "victim." The essence of life in a small town, the whole scene was, and unfortunately a few years later, Barber Bob died suddenly of a heart attack. There was no one to replace him. His big chair eventually got discarded somewhere in the town dump. Only that big circle in the boardwalk remained of that time. Sheriff Waters continued his walk, a sour feeling in his gut.

Near the general store, on the opposite side, he paused again. Another memory began to materialize, and he sized up an area of 8'x8' upon the gravel near an old horse's hitching post still intact. Many more summers ago, long before the advent of "Barber Bob," a finely sanded, oak booth stood here. Indians, from both in town and the Reservation, and usually attired in drab-colored dresses or cheap corduroys and flannel shirts, would sell arts and crafts from this very spot, and often from sunup until sundown. People like Walks with Moon, "Big" Two Rivers, and Running Fox would carry armloads of paintings, pottery, jewelry, and weavings of splendid textures to the booth everyday in hopes of making a few sales and a whole lot of new friends. Often the boardwalk would be covered with overflow product, creating hazardous foot traffic, and yet adjacent merchants were unconcerned. The little Indian booth was a curiosity—a word of mouth draw for travelers in the North Country who may not have otherwise visited Westcreek. It spurred the little town's economy, and sometimes the merchants, themselves, would snoop amongst the handmade wares for that steal of a deal. With a sincere smile, a few friendly words, and some good-natured haggling, a sale could almost always be assured.

Sheriff Waters could see Walks with Moon leaning over the booth and pointing down with excitement at her latest painting: she in her big, flowery smock and she with her very long, straight black hair and deep wrinkles. He could hear her woodpecker-like laugh as a grinning tourist asked for a "2 for 1" special because he was "low on money," but eager to buy. "For you, one painting, ten dollars," he could hear her say. "Two paintings, twenty dollars." She was a tough negotiator, and the tourist honored her terms, purchasing three paintings with eagle, moose, and timberwolf subjects. After a few minutes of warm conversation, the transaction was finalized with a meaty hug. A very meaty hug. It was always that way.

Eventually fewer and fewer Indians brought their arts and crafts downtown. At one point, the oak booth was dismantled altogether, used as firewood by the McGreggors during an especially cold winter. Sheriff Waters bit the side of his cheek.

At the very east end of downtown, he concluded his walk. He stopped suddenly. He pivoted a bit lackadaisically and stared back at whence he came. His brows narrowed.

When was the last summer festival in Westcreek, he wondered? Where was the last community picnic held? And why were the town parades always so short? Sheriff Waters was quite partial to parades, you see.

The most intense of memories came. The past suddenly came to life in front of him and like an internal projector gone screwy—very engrossing, very three-dimensional, it was.

Unable to recall the exact date or even the time of day, the good sheriff began observing a procession of floats and cars and people drifting through his body, at a snail's pace, and moving east to west. Like ghostly images atop the gravel, he could see garden tractors and small log skidders pulling old hay wagons decorated in wild flowers, paper-mache, posters, and ribbon. Float themes were recognized, from celebrating the great outdoors to remembering pioneer life to telling the tale of Paul Bunyan and to that associated with a particular local business. Each float was made rather cheaply, often rocked uncontrollably from side to side, but was nonetheless a source of pride for those who rode and walked beside. Sheriff Waters could see the pride in their tall stances and confident steps. He could see it in their eyes that sought to make contact with those that rose from the ashes and lined the street. He could hear it in their excited chatter amongst themselves.

The lawman watched an occasional, classic car drive through. "Pinky" Peterson, a jolly old man with thick rimmed glasses and snow white hair, along with his much plainer sons, showcased his white '56 Chevy, his blue '69 Corvette, and his fire engine red '39 Ford Pickup and to the citizenry of Westcreek. With horns beeping, he and his progeny swayed in and out of the procession, waving to all. Waving to all. Sheriff Waters could almost smell the rich exhaust. He could almost feel the crowd's interest.

Finally, people were seen in the parade, some dressed plainly, some dressed lavishly. Spotted were bankers in business suits, mothers in aprons, Indians in T-shirts and jeans, a heavy set woman in a showgirl costume, a skinny man dressed as Santa but in shorts, and scads upon scads of clowns in bib overalls, their faces colored red, yellow, blue, or orange, or some combination of all and in a sort of jigsaw pattern. Come one, come all, it was, and everyone joined the merrymaking.

The clowns threw Tootsie Rolls to the children scattered here and there along Main Street, but rarely was a candy caught. You see, the transparent children were terribly distracted. They had high expectations of something to come. Their little eyes were big and ever focused on the west, some jumping like popcorn to see above adult heads. Their little ears were ever listening, just waiting for a particular sound, a particular signal, a particular calling.

The good sheriff's internal movie playing out suddenly scored a wolf's cry, a piercing howl that came from the now dilapidated and singed gazebo. With lightning quick responses, he saw the children dart away from the crowd, sometimes bumping each other or an unsuspecting adult. A second could not be wasted. In a mad dash, the little people jockeyed for the best possible seats. A magic show was about to start.

And the children's faces. Once inside the gazebo. They were of many colors and many joyful expressions. A collage of images overlaid the film still rolling: of a Black boy almost in tears, his smile wide and of few teeth; of an Indian girl hiding behind long, black bangs, her eyes bashful but twinkling; of an Asian teenager, his brows arched high atop his forehead, the tricks unbelievable; and of a White teen girl, her chin dimpled, her cheeks rosy, her nose flattening out. So many faces were seen, so much happiness, and it was all due to one, old Indian in a top hat, cape, and cane.

Suddenly that internal projector switched off, the ghosts returning to his body. And the images of the children faded. Sheriff Waters simply remembered Decoreous.

He and his roly-poly frame, his dark, dark complexion, his soft, warm eyes, and his shuffle-like walk—the lawman considered Decoreous a friend. More than his words of support during troubled times, more than his ever-present willingness to lend a hand, though frail, and more than his tireless energy when educating young and old about Indian culture, both past and present, it was his way with touch that was most remembered and sorely missed. The old Indian's ability to calm a colicky baby with the brushing of his fingers across its cheeks, his ability to lessen anxieties and befriend a newcomer to town and with a slow, deliberate handshake, and his ability to lift worries from the shoulders of an ineffective sheriff with a gentle embrace— the whole lot of it. And more. At one point Decoreous was a major fixture in town—the blood in Westcreek's beating heart. He was not only a respected elder of the Ojibwe First Nation, but a respected elder in the White community, as well. Entertainer, friend, leader—that was Decoreous.

So what happened, the good sheriff thought? How could a man so revered become so despised and in a matter of hours? Did he really burn the ol' Krebs place and scatter Indian artifacts everywhere? Or was Jake behind it all, as originally suspected?

Sheriff Waters kicked at the gravel and pondered further. So many unanswered questions loomed: What ever happened to the handgun that took three men's lives? Was their deaths an internal matter or was someone else involved? And why was more Indian artifacts found?

And firearms—why were there so many accidents in the valley involving firearms? So many questions. So few answers. And even fewer people and places to investigate.

Alone, amidst ruins and feeling inadequate, Sheriff Waters wished selfishly, simply, for a warm embrace. A special touch.

He bowed his head. He breathed deeply. Then he dragged himself back toward his pickup. Homecoming was over.

He wouldn't get far, however. A loud whisper from somewhere startled him.

"Sheriff," a male voice said. "Sheriff, help me."

It seemed to be coming from the north, and so the puzzled lawman faced that direction, scanning the horizon. "Hello?" he shouted. "Who's there?"

"Come to me now. Help me."

Sheriff Waters did not recognize the voice. He began pinpointing its location, however, that being within The Great Forest and about half way up the valley. He stepped cautiously forward, through and around debris, and to the back side of downtown. His eyes kept searching.

"Where are you?" he shouted even more loudly. "Tell me where you are!"

"Help me. Help my people."

Sheriff Waters bolted for the edge of The Great Forest. Scenarios were running through his head: What if someone was left behind during the evacuation and was lost in the woods? What if one of Jake's men was hurt or trapped somewhere, clinging to life? Or what if the Johnson boy was alive, after all?

Fumbling his way through the trees, he entered the forest for a fourth time and with a sense of urgency. He had to find the voice.

And nature would prove to be much kinder.

"Come to me, Sheriff. Discover our secret."

The clearing. Visually, and from a certain perspective, it became less of gravel and a giant rock, less of churned earth and bone, and more of one dark, abandoned, mysterious mine. Sheriff Waters came from the southeast, his heart pounding, his sweat streaming. Struggling to keep afoot, he watched and listened carefully, hoping to support an internal hunch. Then the voice spoke again.

"Help me. Help my people."

The good sheriff felt a surge of adrenaline. He was right: someone was within the mine. But how far back? How deep? And in what kind of shape? Continuing to climb, and sometimes having to walk on all fours just to keep up momentum, he stumbled across a forgotten lantern lying sideways in a clump of stones. It might be salvaged, he thought. Sure its metal was scraped and dented, its glass cracked and cloudy, but its tank was half full of kerosene. Sheriff Waters raised and lowered the thick wick to a proper setting, he patted his pockets roughly for a lighter, and then he set the lamp on a level, flat rock. First flick of the lighter—the wick didn't take. Second attempt—same. Finally, with a third, more determined flick, some little cinders appeared on the tip of the wick, and pretty soon the lantern began to glow. The lawman smiled, briefly. He wouldn't have to search blindly within the tunnel.

Reaching the sort of apron to the mine, he became still, an eerie chill rising slowly up his spine. You see, a sudden, cold wind floated out to greet him. A constant, low-pitched hum heard from deep within rattled his ears. And spindly vines, dangling without life across the opening, swayed together in an almost hypnotic rhythm. But Sheriff Waters kept his focus. He had to find and assist whoever was inside. So swallowing a bundle of nerves and gritting his teeth, he searched the darkness.

"I'm here!" he called out. "Where are you?"

The voice ceased.

Twenty yards in and the cold wind became colder, the darkness darker. Beginning to shiver and about to shiver more, he pushed the lantern out away from his body, hoping to spy whatever may lie ahead. But the glow was just too dull. He tripped into and out of small holes in the dirt. He bonked his head several times on wooden beams that sagged downward under the pressure of the earth above. One beam even sat diagonal in the tunnel, and so the lawman had to crawl underneath in order to continue. And he grazed the obstacle. With his wide back, he bumped the fallen support, and a shower of dirt and little rocks came down, thinly encrusting his body. He fully expected an all-out cave-in, and silently he said a quick prayer of thanks. Then he shook his back a few times and went on.

"Hello, hello?" he said with a bit more concern. "Can you hear me?"

No response.

Forty yards in. Sheriff Waters wiped the sweat from his forehead. The humming noise was becoming louder, the light at the mine's entrance and behind was like a keyhole, and for the first time he questioned the existence of a rescuee. What happened to the voice, he thought, stepping forward with slight reluctance? Was the person unconscious or dead? Was the voice just all in his mind? Or was he being lured toward some kind of trap and for some unknown reason? The good sheriff considered all possibilities.

Then suddenly, he lowered the lantern. Peering far, far ahead, his mouth gaping open in awe, he locked onto a sight of wavering light. Orangish in color, it was, sometimes solid, sometimes faint. Intrigued, Sheriff Waters advanced more quickly, his steps little so as not to falter.

Sixty yards and the orangish color grew in both intensity and depth. A warmth was felt, coming in waves, and the lawman gradually became aware of multiple light sources, not just one. Where the tunnel ended, where the mine was officially abandoned many years ago because of money shortages, a hoard of wax-dripping candles were placed on little wooden tables or squished into metal holders or stuck into holes within the mine walls. Someone or something had erected a sort of shrine, and as Sheriff Waters approached, the flames seemed to wiggle more and more, as if excited.

He studied many of the candles and wondered: Who did all this? Who tended to the shrine's upkeep, for some candles were much longer than others and little wax buildup was evident on the tables? As if concerned he might extinguish some of the flames with his movements, he bent slowly, setting the lantern down upon the floor.

Then he studied the walls and slightly raised ceiling like an archaeologist making a new discovery.

Etchings were everywhere, you see, pressed into a clay/soil mixture. Stick figures chased deer with bows and spears; they played with bear-like creatures; chasing suns, they ran with large birds; they sat before teepees colored red and yellow, maybe sharing tales; and they bowed before great beings that rose from fires. All around Sheriff Waters, from the lowest point on a wall to the very middle of the ceiling, miniature scenes could be found of a long ago culture. Very long ago. The good sheriff mumbled to himself in some kind of amazement. He took a white hanky and rubbed his face and neck. And there would still be more to his discovery.

A draft was felt near his ankles. It was warm and then sometimes hot, and so he turned about, staring downward, trying to locate the sort of heater. On the north wall he found a 4'x4' hole. It was squarely cut, pulsating with even more dynamic, orangish light, and humming loudly. Sheriff Waters got down on his hands and knees and with difficulty. With some reserve, he crawled through the hole.

"Hello?" he yelled. "Anybody in here?"

Silence.

If the former room was indeed a shrine, then the latter could be considered a cathedral. The good sheriff entered a monster of a space. It was like a miniature dome, precisely carved out, and rows upon rows of candles lined the walls from his immediate left all the way around to his immediate right. He stood numbly, breathing in the rooms sheer size, its overpowering aura, its majesty. Humbly taking a few steps, he twirled about, throwing back his head. On the ceiling, more etchings could be seen, much larger than before, and they usually depicted spirit life—a celebration of it. Sheriff Waters moved further into the cathedral. The middle was treasure-ridden.

On tiers rising upwards in a sort of square pyramid, a bounty of wonders lay before. Old metal buckets spilled over with gold bouillon. Necklaces, earrings, and rings of sapphire, garnet, and diamond were attached to or draped over upright, taught weavings of deep color and pattern. Thin ceremonial robes and extravagant animal-like costumes served as soft seats for both large and small vases, each intricately painted. And there were weapons. Bows, arrows, spears, hatchets, and daggers were scattered here and there, meticulously fashioned and proudly displayed. All items seemed to be placed with care. All items seemed to be arranged with some sort of meaningfulness. All items and tiers seemed to crescendo toward a small landing that supported the littlest of little wooden tables. Sheriff Waters drew closer. He saw something of interest on that single, wooden table.

Driving himself into a sprint, he bounded his way up and passed the precious metal, up and passed the jewelry and cloth work, up and passed the clothing and ceramics, to that top level, hovering over the stained piece of furniture like an Indiana Jones character finding a most fantastic relic. His breathing bordered on asthmatic. His skin felt tingly. His left arm ached. Tending only briefly to such a sudden, physical condition, he leaned upon the table for support. Then with a shaky hand, he grabbed for a small handgun. It quaked his stomach.

It was a small weapon, .38 caliber, cold in feel and of lightly colored metal. Its grip was quartz and smeared with blood. Sheriff Waters eyed the elusive gun like it couldn't possibly be real, twisting and turning it in every direction. He gasped. And that's when a voice called out.

"Find something, Sheriff?" the voice said, much deeper and with more growl than before.

Sheriff Waters looked to the four-by-four hole. He was surprised, a hooded figure in a large robe of earthen tones standing there. The figure did not move, and Sheriff Waters climbed down from the pyramid, carefully, gun in hand but with no threat.

"Who are you?" he said.

"A chief," the figure replied, shortly. "Now what are you doing here?"

"I heard someone calling for help."

"Who?"

"I don't know. It sounded like they were somewhere back here. I searched. I didn't find anyone." The good sheriff glanced at the ceiling and treasures. "What is this place?"

The figure responded a bit more calmly. "A throne room, you might say. Fit for a king. It's all the valuables left of my people. I am charged with guarding them."

"Are you from the Reservation?"

"No."

"Are you from the valley?"

The hood jiggled as the figure laughed softly. "Yes. I lived close to you for many, many years."

Sheriff Waters kept a good deal of personal space between he and the mysterious man. With a suspicious tone and his face puckered with curiosity, he cocked his head sideways, his eyes never drifting from the dark space within the hood. "Then I know you?"

As if in slow motion—very slow motion—the figure pulled back the hood. "All too well, Sheriff. All too well."

"Amos!" Sheriff Waters spat with a huge sigh of relief. "My God, it's you! Jesus Christ, you had me scared for a minute!"

And, indeed, it was the old Indian. He stood tall, never appearing more sober. His face was clean-shaven, serious, but with still a look of craziness in the eyes, all the same.

"Why did you sneak up on me?" Sheriff Waters asked.

"To try and catch a thief." Amos nodded at the handgun. "What do you have there?"

Still trying to catch his breath, the lawman fiddled with the weapon like he still couldn't believe it existed. "We searched everywhere for this. It was crucial evidence in our investigation. How did it get here? Why was it sitting on a table?"

Answers did not come forthright.

Amos walked forward and passed Sheriff Waters like a proud proprietor in a one of a kind store. "You've found the greatest treasure this room has to offer. A simple gun. A little pistol responsible for making me a chief—a guardian over these hills. Why shouldn't it be given a place of honor?" He spun around with sudden anger, his jaw shaking. "Do you know how many years I waited in that miserable hole you call a town? Waited for my calling? My opportunity to lord over all that you see? Twenty years. Twenty years. I was nothing to my tribe because of the Blackfoot family—Decoreous, his son, his grandson. They would all be chief before me—it was written. But now they're gone. And the tribe, the spirits—they depend on me. My calling was loud and clear. And I shall be the last."

Sheriff Waters increased personal space. Confused and a bit concerned, he backed away. "Did you kill Bull and the twins?"

"No!" the sudden guardian said forcefully. "I didn't have to. Their greed for treasure killed them. I simply made use of their deaths. I hid your murder weapon and waited, waited for your Indian-loving town to help me. You were all little pawns in a much greater game." He stepped solidly—precisely toward Sheriff Waters and with a slight smile.

"Click-click-click… BANG!" And the handgun fired, the trigger untouched. A single bullet ripped across the monstrous space, followed by a second. The good sheriff dropped his critical evidence like he had been bitten.

Laughing full-bodied, Amos continued. "I simply caused an accident every so often, a mere magician's trick; I burned a home to the ground; I dropped a few spears and hatchets near a couple of tragedies and let you and your people do the rest. It was only a matter of time before I would became the most powerful man in the valley."

"Look at me, look at me!" he urged. "I hold a position of great respect within my tribe. I watch over our dead. I command wondrous magic you can only begin to understand. And I guard a treasure too valuable to ever calculate in money." He smiled maniacally. "And what did it cost? A dying town? A few meaningless lives? The reputation of a sheriff?"

"You used us, Amos," Sheriff Waters said shyly, taking another step away. "We were your friends. We gave you a home when you had nothing. We trusted you."

"You trusted me to fill a role! Of a drunken Indian! Of a fool! A man for your amusement. Twenty years. Twenty years. But now who's the clown? Now who has the control?" Amos ended with squinting eyes.

And Sheriff Waters became extremely uncomfortable. He

retreated a third step, his person bumping the 4'X4' hole. "What's gonna happen now?"

"Tell me again about this voice your heard. Who was it?"

"I told you, I don't know. I swear. It just disappeared."

Amos growled, as if annoyed. "Then you serve me no further purpose. As I said, I came here to catch a thief. I've done so. Now the thief must be punished."

As if fueled by the old Indian's words, Sheriff Waters took off like a lumbering bear, crawling back through the hole, tipping over the lantern and spilling a small amount of blue fire. In the middle of the shrine, trying to stand and getting his feet all tied up, he fell face first into the dirt. He lay vulnerable.

"Get up and run, Sheriff!" Amos teased. "Run for your life!"

Then phantom winds picked up. And from the cathedral. Whistling sounds and breathtaking gusts of air raced at and beyond the good sheriff. White ceremonial robes and coyote, moose, and deer costumes came along for the ride, either slapping him with flimsy sleeves or biting him with worn jaws. It was much like an open dryer gone haywire, and Sheriff Waters tried his best to at least get to his knees and defend. That's when vases presented a new challenge.

Of red and blue and green and yellow line patterns, they collided with his forearms and skull with solid "Clinks!" Showers of clay particles sprayed about. One vase, larger and thicker than the others, connected with his right wrist, snapping bone. He moaned. He bent over, hiding his head and protecting his wounded limb.

And then the projectiles stopped coming, the winds slowing. The air suddenly returned to normal.

The good sheriff took a peak. He saw Amos standing stiffly by the hole, within the shrine.

"What's your great White solution now, Sheriff?" the transcended Indian asked. "How will you save yourself?"

Sheriff Waters winced in pain. He could think of nothing.

And then a sweeter voice returned, more prominently than before. "Show us the light, Sheriff," it said. "Show us the light."

"Who's there?" Amos blurted out.

As if suddenly succumbing to a bright idea, the desperate lawman stared intensely at the toppled lantern. Snatching the handle with lightning quick reflexes and with his one good hand, he reared back, straightened and tensed his arm, and then flung the lantern with all his remaining might. It struck the stoic Indian above the right breast, dribbling down blue fire and upon the robe.

Amos laughed. "Foolish sheriff. You can't hurt me." Chanting in the Ojibwe tongue, he felt for the web and plucked a string. *"Béka ki ashkote,"* he said calmly. *"Béka ki ashkote."* No response followed.

Instead, a horrible clatter—like a freight train rolling—came from the mine opening, inward. The sound steadily increased and vibrated the tunnel. A hundred or so spirits stormed the shrine. They flew as if pissed, funneling around Amos and fanning the flames.

"No!" Amos cried, hobbling about and waving his hands. "Stop this instant! I command you! What's happening?"

Sheriff Waters coward near one of the tunnel walls. He saw blue fires become orange and spread further down and across Amos' body. He saw Amos fall into a table of candles, igniting his hair and face. Shocked by such a turn of events, he saw the spirits flying faster and faster around Amos, transforming him into a human torch.

"Save me, save me!" the new chief screamed in bloody murder, slumping to the ground.

And then it all came quickly to an end.

The spirits streaked out of the tunnel, Amos becoming still. The skin upon his face began to melt. His blood boiled and then dried. And his bones scorched. A sort of king had seemingly fallen from his throne.

The lawman watched the burning body for some time and with both bewilderment and horror. Then, as if scared he might wake the dead man, he tiptoed away, sliding his big frame up the tunnel side, his broken wrist chicken-winged against his stomach. The scene was emotionally disturbing, and it was his eyes that were slowest to leave.

He hurried down the tunnel. Reckless and jostled by the uneven floor, he impatiently sought out forest air. Light appeared. A dot, far in the distance was seen, and he moaned. The dot became basketball in size, and he mouthed some sort of personal motivation. The basketball became a crude doorway, and his eyes began to tear. Finally, building up to a tubby man's jog, he exited the darkness and entered a world of pure shine, falling to his knees upon the mine's apron. The sun felt warm and nourishing upon his face. His breaths became deep and rejuvenating. His skin was cooled by the gentlest of breezes, and there would be something more within the little wind. Much more. The breeze seemed to embrace the lawman.

Sheriff Waters felt grabbed. It was like he was suddenly surrounded by a pair of firm, but soft arms, and then pulled toward a sort of invisible chest. The whole sensation was tender, reassuring, soothing, and the good sheriff began to recognize the feel of that chest. He went limp, an almost hand rhythmically rubbing his shoulders. Closing his eyes tightly, he convulsed with at first little sobs and then, eventually, deep crying, the very pit of his gut rattling unrestrained. Over and over it rattled. Over and over. Sheriff Waters was becoming cleansed. And he was held there almost in thin air for what seemed like hours. But time was of no matter. It could have been days, for all he cared. After all, a lost friend had returned, even if just for a while. A lost friend with a very, very special touch. An embrace. Sheriff Waters had done good.

An investigation into four mysterious deaths could now be brought to a close. Events of that night were better understood, as were all that recently occurred within the valley. A small town sheriff now had time to fully grieve over what and who had been lost. His job was finished.

Almost finished, that is.

THE
REPORT

In St. Paul, Minnesota. In a capital building of white stone and gold. In a governor's office of plush carpeting, tall bookshelves, and deep back, leather chairs. And on a desk of polished mahogany, a manila envelope lay, recently delivered. It was quiet, so very quiet inside the capital. It was early in the morning, before the arrival of the governor and his staff, and within the envelope could be found a sort of catharsis. Sheriff Nathaniel T. Waters answered to the authorities. In a twenty-page, typewritten report, he explained the events and circumstances precipitating his frantic call for the National Guard. Further, as best he could remember, and with approximate names and dates, he documented over fifty acts of unlawful behavior on behalf of himself and Deputy Jake Flint. Such acts included partiality in the line of duty, police brutality, cover up, and insubordination.

Attached to the first page of the report, written in perfect penmanship, was the following letter:

Dear Governor,
Our town wasn't a bad place to live. We weren't monsters. Matter of fact, we could've been your neighbors, your mothers and fathers, your sisters and brothers, even your sons and daughters. It's just that we grew tired of ourselves. With little money, fewer and fewer jobs, more friends and family leaving than coming, and unable to see beyond these valley walls, we remembered too much about the past and differences in people. We tried making ourselves feel better, the easy way. We let anger replace our joy, harsh words replace our laughter, and hatred replace our compassion. It brought us closer

together, but for the wrong reasons. Please forgive us.
As chief law enforcement officer in Westcreek, I stand ready to face any and all charges you may bring against me.
With terrible regret,
Sheriff Nathaniel T. Waters

And the good sheriff—his cancer was cured.

Printed in the United States
28854LVS00001B/43-45

9 781413 756258